THE BONE WITCH

IVY ASHER

Copyright © 2020 Ivy Asher

All rights reserved. This book or parts thereof may not be reproduced in any form, stored in any retrieval system, or transmitted in any form by any means—electronic, mechanical, photocopy, recording, or otherwise—without prior written permission of the author, except in cases of a reviewer quoting brief passages in a review.

This is a work of fiction. Names, characters, places, and incidents either are the products of the author's imagination or are used fictitiously. Any resemblance to actual persons, living or dead, businesses, companies, events, or locales is entirely coincidental.

Edited by Polished Perfection

Cover by Book Covers by Seventhstar

Chapter Heading by Ricky Gunawan

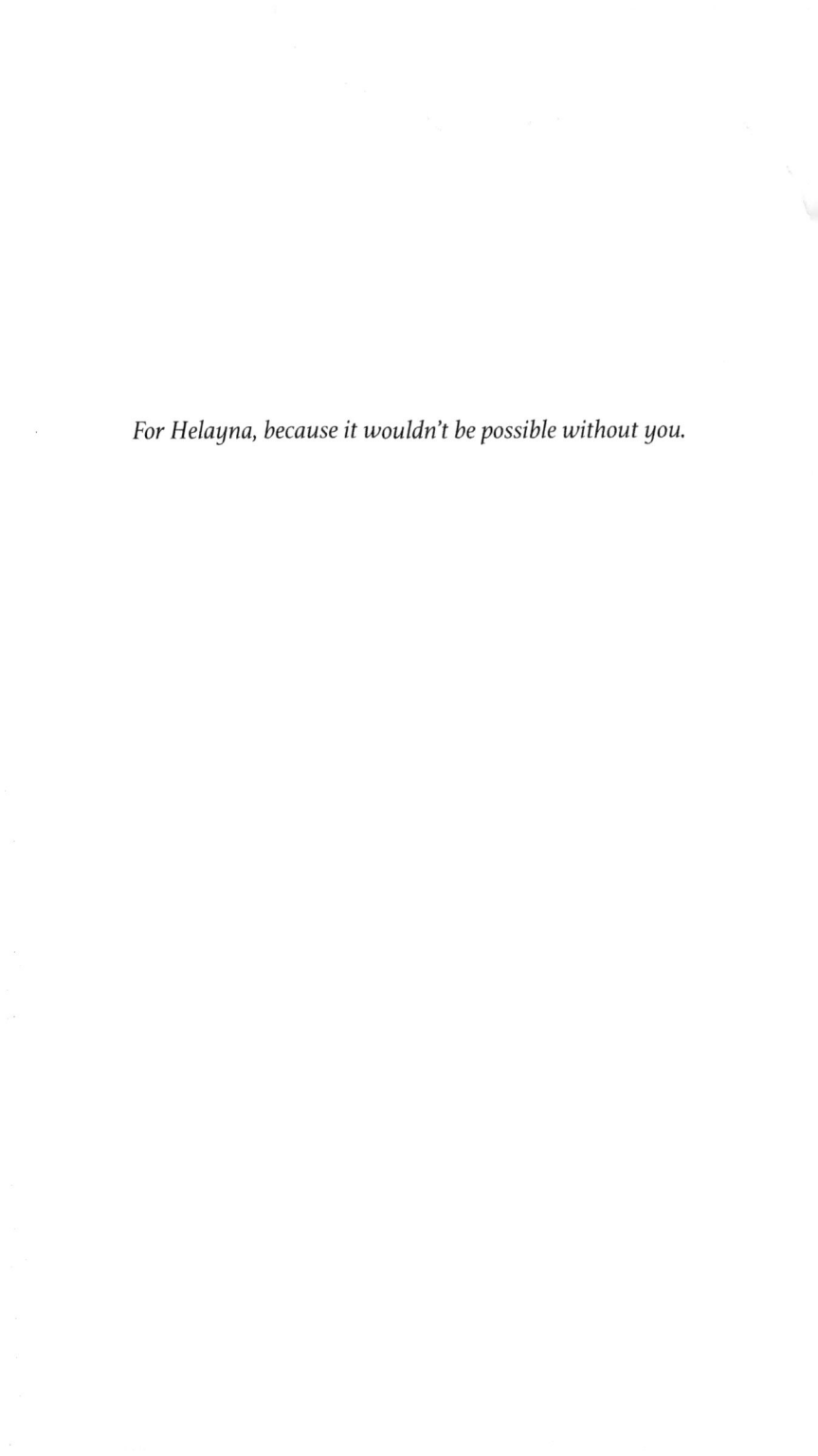

For Helayna, because it wouldn't be possible without you.

1

My feet ache as I plod up the cement stairs that guide the way to my third floor apartment. Each step saps the last vestiges of my energy, and I'm ready to call it quits halfway up the concrete flight. Step number seven is starting to look awfully cozy, I tell myself, and I would be saving the food delivery guy from having to trek up this Everest to deliver the shrimp scampi I just ordered.

I chant a steady stream of *I think I can*, while promising my tired muscles and barking feet a warm bath and a soft bed just as soon as they get us through the front door. I groan and make a note to find a ground floor apartment before accepting any more double shifts.

I am bone tired.

I had three cancellations today, which means I had to take walk-ins. This would normally be fine, except Leann called out sick, and her appointments were divided up between the masseuses that were there. I, of course, got stuck massaging the woman who smelled like garlic and the dude who kept fishing for whether or not I was going to give him the happy ending he was hoping for.

Ugh.

I need to find a new job. Or better yet, I need to open up my own place instead of working for an evil massage chain. Too bad rent is exorbitant, and trying to run an *I'll come to you* massage business is just asking to be seen and treated like a sex worker.

Finally, I crest the top of the stairs, but my arms hurt too much to raise them in triumph. With a tired huff, I shove my key into the lock and shoulder my front door open. I'm so ready for a glass of wine, my just big enough tub, and some *Witcher*. Lord knows I need a healthy dose of Henry Cavill in my life to remind me why I shouldn't look into becoming a lesbian.

My purse slides down my arm like it too is exhausted and can't wait to veg out. A clang fills the quiet of my apartment as I drop everything onto the black entry table and pull in a deep inhale of home. The scent of wisteria and lemongrass settles in my lungs, and the stress of work starts to sluff off my shoulders. A twinge of pain shoots through my back as I step deeper into the comforting smells of my cozy apartment. I snort at the irony of needing a massage to help combat all the aches and pains I have from *giving* massages for a living.

Today's need for Tylenol is to be blamed on Mr. Nobo. He was my last massage of the day and the one who pushed my aching back over the edge. I mean, good for him for being so fit at his age. If *silver fox* was my thing, I'd be all over that and then some, but I *hate* massaging ripped guys. Don't get me wrong, I love muscles. *Nice body* definitely ticks off a big box for me when I'm on the prowl and hunting for a bed buddy for the night. But getting knots out and relaxing all that muscle, it's like the worst kind of hardcore workout, and Jillian Michaels I am not.

Thoughts of shrimp scampi float through my tired mind

as I head toward my room. I should be able to fill up the tub and get Netflix streaming on my tablet just before dinner is delivered to my doorstep. Eagerly I start to strip down. I pass the espresso-colored table nestled in my dining room when out of the corner of my eye, I spot something that was not there when I left this morning.

Perched dead center in the middle of the dark wood is a deep purple velvet pouch. I freeze at the sight of it, and my blood runs cold. Dread floods me as questions try to burst through my mind like faulty fireworks. My head shakes back and forth like the simple *no* motion will undo what I know in my gut has already been done. I retreat away from the table, putting as much distance between me and the curse that's just sitting casually, uninvited, in my dining room.

"Fuck, fuck, fuck, fuck, fuck!" I screech, like some sailor-blessed exclamation will scare the bag away, erasing this moment and everything I know is about to happen.

But how?

Why?

Did they get lost on the way to their true home, stop to take a nap or something?

I mean, I get it, I've had a long day too, but as much as I want to think that there's been some kind of a mistake, deep down I know that's *not* how this works.

I scramble for my purse. Phone. I need my fucking phone. The trill of my ringtone suddenly fills the panic-laced air all around me, the sound like a cannon going off in the eerie quiet of my apartment. With shaky hands, I scramble to open my bag. I finally find my still ringing phone but drop it in the process of trying to accept the incoming call. The phone goes quiet as it clangs against the floor, ominous silence once again filling my apartment like a dense fog. I clamber to pick it up. Adrenaline slams into me like a sumo wrestler, and with a trembling grip, I open up my recent calls and click my cousin's number.

My alarmed gaze lands back on the velvet pouch. I pinch myself and blink profusely, testing that I'm not currently hallucinating or somehow passed out and experiencing a fucking nightmare. My call barely makes it a full ring before a silvery tenor voice answers.

"Leni? Did you hear?" Tad demands, out of breath and in place of the friendly *hey you* that he usually greets me with.

"They're here," I choke out, cutting off whatever he's about to say. "They're fucking here!" I shout into the phone, you know, just in case he didn't hear me the first time.

Tad goes silent, stunned by my panicked revelation as much as I am.

"Holy shit," he whispers reverently, and I nod in agreement regardless of the fact that he can't see me. We're both silent for a beat. "Gwen is going to shit kittens," he finally blurts, and I begin to massage my temples.

Shit. I didn't even think about that.

I shove that thought in a drawer and close it. One messed up thing at a time. "How is this happening?" I whisper, awe slowly filtering in and filling up the cracks in my soul not currently cemented by shocked dread.

"Ma just got the call ten minutes ago."

"How?" I ask as comprehension shoves through my surprise and worry. The dots start to connect, and reality walks up to me and cracks me one right in the nose.

"They said she died in her sleep."

"Did the necros smudge?"

"Yeah, no traces of outside magic. It was definitely natural causes," he reassures me.

"Fuck," I concede, closing my eyes and dropping my head back in defeat.

"Lennox Marai Osseous, you watch your language," Aunt Hillen orders, and with an exasperated growl, I pull my phone away from my ear and make a strangling motion at it.

"Why am I on speaker?" I demand of my cousin, but he ignores the question, instead whisper-shouting, "She has them," to his mother.

"Well, fuck," Aunt Hillen exclaims with a shocked gasp, and I immediately choke on an astonished laugh. I hear Tad coughing with his own amusement. I don't think either of us have ever heard her swear before. If shit wasn't currently hitting the fan and spraying all over the place, I'd be pressing the record button and trying to get her to say it again.

"I have to call Magda!" she declares excitedly, shock still evident in her tone. "I bet she and Gwen are searching every nook and cranny right now, looking for the pouch."

Smug satisfaction rings in my aunt's tone, and I know the rest of the family is going to love that Magda and her prissy little shit of a daughter aren't going to get their hands on the bones and subsequently the power that comes with them. I suppose that should be some small consolation, but internally, I'm begging the gods to choose anyone else but me.

I catch a hurried, "Congrats, Leni," before my aunt disappears, off to become the bearer of bad news that she's always wanted to be to the snooty side of the family.

Tad chuckles at his mother's hypocrisy, and even I crack a small smile despite the clusterfuck I now find myself square in the middle of.

"I think you just made my mother's decade, Leni. Shit, I guess I now have to call you Lennox, or would you prefer *Oh Powerful One* instead?" Tad teases.

"Supreme Being will do," I deadpan as I try to fight off a

new wave of bewilderment and vexation. "Crap, everyone is going to get all formal with me, aren't they?"

"Well, being that you were just chosen as the next Supreme Boner, oops, I mean Supreme Osteomancer, I'm going to go with yes."

Hearing him call me that is beyond weird, and what's scarier to me is that there's something inside of me, something I've never looked at before and don't want to acknowledge now, that feels right. I'm the next Bone Witch.

A frustrated groan climbs up my throat, and I drag my palm down my face. "What the hell am I going to do? Can I ask for a revote or something?" I query, not even caring about the whine dripping thickly off of every word like cold molasses. I sigh and ask what everyone else will be thinking when they find out what's happened. "Why in all the universes would the bones choose *me*?"

I slide down the wall next to my entry table until my ass meets the floor; it's as though I'm being pulled down by the weight of all of this as it settles heavy like sandbags on my shoulders.

"You know how this works, Lennox. We all do. You knew someday Grammy Ruby would pass away and the bones would choose one of us to take her place," Tad reminds me, his tone tutorial before it dissolves into sympathy.

"Yeah, but we *all* thought it would be Gwen. Magda's been going on and on about how she's been a gazer since she was seven."

I rest my elbows on my knees and press my head against my forearm, cocooning myself in defeat and mourning all the plans I had for my life.

"All that bitch can gaze is the inheritance that comes with that purple pouch of bones, the rest is smoke and mirrors. Leni, the bones wanted you. They wouldn't be there if you weren't the one." He pauses, and I hear what sounds like a stifled chuckle.

"This isn't funny," I argue.

"Well, that's not exactly true, Mighty Bone Whisperer, but I'm laughing because I went all spirit guide on you, not because you're the chosen one. I'm like the Hagrid, Obi-Wan, Haymitch, and Khloe of your story, and *that* is hilarious."

"Khloe?"

"Damn right. She's the most logical and badass of the Kardashian clan. She'd totally be a spirit guide if given the opportunity," Tad defends as though any of that makes sense.

"I'm like a hot Yoda! And trust me, Leni, if the bones want you, then you they shall have. There's no fighting this," he declares with an adenoidal voice that sounds more Kermit than Yoda.

"Isn't there?" I plead.

"Remember all the stories about great-great-great-grandpa Lown and how he tried to avoid his duty? It gets you in the end no matter what you do."

Thoughts of the ancestors who tried to shirk their selections flash through my mind. Lown choked on a rib bone one night in his bed. Weird thing was, he was asleep when it happened. That, and the fact that the man was a vegetarian, amped up the mystery to outsiders. But the family knew that either you honor the bones or they'll find the next in line who will.

I pick up my head so I can stare at the underside of my dining room table. At where I know a bag filled with blessed bones sits just on the other side. Their presence marks my selection as one of the few remaining Osteomancers in the world. It decimates all the hopes and dreams I had for my future. One purple pouch, and life as I know it is fucking over.

Desolation and worry roost in my chest. *What the hell am I going to do?* Tad is talking, but I can't tune into what he is saying. All I can do is slowly get up and reluctantly close the distance between myself and the unwanted bones that are encased in purple velvet on my table. The bag looks so unassuming. So faultless. But I know nothing could be further from the truth. The bony contents will awaken the dormant abilities in my marrow and unlock a world of secrets, the likes of which I can't even begin to fathom.

It's not the letter to Hogwarts I spent my middle school years hoping would drop down my chimney though. This bag of bones leads only to a life of servitude, suffering, and societal rejection.

The aroma of patchouli, singed cedar, and sugar cookies fresh out of the oven waft out to me as I reach for the bag. All at once, it's as if my grandmother is here, lending me her strength and encouragement. Warmth envelops me, and I'm reminded that the presence of these bones means that she's gone now.

A hollow ache starts in my chest, the reality of her death trumped by the appearance of the velvet pouch on my table. Shame fills me, and I pull in a sharp breath, emotion stinging my eyes. It doesn't feel real.

My grandmother's face pops up in my mind. Her lined tan skin and thick gray hair, cut short because *who can bother to try and tame curls in their old age,* she would complain. Her hazel eyes and the way they would flicker from stern seriousness to mischievous to kind glimmer in my memories, her time-thinned lips tilting up in a sassy smile.

I'll never again walk into her incense-soaked shop to be greeted by her sharp wit and knowing way. Her slender and sinuous arms won't wrap me up in a strong hug that squeezes all of my problems into nothing. Her sure, comforting voice will never call me on the phone to check in or to ask for help with sourcing ingredients because technology just wasn't in her bones. Her gumption, her light, her give no fucks way, all...gone.

My Grammy Ruby is no longer in this world, and I'm not sure how to navigate that loss let alone the looming legacy I've been bestowed because of it.

Tad's voice pulls me from my thoughts, and I look down to see the phone still clutched in my palm. I pull it back to my ear, sadness settling like hardening cement in my chest.

"I can't believe she's gone," I whisper hollowly, the truth of it taking root and changing everything. Whatever Tad was rambling about immediately comes to a stop, and he's quiet for several beats.

"I know. It's weird to think of a world without her grumpy ass in it."

I snort out a laugh, not able to help myself. Amusement trickles in to mix with the sorrow I'm wading through, and I cling to it like it's a life preserver. "I probably shouldn't be so shocked, she's been telling us to fuck off and let her die for at least ten years," I recall with a despondent chuckle.

"The old bat is probably laughing her ass off right now," Tad teases, but I hear the melancholy saturating his tone.

"Do you think she knew?" I ask him after a weighted moment of silence.

I find myself looking back at all of my interactions with my grandma and analyzing them with a new lens. Every time she smiled at me with an interested glint in her eye or deposited a curious bit of random wisdom, did she know the bones would end up on my dining room table one day?

"Lennox!" Tad shouts at me, his demanding tone pulling me from my thoughts. "Did you hear me?"

"Huh?" I ask, the single syllabic sound requesting he repeat whatever it was that I missed.

"Have you sealed yourself to them yet?"

"The bones?"

"No, to Stephen James," he snarks, pausing for dramatic emphasis. "Of course the bones!"

I reluctantly swat away visions of the tattooed model my cousin and I both spend many an hour on Insta drooling over, and focus on his point.

"No. I spotted the pouch, freaked out, watched my life crash and burn like a downed plane, and then called you."

"Lennox, what the fuck?" he chastises. "Ma, don't start with that shit," he defends against my aunt's squawking in the background. "Leni has unsealed bones sitting in her house," he rats.

There's a scuffle on the other end of the phone before my Aunt Hillen's voice comes screeching through the line. "Lennox Marai Osseous, what in the name of goat balls do you think you're doing?" she mom-yells at me.

I flinch. She pauses like she actually wants an explanation.

"Um, waiting to see if the bones will choose someone else?" I respond, only half joking.

Aunt Hillen gasps, and I cringe against the sound.

"Leni, it's *you*. You're the next Osteomancer. Stop messing around and take it seriously just like you've been taught your whole life to do." With that, she hangs up on me.

I pull the phone away from my ear and stare at the lit up screen until it blinks black. I set the phone on the table and then stare at the velvet pouch, indecision warring with what I've been raised to do in the event that this ever happened. I take a deep fortifying breath and reach for the bag.

Fuck my life...here goes nothing.

2

Voices echo in my mind as I run through every lecture I've sat through my entire life about what to do if the bones were to ever choose me. First, immediately seal them to you or risk them falling into the wrong hands and damaging our line of magic to infinity and beyond. Second, bind a familiar to help protect and stabilize any and all abilities that will show up over time. Third…shit, what was the third thing?

I tick off the numbers on my hand over and over as I will my mind to deliver the information I know it has stored somewhere inside of its tangled recesses. Third…add a bone to the pouch that represents me and my reign.

Relief fills me as I remember that step, and then I cringe as understanding sinks in. Yikes, where am I supposed to find a bone to do that? Does it have to be a human bone, or can I hit up my local fried chicken joint, eat a drumstick and call it a day? My stomach rumbles hungrily at the thought, but I dismiss it and focus on the last major task I need to tackle.

Fourth, take over the shop and guide anyone the magic chooses. Sounds simple enough, but I have a sinking feeling it will be anything but. There's more to it all: inheritances, abilities that will just show up like unwelcome relatives, dealing with the Order, but these first four tasks are the big ones.

I groan like a five-year-old on the verge of an epic whine-fest. It takes all the maturity I've mustered in my thirty years of life to not stomp my foot and start making claims about how life isn't fair. I grudgingly pull the velvet pouch toward me from the center of the table and take a deep empowering breath. I untie the black thread at the top of the bag that keeps it cinched shut. Amber, black currant, and balsam rise up to greet me as I pull it open, and it feels like a balmy blanket of power was just thrown over my shoulders.

Small bones and bone chips from larger sources sit ominously at the base of the pouch, each one with a symbol or set of symbols carved into them. I don't know what any of it means yet, but I will the moment I spill my blood on them and seal their magic, their history, to me. I reach out and trace a bone chip that has a diamond shape carved into it. There's a slash through the rhombus and what looks to be bolts of lightning at each of the points.

I run my finger over every marking, hypnotized by the hum of power I feel in them already without any kind of forged connection. Goosebumps sprinkle up my arms, and a shiver crawls through my body. Shaking my head to clear my ominous thoughts, I bring the pouch of bones with me to the kitchen. I root through my utensil drawer until I wrap my palm around a steak knife.

I don't waste any time pressing the blade to my hand and slicing a cut right along the heart line of my palm. I may not love that the bones chose me, but I've done enough fucking around. Tad and Aunt Hillen are right, it's time to get down to business. Blood flows from the wound and pools in my palm. I position it over the opening of the deep purple velvet bag and slowly tilt my hand, my fairy pool of hemoglobin spilling over. I hold my breath as my essence drips down to coat the top of the bones, stamping them with all that I am and claiming them as mine—however reluctant that claim may be.

I watch, surprise striking through me, as the red spatters of my blood slowly disappear as though the bones are soaking it all up and claiming me right back. A thunderous crack rends the air. I'm yanked from where I'm standing in the kitchen, leaning against the counter, dripping ichor all over a bag of bones, and slammed up against the ceiling by a powerful, unseen force.

It knocks the air out of me, and I gasp and struggle to fill my lungs as a soul-freezing cold crashes through my body. My skin pebbles and simultaneously burns from the frigid assault. Frostbite feels like it kisses my every cell, and my lungs are entirely too empty to support the scream that I feel in my soul from the pain.

Voices explode all around, thousands of whispers swirling and zooming past me, making me disoriented. I can't seem to latch on to anything they're saying through the arctic agony. Black spots sneak into my vision, and if I didn't know better, I'd think I was about to die, suffocating on nothing, frozen from the inside out.

My vision clicks off, and the images of my kitchen are replaced by faces. They flash by so quickly it's hard to focus on any individual one, but after a few seconds, I start to notice similarities. High cheekbones, similar jawlines, uniquely colored eyes. They're my family. The Osteomancers that came before me.

When finally my Grammy Ruby's face flashes by, disappearing all too quickly, the images suddenly morph. Bones being shaken and splayed for reading after reading flicker in front of me. Everything else is dark except for the bones, their markings, and the talismans that help guide the readings. I feel as though knowledge and power are coaxed out of me with each flash of a reading. Suddenly I know what they mean. I know the right way to interpret each cast of the pouch's contents. Abilities braid themselves into my soul, but the raw power of it all is so overwhelming that I can't see clearly what the infusion of ability will allow me to do.

Gravity kicks in out of nowhere, and the next thing I know, I'm falling to the floor from the ceiling, a painful splat overtaking all of my senses. I lie there, stunned and silent until a desperate gasp rips through the quiet. I finally manage to pull a frigid breath into my chest, only to release a pain-filled groan as I exhale. My cheek is plastered to the laminate floor, and all I can think is that I need to sweep under my cupboards...oh, and what the fuck just happened to me?

I could be paranoid, but I'm pretty sure that my ancestors just bitch-slapped me for my ungrateful response to being selected.

Message received, ancestors, message fucking received.

I give myself another minute and then unpeel my pancaked body from the kitchen floor. I feel like I've aged a hundred years. And like a semi just hit me. Pretty sure that semi was hauling pepper spray that just so happened to leak all over every inch of me, because ouch. The stinging sensation thankfully starts to recede, and I pull myself up. Shakily, I lean against the counter for support as I try to regulate my breathing and convince my legs that they don't have to act like we're Bambi on ice.

I stare down at the bag of bones. The bone that has the slashed diamond with bolts of lightning at each corner is still sitting on the top of the pile, and words like *obligation*, *honor*, and *gratitude* float to the surface of my mind like I'm a

Magic 8 Ball supplying the answer to a question that was just asked.

I cinch the pouch of bones shut and throw my head back to the heavens. "I get it, okay!"

I look down to the ground beneath my feet and repeat myself, because fuck knows some of them are surely down there too. When my legs feel less like jello, I stomp toward the front door, my reflection in the mirror hung above my entryway table catching me off guard. I pause mid-step, my mane of dark-chocolate and cinnamon-kissed curls definitely having seen better days. Oddly, my tawny-beige complexion has a glow to it that wasn't there before, the golden undertones of my skin alight, vibrant, and making me look entirely too radiant for how crappy I feel. Toffee-colored eyes stare back at me, and they're filled with shock, wonder, and doubt.

I stare at myself for a moment, trying to see a woman that is ever going to live up to the legacy that just dropped like an anvil on her head, but no matter how hard I search, I can't find her.

The mirror doesn't take on any magical properties, declaring me the fairest of them all or answering any of the questions swimming in my gaze, so I turn away, shakily grabbing my purse and keys from where I previously deposited them. I take one last look at the velvet pouch that now owns me and then open my door and step out.

I better find a familiar before these impatient bones, and all the ancestors attached to them, zap me again.

"*Fucking rude, if you ask me*," I grumble under my breath as I shut my door and lock it. Then I warily look around, hoping none of them actually heard that. The last thing I need is to get brained by something as I trudge down the stairs in search of a familiar like a good little Osteomancer is supposed to do.

I rub at my eyes with my palms and groan pitifully. I'm seriously going to suck at this so bad. Maybe the bones chose me purely for amusement. Maybe the ones who have gone before me were in need of a little pick-me-up, and it's all about to happen at my expense.

A moth dive-bombs me, and I swat at it and squeal, ducking and tripping down the last couple of steps. Bastard bugs. Oh god, please don't let my familiar be a moth—or worse, a ferret. I have a hard enough time finding decent guys without a pet that smells like piss following me around all the time.

"No goldfish!" I shout out like I'm beating my ancestors to the potential comedic punch.

A man gives a scared yelp, which makes me scream because I didn't see him rounding the corner. I watch as the shrimp scampi I was looking forward to goes flying out of the bag clutched in the startled delivery driver's hand. Its trajectory arcs up for a moment before it plummets to the ground, breaking open to spill its delicious contents all over the sidewalk. A piece of shrimp lands on the toe of my boot, and I look down and stare at the mess while the delivery guy groans and starts to rant at me.

I sigh, open my food delivery app, and tip him twenty bucks before walking away without a word. Yep, that about sums up my life. Now off to find a familiar that I hope like hell isn't a shrimp or any other kind of crustacean.

"Where are you?" Tad asks me, judgment oozing from his tone as he answers my call.

"Where do you think I am? I'm at a shelter, working on step number two. The problem is that I can't remember what I'm supposed to do after I find it," I confess to my cousin as I walk slowly down the line of plexiglass-enclosed cages that are filled with various cats.

"Where's your guide book?"

"At home. Can you please just get yours and tell me what the hell I'm supposed to be doing?" I plead, hoping my desperation will motivate him to be fast about it.

"Why is it at home?" Tad asks instead as I give an orange tabby that's giving me the stink eye a wide berth.

"Well, after being magically tazed when I sealed the bones to me, I was kinda in a hurry and forgot it. Can you *please* just remind me what it says about familiars?" I beg, and I can practically feel the head shake Tad is doing on the other end of the line.

The distinct sound of him clomping up the stairs to his room has me releasing a relieved exhale. I knew I would be bad at this, but my level of suckage is surprising even me. I need to up my ginkgo biloba because I'm struggling to recall any of the things that have been hammered into me since practically birth. I forgot that I even owned a book that details what to do if this ever happens, *that's* how bad I am at this.

I wait patiently as I hear Tad rustling around on the other end of the phone, and lean in closer to an adorable calico kitten that's lapping up water from a stainless steel bowl. I smile and swallow down the *awww* that I'm just about to voice when the kitten looks up at me and immediately arcs its back and hisses. Every hair on the kitten fluffs out to stand on end, like each individual follicle is offended by my presence, and I quickly back away from the angry little furball.

Sheesh.

"Okay, I'm paraphrasing here," Tad starts. "But it pretty much just says that you need one, it can be any living thing, and you'll get all tingly when you find a good fit for you," Tad tells me, and I can hear the flipping of pages as he scans his guide book for any more useful information. "Yep, that's it aside from the incantation to bind a familiar."

Words and their cadence pop into my mind unbidden, and I immediately recognize the very incantation he just mentioned. Weird. Maybe my brain is just rusty and not useless like I thought. Tad starts to read the first line of the binding.

"I know it, don't keep going!" I shout, hurrying to cut him off before he completes the incantation and accidentally makes Small, Poofy, and Ragey my next familiar. He stops and I press a palm to my chest. That was close. I back further away from the still angry little kitten.

"Thank you, Tad. I'll let you know if I find one."

"Better hurry, it's almost seven, and I'm sure pet stores and shelters will all be closing soon."

Panic flares through me, and I hang up the phone before he can say anything else, and hurry on with the task at hand. I scan the rest of the cat cages hopefully and continue to make my way through the feline portion of the first shelter that popped up on google. Like some weird Peeping Tom, I peer into every cage, my eyes intense and my body expectant. I stare and I wait for the tingles that are supposed to come, but after my second round of creeping out the cats, nothing happens. I sigh tiredly and accept that finding my familiar at the first place I stopped was probably wishful thinking.

I leave the cat enclosure, defeat echoing in the tap of my steps against the polished concrete floor. I rummage through my purse for my keys and pull up on my phone a list of other shelters or pet stores I can try to get to before they close. A cacophony of frantic barking pulls my attention away from the maps app I just opened. I look up and see rows of kennels with a myriad of different-sized dogs in each chain-link pen.

Crap, I must have gone out the wrong door.

I turn to retrace my steps through the cattery and back to the door that lets me leave, but the handle on the door I just came out of doesn't budge. After trying it a few more times, I curse my luck. It's locked. I scan my surroundings, looking for another exit, and wince at the high-pitched desperate barks of the animals all around me.

Pulling my shirt up over my nose in hopes it will block out the smell of wet dog and anxiety that's permeating this place, I start to make my way down the line of kennels in search of a way out of here.

Dogs yap and yowl at me as I pass, and I pick up my pace, the smell and noise becoming more and more overwhelming. A set of double doors that look like they lead to salvation come into view just as I pass a particularly loud kennel. Tingles erupt all throughout my body. I feel like I just stuck my finger in a light socket. I'd bet if I saw my reflection right now, my curls would be standing on end from the electric charge humming through me.

Dammit.

I squeeze my eyes closed, rub at my tingling arms, and throw my head back. "A dog?" I demand. I mean, of course it's a dog. They're needy and stinky and super demanding of things like time and affection. I needed something more independent and loner-ish. Something that wouldn't judge me for not knowing how to take care of it. I was willing to settle for a cat, but really I need a hedgehog or a snake, definitely not some pesky pooch. My apartment doesn't even allow dogs.

I remind myself that it could be a ferret and try to rein in my irritation. The tingling sensation working through my body gets stronger, and I shake my head in denial and exasperation as I open my eyes. *Tad said that the tingles would happen if I'm compatible with a familiar, not that I had to take one just because I went all static cling over an animal.* I take a deep breath at that thought and try to get a better look at what I'm dealing with. I peek hesitantly into the kennel I'm standing in front of, which is when a fucking dire wolf straight out of the pages of an epic fantasy novel chooses to attack from the dark corner of its kennel. The door to its cage rattles ominously as it snarls at me and looks me dead in the eye with a clear message of *I will rip you to shreds and devour you piece by motherfucking piece, bitch.*

It charges the cage again, and I stumble back in fear and slam into another kennel behind me. No fucking way am I taking that monster home. The bones can't be serious.

"Ha ha, ancestors, you've had your fun!" I shout, completely unnerved.

The declaration comes echoing back to me, mockingly, as it bounces off the cement walls of the large room and dances all around me like some playground taunt. I scan my surroundings to make sure no one else is in here witnessing my crazy as it unfurls like a flag in the wind. And that's when I hear a snort coming from the kennel I'm currently pressed up against in my efforts to get as far away as I can from the demon dog across from me. Snarls ricochet off my back as I turn to see what's responsible for the disgruntled pig noises.

My eyes widen with surprise when I find a pair of moon-dust gray eyes looking up at me. It's a dog, but not a breed I've ever seen before. He looks like some kind of pug, bulldog, collie mix with his long hair, perky battish ears, and squished face. His soot-gray coat sticks out all over the place and looks how I just felt, all charged and staticky. He lies there, his moonlight-toned eyes staring at me like he can't be bothered to bark or get excited.

The prickling I was feeling before gets even more intense, once again lapping through my body and making me feel charged and fuzzy. I'm both relieved and anxious at the same time. Yay for the *Game of Thrones* beast not being the one to set off my spidey senses, but it's still a *dog* that's giving me the familiar feels.

A clang sounds around me, and I jump, startled by the loud noise. I spin around, hoping that wasn't just the sound of the rabid fucker's lock breaking on its door behind me.

"What are you doing back here?" a shrill voice demands, and a reedy woman stomps her way over to me.

I throw my hands up like I'm under arrest and take a step back. "I was in the cat area and went through a door that led me here. I tried to get back, but I was locked in here," I explain defensively.

She shakes her head. "Sorry about that. I thought we got that door fixed. If you're looking for a dog, these are not the ones you want. They're all unadoptable. Follow me, I'll show you where the available dogs are." She moves to walk away, and I hesitate to follow her.

I don't want a dog, but I also don't want to be looking around for days or risk that my ancestors might throw something worse my way. As much as I hate it, I also can't help feeling a little bad for the pet reject. I look down at the gray four-legged Ewok, my senses confirming that he's the one, and sigh.

"Wait. I want to take this guy," I announce to her back, rolling my eyes at my luck.

I look for a name tag or something on the little gray dog's kennel and spot the name, Hoot. The woman turns, her gaze following my pointed arm to Hoot's cage, her brows furrowed with concern.

"I know he's cute, but he won't play or interact much with you. He seems to only be interested in sleeping and rubbing himself on things. He's been adopted and brought back multiple times," she warns, clearly assuming all of that information will have me rethinking my decision.

What *she* doesn't know is that his laziness and lack of interest in being a *pet* isn't a deterrent for me, it's a selling point.

"I'm cool with that," I chipperly admit. "I'm not into all that dog crap anyway," I confess, which just makes her eye me warily.

She looks at the squat, flat-faced dog sympathetically and then back to me. With a shrug, she walks back to where I'm standing in front of the little dog's kennel. "There's a lot of paperwork to fill out. If you qualify for adoption, then I'm fine with you trying your luck with him. He's going to be put down in a couple days anyway, maybe this is the last chance he deserves."

A hopeful smile sneaks across my face, and Hoot gives an indecipherable snort. Looks like I just found my familiar.

"Hear that ancestors? Step two is in the bag," I announce happily, hoping that they appreciate how quickly and obediently step two went.

"What's that?" the shelter worker asks, a hint of concern in her tone.

"Oh, nothing," I reassure her with a chuckle that I hope makes me look friendly and normal and not unhinged. Judging by the look she gives me before she continues on, I'm not completely successful. I brush the judgment off and internally high-five myself. Step three, here I come.

3

I watch Hoot out of the corner of my eye. He's sitting in the passenger seat, his head resting on the doorframe as though it's just too heavy to hold up. The window is down, and the wind is making his jowls flop around in a way that would be cute if I liked dogs. I'm worried he's going to make a break for it out the car window, but so far he seems chill and pretty content to sloth along wherever I want to take him.

We've been bound to each other for about twenty-four hours now, and it's going about as well as I could hope. He wasn't fazed in the slightest by the incantation or power that swept over both of us when I linked him to me. In fact, I'm pretty sure he snored through most of it. I did discover, mid-shower this morning, that he has a weird penchant for wanting to rub himself all over my dirty underwear, but I suppose we all have our kinks.

The overwhelming scent of rotten eggs fills the car, and I groan and cover my nose with my shirt. I glare at Hoot, who couldn't give two shits about the ass bombs he keeps dropping. I have the sneaking suspicion that he was adopted and returned because of the Bog of Eternal Stench that lives in his ass and not the mellow way he has about him. Gagging, I quickly roll down my window to combat the reek. So much for pretty curls today. I'd rather sport a lion's mane at this point than breathe through the noxious fumes my familiar likes to bestow upon me. My eyes start to water, and I fan the air in front of my face to help dilute the smell.

"Couldn't have crop dusted me back at the shelter and warned me about what I'd be dealing with *before* I bonded my soul to yours?" I grump as I wipe the fetor-induced tears from my eyes. He gives a snort that I swear feels like a *you're stuck with me now, witch*.

Shaking my head, I turn the fan in the car to high in an effort to help dissipate the stink trying to settle into my upholstery. I steer into the parking lot of my grandmother's shop and take it in as I pull slowly into the spot marked with a sign that reads *Owner*. Melancholy seeps into me as I turn off my car. I take a moment to stare at what used to be Grammy Ruby's place, knowing that as soon as I walk through the front doors, it all becomes mine.

Hoot is tight on my heels as I step out of my car and reverently stand in front of the whitewashed brick building that houses the *metaphysical* shop on the ground floor and an apartment above. I'm supposed to move in here, but the thought of taking over my Grammy's home so soon makes me feel uneasy. So I don't plan on actually doing that until my apartment catches onto the whole dog thing and kicks me out, leaving me with no choice. The building is old and charming, but it's been taken care of and kept up. It sits on the end of a cozy small-town-feel kind of street with other quaint shops speckled here and there.

We get a steady trickle of tourists because we're not too far away from Salem. Hotels and B and Bs are occasionally cheaper here, so a lot of visitors like to stay and make the drive or ferry ride over to visit the more exciting cities next to us here in Marblehead. I have the option to pick up shop and move anywhere I want, but I just can't picture wanting to be anywhere but here. The trees, the ocean, the Massachusetts accent, what more could a girl need?

It's weird how much has changed in the last day, and yet this place looks the same. I don't know what I expected when I was driving over here; I thought it would feel different maybe, but strangely it feels like it always did to me. Grammy Ruby was a minimalist and didn't like change. I know it won't take long to clear her things from both spaces and take them over with mine, but it feels wrong. I know the bones will forever connect me to her, but I'll miss her immensely. Packing up her life isn't going to feel good. I know she was ready to go, but selfishly *I* wasn't ready. I'm still not.

The closing of my car door echoes around the empty street as I prepare myself for the next task at hand. The shop's name, The Eye, sits white and pristine above a fig-colored awning. The large windows bordering the front doors announce *Psychic Readings* in text so large that it's readable from the two-lane street as you drive by. There's a sacred geometric shape stenciled in the background that looks like a large flower, but if you study it closely, you'll see that each line of the drawing is composed of a bone. I finger the skeleton key on my keyring that opens the shop, batting away the feelings of inadequacy and intimidation.

I can do this. I can honor the call of my ancestors.

I steel myself and grumble internally to *stop stalling*. No amount of standing out here and staring or reminiscing is going to change the fact that I'm the line's Osteomancer now. I need to stop focusing on how hard this is going to be or how bad I'll feel about it and find a way to make it work. With that, I straighten my spine and walk confidently to the front of the shop. I slip the key into its partnering lock, and with a snick, open the doors to the rest of my life.

Incense, sage, and verbena greet me as I step into the sunshine streaked space. My gaze roams over the different stones and crystals on display, either for sale or positioned in the shop for some other purpose. Dried herbs and other bottled ingredients take up a whole wall to my left, housed on rustic wood shelves that could use a good dusting. A saffron-hued curtain separates the main part of the shop from the area where Grammy Ruby liked to do her readings. I breathe it all in, and for the first time since the bones appeared on my dining room table, I feel a little hopeful.

Each generation of Osteomancer makes a shop their own, moving, updating, and tweaking things as they see fit. Sometimes they come in and overhaul everything, sometimes they change nothing. I've been here mere seconds, and already I can envision iron and glass shelves, blond hardwood on the ground, and a sleek neutral color palette with a warm inviting feel. Massive cushions should be positioned around the place for customers to relax on while they page through magic books or pick out their next tarot deck. I picture potions and tinctures packaged in modern glass bottles, with my family's sigil pressed into wax on the seal. I may not be ready for all the magic and mayhem that comes with this new title, but the redecorating, I can definitely handle.

I step past the rows of shelves in the middle of the shop and step through the curtain that leads to the reading area. I immediately imagine antique barn-style doors to close off and separate the space instead. Light streams through the sheer curtains and settles on a large round ebony table that sits in the middle of the room. I won't be the one to remove it as it's been a fixture in my family's shop for more generations than I could count. I make a note to get some colorful armchairs for this area and to look at some textured wallpaper options. I want a cozier vibe back here as opposed to the ominous feel it has now with all the dark purple and black. It's time to bring this psychic crap into the twenty-first century.

The wood of the stairs groans under my weight as I start up the flight that leads to the apartment above the shop. A familiar tinkling sound of the chimes above the front door reaches me, and instead of going up, I turn on the spot and rush back down.

Shit. I must have forgotten to lock the doors.

"Sorry, we're closed," I announce as I burst through the saffron-colored curtain and rush toward the front of the shop to intercept whoever just walked in.

"We'll be open in a couple months..." I continue, but when I exit the potions aisle and turn toward the front door, I smack right into a large, hard chest.

An *oomph* escapes me, and I stumble back, ricocheting off a wall of pure muscle. Large hands grab me by my shoulders and keep me from ass-planting myself on the linoleum floor. I press my palms against man pecs to steady myself, and then I look up. And up. And then up a little more before finally settling my gaze on what is probably the most attractive face I've ever seen.

I just body checked Joe Jonas's hotter, beefier, and more masculine looking older brother. Creamy olive skin, hair the color of rich freshly ground coffee, a five o'clock shadow I want to lick off his perfectly angled jaw. The man's bright moss-green eyes look me over, and I'm so close to him I can take in the small ring of gold that circles his pupils. He has a scar that starts a couple inches above his left eyebrow and slashes down his face, stopping just under his cheek. The large scar does nothing to take away from his overall gorgeousness. If anything, it adds a more feral vibe that I suspect any red-blooded woman would find utterly irresistible.

I stop teetering long enough to realize that I'm gawking. I should probably say something. Perhaps a *sorry for the pinball impression I just did against your rock hard body*. But nope, no words come out of my mouth; instead, I just continue to gape at him. At some point, and I couldn't say when, I started to pet his chest. The button-down shirt he's wearing is incredibly soft, and I wonder what the material is, because it's entirely too lush to be cotton.

Realization dawns on me, and I snatch my hand back, stepping away from the physical manifestation of all of my best dreams. I back up, his strong grip falling away as I put distance between the two of us. A part of me, one I like to call my inner fiend, really wishes he would have just kept holding on. That same part of me is really hoping he'll pin me against a wall and show me what he's really all about, which is exactly why *it* gets shoved to the far recesses of my deranged brain and ignored for the more logical and socially acceptable parts that can be trusted to deal with a complete stranger.

"Hi. Um, super sorry, but we're closed. I must have forgotten to lock the door when I came in to do inventory. We should be open again in about a month, give or take maybe another month. I really, *really* hope you'll come back for whatever you need then. We'll do a grand re-opening with all kinds of fun things...and coupons..." I finally get a hold of my runaway mouth and stop talking.

Coupons? I want to crawl into a corner and rock back and forth until the mortification goes away. I'm pretty sure I also just said *really* twice. Well, *that* will become a moment I relive late at night when I'm trying to go to sleep but instead rehash every dumb or embarrassing thing I've ever done in my life.

He smiles at me, flashing his straight white teeth, and I force myself to take another step back in hopes it will keep me from being further twitterpated by whoever he is and whatever he wants.

"Are you Ruby?" he asks, a glint of confusion and interest in his swirling green gaze. "I'm Rogan Kendrick, we spoke on the phone earlier this week."

"Oh," I coo loudly before I can stop myself. I clear my throat and try to wrangle my hormones. "Yeah, no," I start again more somberly. "I'm her granddaughter Lennox. I'm sorry to tell you that Ruby passed away...yesterday actually," I inform him somewhat awkwardly, as a plume of sadness settles over me like my own personal rain cloud.

Surprise, disappointment, and then strangely defeat seeps into his quagmire-kissed gaze at my announcement, and his shoulders slump as he steps back and runs his fingers through his silky hair.

"I'm so sorry..." I offer, when I see how upset he is by the news. I immediately want to ask how he knew my grandmother, but then I recall that he didn't know what she looked like so he couldn't have known her well enough to warrant this level of emotion at hearing that she's died.

I watch as his eyes move around the shop and land on the velvet purple bag of bones I set by the register when I walked in. His gaze flashes to mine, a flicker of hope burning on a wick of desperation in his stare. And then he goes and ruins all of his gorgeousness by looking deep into my eyes and saying, *"Tedas ruk shaw aus forin ve* Osteomancer. *Ise hiruse ou fooiq tork shin iei."*

Warmth licks up my body to wrap around my wrists, neck, and ankles. My eyes widen with shock and then betrayal, as I recognize the first half of the incantation he just made. I spoke those very words myself to Hoot when I bound him as my familiar. My Mancer is as rusty as a battleship at the bottom of the sea, but aside from this asshole claiming me as his familiar, he just bound me to him in another way. I only recognized a couple of words, but it's enough that panic and rage are now surging through me, and I'm about to get my money's worth out of the years of kickboxing classes I've been taking.

I don't know what Rogan Kendrick expected me to do when he violated magical law and bound me to him, but judging by the way he crumbled like a cardboard box, me punching him in the stomach wasn't it.

"What the fuck?" I demand, outraged as I go for a follow-up knee to the face.

He leaps back, saving his head from my patella and his dick from my Converse by mere inches. He slams into a shelf of lace dream catchers and crystals, hitting it so hard that it comes crashing down. I dive to get out of the way of the large wood shelves, just barely missing being clipped by them. Rogan stands up on the other side, annoyingly recovered from my hit, and glares at me.

He. Fucking. Glares. At. *Me*.

I pick up a candle and chuck it at him, following that up with another candle and another. He's dodging and batting away projectiles, while Hoot just lies in the corner, calmly taking in the show.

"Please, just hear me out?" Rogan pleads when I almost brain him with a glass bottle of love potion. He eyes the shelf I'm pulling my missiles from, and we both come to the same realization at the same time: I'm about to run out of things to throw. There are shelves of incense behind me, but they don't pack the same punch that potions, rocks, and candles do. I reach for another glass bottle, and the next thing I know, I'm being tackled. He just leaps over the tipped bookshelf like a graceful cat, and down I go like some grasshopper that didn't even know it was being hunted.

Sonofabitch.

This soul-stealing bastard is heavy, and I'm suddenly cursing all the muscles that I was just drooling over. Should have fucking known he was too hot to be trustworthy. It's always the pretty ones you have to look out for, my Aunt Hillen has always warned. Hate when she's right. Rogan pins my wrists down on each side of my head in a way that would be sexy if he hadn't just stolen me and connected us forever. I struggle against his hold, panting and screeching like a vengeful banshee from the depths of hell, but neither Rogan nor Hoot seem to be fazed at all by anything that I'm doing.

"Just listen to me," Rogan grunts as I struggle to get free. "I need help. All you have to do is help me, and then I swear your life is your own again. This doesn't have to be permanent if you'll just cooperate."

"If I'll cooperate?" I seethe. "I'm going to kill you and grind your bones to dust. Then I'll curse them so that you come back every week just so I can kill you again. I'm going to spend my entire existence making you suffer," I snarl into his face. And just when I think I can't get any madder, he goes and gives an amused smile at my threats.

"No, Osteomancer, because what happens to my soul, happens to yours. What happens to my bones, happens to yours. We are bound now, and unless I remove it, there isn't a thing you can do to change that."

Betrayal and terror bubble up in my throat, but I swallow it down and headbutt him. I wasn't quite prepared for how badly that was going to hurt, but neither was he, and we both let out pained groans and shield our faces. My forehead is throbbing, whereas he's holding his nose.

"Lennox, please. I'm begging you. I need your help, and you don't know it yet, but you need mine," he tells me, his deep voice a hint more nasal.

That probably has something to do with the blood I see seeping through his fingers. Good. Hope I broke his too perfect nose. At that thought, he reaches out to me with a bloody hand and smears crimson ichor down my chest.

"What the fu—" I bellow at the same time he growls, "*Seno.*"

And then, just like that, I feel consciousness drain away, and everything goes black.

4

My head aches and I feel like I've been sucking on dry cotton balls. "I Put a Spell on You" starts playing quietly, and I'm too befuddled to figure out why it's playing or where it's coming from. I peel my eyes open, confused. Dark purple walls and familiar smells offer comfort and reassurance as I take in my surroundings, and then my eyes land on him.

I should feel relieved at the fact that I'm still in Grammy Ruby's—I mean, my—shop and not in some dank basement, chained to a wall, but all I can feel right now is pissed. Well, that and like I just went ten rounds with a grizzly bear.

Ugh. What did he do to me?

I let out an irritated groan and try to sit up as the song ends. I notice that the soul thief is currently holding Hoot and scratching him behind the ears. Hoot—being the traitor that he is—is loving it. My growl sounds more akin to a groan as I push up from the onyx table that my ancestors have used for their readings for longer than anyone knows.

"Put him down," I order, glad that I sound more annoyed than pained.

Rogan studies me for a moment, and I can't discern if

he's checking that I'm okay or looking for weaknesses. He pulls Hoot up to his face and kisses the top of his head and inhales deeply.

"Did you just get a bath, little buddy? You smell so good, you handsome little tater tot," he coos at him.

I bite back a scoff as I watch Rogan kiss him again. Hoot rubbed himself all over my dirty underwear while I was in the shower this morning. The only thing he smells like is eau de mon vagina. Rogan's eyes never leave mine as he gives Hoot one last rub down and then sets him on the ground. Hoot snorts and trots out of the room, and I feel some of my worry and tension drain as my familiar moves far away from this man.

"So I guess the *what happens to my bones happens to yours* is a load of crap since you don't look like someone just knocked *you* out," I grumble as I try to talk my muscles into helping me move.

"I said what happens to *my* bones happens to yours, not the other way around. I bound *you* to me, not me to you. That's how a familiar bond works."

"I thought you couldn't do that with humans?" I growl as fury rocks through me. I use it to fuel my movement.

I scoot off the ebony table, feeling a little too *virgin sacrifice* perched atop it to find out what the hell is going on. Rogan's moss-green eyes watch me intensely as I get to my feet. I take a second to test my weight to ensure my legs don't crumble beneath me, and just when I'm sure that I'm good and ready to ball my fist and take another swing at his too handsome face, his smooth voice stops me.

"I'll put you out and wait for you to wake up as many times as I need in order for you to hear me," he threatens, but he says it in such a silky assured way that it takes my mind a moment to get past his tone and focus on the context of his words.

Tensing, I narrow my gaze at him and contemplate if I can run out the door and get into my car before this big asshole can catch me.

He tsks at me as though he can see my thoughts painted in the air clear as day.

"Can you read my mind?" I demand, frustration and helplessness overflowing in my veins.

"No, but I can read your face. And yes, you can create a familiar bond with humans and, like in this case, with other witches. It takes a level of power most magic users don't possess anymore, which is why they've outlawed the practice. It was killing too many of us."

His arrogance grates on my last nerve, and I'm not even sure how to respond to anything he just said. "Who are you, and what do you want?" I snap.

He leans back in the obsidian velvet wingback chair that my Grammy used to love. I try not to give in to the anger that surges in me as he makes himself comfortable in it, and focus on what to do about him.

There are rules about familiars, and this guy just admitted to breaking most of them. If I could just find a member of the Order and report him, I should be good. They would know what to do, how to fix this. The only problem with that is, I have no idea how to find one. I don't have the foggiest clue how any of this really works, because I've been a damn Osteomancer for less than a day.

"My name is Rogan Kendrick," he starts, pulling me from my powerless thoughts. "I'm sorry to do what I did to you, but you need protection, and I need your help. We're running out of time."

I cross my arms over my chest and cock an eyebrow, silently saying *go on*.

"A week and a half ago, my brother disappeared. I'm trying to find who took him, and for that, I need your help."

Empathy swells in my chest, but I remind it that this guy just broke magical law and bound us together without my consent, so it can just fuck off. "What is it that you think *I* can do?" I snap, half irritated with him and half irritated with how quickly I felt bad for him despite what he's just done to me.

"For starters, you can tell me what you get from this," he explains, reaching into his back pocket and pulling out a small plastic bag, containing what looks to be a light gray powder.

"And it never occurred to you to just ask me to help you with that?" I demand, pointing to the bag in his hand and trying really hard not to punch him again.

"That's initially what I hoped Ruby would do. That's why I came out here. But when you said that she had died, I worried that they had gotten to her somehow and that you would be next," he defends, and my brow furrows with confusion.

"Who is *they*?"

Rogan pushes out of my grandmother's chair and runs a hand through his hair. "I'm not sure," he confesses, deflating slightly, and alarm bells go off in my head.

This dude is mental. I've been attacked and bound to a man that is certifiable. Oh goody.

I take a step back, and his eyes narrow. Of course he has gorgeous long black eyelashes framing his already captivating green eyes. He's the most dangerous *lure* I've ever seen: mouthwatering on the outside with a crunchy batshit-crazy center.

"Don't look at me like that," he growls.

"Excuse me? You waltzed into my shop, magicked me, and dropped your crazy right on the ground for all to see. I'll look at you any damn way I want to."

"I'm not crazy, and I'm not wrong. Something is going on

in the magical community. Someone is taking our kind. There are four Osteomancers on the northern continent—know how many of them are missing?"

I gape at him, not sure what to say.

"All of them except you."

"You're an Osteomancer?" I ask, surprised by the discovery. I figured we'd give each other the tingles or there'd be a *knowing* sensation that would come over me when I was near another witch.

"No. I'm a Hemamancer, my brother is the Bone Witch in the family."

It takes me a moment to mentally flip through my lessons as a kid and figure out what that means.

He's a Blood Witch.

I guess that explains what he did earlier when he knocked me out. "Wait, you can have more than one kind of magic in a bloodline?" I ask, shocked.

He gives me an incredulous look, like he thinks my question is somehow mocking him. "Did your grandmother not teach you about our world?" Moss-green eyes take me in with concern, and there's a definitive spark of judgment in his gaze.

"She tried." I pause, feeling sheepish and hating it. "Everyone in my family thought the bones would go to someone else. I didn't think I needed to pay much attention," I admit.

"So you don't even know what you're doing?" he demands dubiously, looking around as though he's now questioning what he's gotten himself into. He shoves the plastic bag with powdery remnants back into his pocket and starts to pace.

Technically he's right, but the way he's acting right now bothers the crap out of me. Yeah, I'm rusty and massively underprepared for the task at hand, but it's not like all hope is lost. I'll get there...eventually.

Warmth moves through me, and I can't help but feel like it's an *atta girl* from my Grammy Ruby. A small smile ticks at the corners of my mouth as the sensation washes over me, and a confidence I've sorely been lacking settles in my soul. I square my shoulders and step in Rogan's path. He's forced to stop pacing and look at me.

"Are you kidding me?" I demand. "You barge into *my* life, take things without asking, and now you're going to throw a fit because those things don't work exactly how you want them to. What kind of spoiled little shit are you?" He balks. "It's going to take me a minute to get my magical feet under me, so to speak, but I will, asshole, and so help me god, you will rue the day—"

Laughter cuts me off, and I stare open-mouthed at Rogan as another chuckle slips past his lips. What is with this guy and thinking threats and rage are funny?

"Did you seriously just say I would rue the day?" he asks.

"Are you okay?" I query. One minute he's pissed and pacing, and the next he's unhinged with amusement. Yep, definitely crazy. Another round of chuckles overtakes him, and I roll my eyes. "Listen, I'm clearly not who you were hoping for, so why don't you just lift the binding you put on me and be on your merry way. I'm sure you can find another Osteomancer to help you with your little problem." I gesture at his pocket, the one with the baggie and the questionable contents.

Rogan sobers, and the odd look that just flashed through his eyes gives me pause.

"You do know how to lift it, don't you?"

A red flush creeps up his neck, and my eyes go wide.

"You're seriously judging me and my Osteomancer proficiency when you're going around using magic you know nothing about?" I shout at him, stepping closer threateningly.

"I know how to use it," he retorts. "Just not how to undo it. And proficient or not, you're still my best hope." He pauses for a beat and fixes me with a determined stare. "You're mine, Bone Witch, until I say otherwise."

My fist is connecting with his jaw before he can even blink. Pain explodes in my hand, and I make a note to yell at my kickboxing instructor. Never once did that prick warn me about how badly it hurts to hit something without gloves on. Rogan's face whips to the right with bone cracking speed, but I'm reaching for the metal rod that Grammy Ruby keeps by her chair to shut the curtains so she doesn't have to get up to do it.

Rogan pulls me back, but I just get my fingers wrapped around the weapon as he does. I swing like my name is Hank Aaron, and connect with his shoulder. He lets me go, which makes me stumble back as he yelps and grabs his arm with his uninjured hand, but I don't have time to feel bad. I need to incapacitate him as much as possible and get the fuck away.

I swing for his leg, and it does the trick. He's down on the ground like a crumbling tower of cards, and I'm sprinting for the door. Yellow curtains billow in my wake as I shove them out of my way and run out into the main part of the shop.

Witches. What binds witches? I shout internally at myself as I search the shelves of the shop I played in when I was a kid. Salt is for demons, ash for angels... I reach the right bank of shelves and search through the bottles, hoping it will come to me.

Witch hazel, no. Turmeric, no. Wormroot, ugh! Frantically, I shove bags and bottles aside in search of something that will help me. Laurelwood...yes! That's it. I reach for the bag of wood chips just as I'm tackled from the side. I go down like Jim Halpert in that Office meme, wide eyes and all. The bag goes flying from my hand, and once again I find myself on the floor of my shop with Rogan's big ass on top of me.

I don't waste time with screaming and swearing this go-round. Instead, I muscle myself toward where the bag slid. I don't care if I have to drag him all the way there, I'm getting to the bag of laurelwood. Hoot wakes up long enough to see that we're there and then lies back down and promptly goes back to snoring.

"Lennox, stop," Rogan growls at me, his strong arms wrapping around me as though he's readying himself to pin me down.

I spot a pile of pink grains and reach out to grasp a handful.

"I don't want to hurt you, please!" he commands again.

Twisting in his hold, I shove my palm full of Himalayan salt right in his eyes. He shouts and bats my hand down, rubbing the sting from his vision as I wiggle away. The bag of laurelwood slides inches further as I scramble for it. I curse and stretch out as far as I can, my fingertips skimming the plastic. Just another inch. Hands grab my hips and start trying to pull me away.

I screech and reach with everything I have. Suddenly the bag is in my grip. I don't know how it happened as I was being dragged further from it, but it's in my grasp. Without hesitation, I flip onto my back as Rogan pulls me closer to him. His eyes are alight with ferocious determination. He doesn't look angry, more like an apex predator about to down the prey in its sights.

Let's see what he thinks about my foot in his neck. I kick for all that I'm worth, and he stops pulling at me to guard himself. He assumes I'm going for a crotch shot, and when his hands drop down, I aim for his neck instead. He gasps and grabs for his throat, and a victorious cheer goes off inside of me. Skittering back, I rip the bag open with my teeth and start throwing laurelwood around his bent over form. My breaths come fast and panic-filled as I scramble to my feet and rush to encircle him before he recovers from my assault. Wood chips fall to the ground in frenzied throws, and just when Rogan looks up at me with promises of retribution written all over his face, I close the circle.

A light moves through the ring of laurelwood, confirming its completion, and unsteadily I step back and exhale a sigh of relief.

He's trapped.

I'm safe.

Rogan watches me, his chest heaving from his efforts to stop me. I want to smile, crow something childish like *take that, asshole*, but the way he's looking at me steals the wind from my overconfident sails. A smile tilts one corner of his mouth, and I watch as he reaches into his pocket and pulls out a small switchblade. The blade slashes down his palm, and he tilts his hand to allow the drops of blood to fall to the floor inside the laurelwood circle.

"Your magic is bound to me, Lennox. Did you forget that?"

Well, shit.

With each vermilion drop, my heart rate picks up. I look around the mess that is now my shop, hoping against hope that somehow the solution to this new problem will be sitting right there in front of me. The Blood Witch starts chanting, and it tears a gasp from my lips as I feel a pull on the magic nestled at my core. A buzzing feeling overcomes me as a current of power flows from my veins into his.

Fuck, is this what Hoot feels when I use my abilities? No wonder he's been trying to choke me to death with his noxious farts. I rack my brain for a way to make it stop, but once again my lack of attentiveness in Witch 101 is coming back to bite me in the ass. I could scream in frustration at being such a shitty witch heir, but my lungs feel cold, and I feel like I'm being stripped of my essence from the inside out.

Words pop up in my mind, disjointed and unhelpful as the Blood Witch pulls on my magic to free himself from my laurelwood prison. I can practically hear Grammy Ruby's voice spouting off the different languages that witches use for their incantations, but none of it is helpful as a flicker goes through the barrier separating me and Rogan Kendrick. I can think of nothing that will give me the upper hand as he siphons *my* magic with each second that passes.

And then it comes to me.

"*Tedas ruk shaw aus forin ve* Hemamancer. *Ise hiruse ou fooiq tork shin iei.*"

Rogan shouts *no* as the last syllable leaves my lips, but the heat that slams into me denies his plea. My feet lift off the ground as a blazing force bows me to its will. I'm all at once consumed by power as I do to him exactly what he did to me. I bind his essence, his magic, to mine, making us both a conduit for each other's abilities. I seal the circle between our souls, and then I collapse in a battered heap on the floor as the power ebbs and I'm left seared inside and reeling.

"What did you do?" Rogan coughs out, his voice pained and gravellier than it was before.

"What you deserved," I retort, my own tone mimicking that of a chain-smoker of fifty years. If he thought I was just going to sit idly by while he treated me like some magical gas station, then he just learned how wrong he was. If you take from me, I'll take right back. I've always been an eye for an eye kind of girl. Let's see him command me now.

Rogan tries to push to his feet, his corded arms shaky

and his legs stiff. On the second try, he finally gets himself upright and fixes me with a glare. I'm still on the ground, and if I have it my way, I'm just going to take a little nap before I'm forced to start cleaning up the mess that's one hundred percent Rogan's fault.

"You tethered us," he accuses, his lichen-laced eyes all the more beautiful for the fury floating in them.

"No, fucker, you did that," I argue, trying and failing to get up myself. No way am I going to let this prick lord over me, disdain dripping from his every word. Maybe I can stand on a downed shelf, bring us closer in height. My arms do their best impression of over-boiled noodles, and I give up. Screw it, standing is overrated.

"*I* created an anchor, *you* tethered us!"

"What the hell does that even mean?"

"Tethering makes our power reliant. They're no longer individual sources of magic, they're linked."

"How is that different from what you did?" I demand.

Rogan releases an exasperated huff, and if I had the energy and Giselle Bundchen's legs, I'd kick him in the throat again.

"Familiars are a one way connection for a reason. We pull magic and energy from them as an extra layer of protection for us. We can also siphon magic and energy into them to be stored in the event that we get overloaded to the point of danger or death. The witch decides and takes or gives what he or she needs. But it doesn't work the same if the link is full circle. Both the witch and the familiar then have control, and that's dangerous. You just tainted a link that was meant for protection, and now calling on the familiar bond will be dangerous for both of us."

Well, isn't that just perfect. I haven't even taken my magic for a proper joy ride yet, and already I've wrecked it.

"Maybe next time you'll think twice about flouting

magical law and pulling crap like this," I lob at him, the accusation sounding impotent and juvenile even to my ears.

He scoffs. "Next time? There won't be a next time for either of us if we don't fix this. I don't know everything there is to know about tethering—other than there are several pages warning against it in my line's grimoire—but it's bad, really fucking bad. What the hell were you thinking?" he demands, reaching down and plucking me from the floor like my mass is completely inconsequential to him. He sets me on my feet, and I'm annoyingly too wobbly to immediately shove him away like I want to.

"*Me*? Are you kidding? This is *your* fault. Nobody ever teach you not to take things that don't belong to you? What were *you* thinking?" I defend on a yell.

"I didn't think you'd do *this*," he shouts back. "Ruby was powerful from what I understand, maybe even one of the most gifted Osteomancers left. I figured her heir would be even stronger, or at least that's how it's supposed to work. I didn't know you were worse than useless."

Wrapping my fists in his T-shirt, I release a threatening growl. "Worse than useless?" I repeat, hating that this conversation has me sounding like a drunk parrot that's only capable of regurgitating the insults he keeps flinging my way.

Is this asshole serious?

Menacingly, I use his shirt to pull him closer. It's a weird move to make, it feels very wild-west-saloon-fight—which isn't my usual style of aggression—but it serves to help me stay on my feet while yanking him around like he's the puppet and I'm the master. Or at least it would if he weren't so damn tall.

"Ruby *was* powerful, and like it or not, I'm the bloodline's next Osteomancer. I *will* get the hang of things, and when I do, do you really think it wise to fuck with me,

Rogan Kendrick?" My voice is even, and I have to school my features so as not to show the raw astonishment I feel over the power that saturates my every word.

A knowing runs through my bones, and my statement rings with just as much prophecy as threat. Goosebumps kiss a trail up Rogan's arms, and a visible shiver licks up his spine. His pupils dilate, the black overtaking the green, and we both stare at each other for a moment, the bottom of his pecs skimming the tops of my breasts with each heavy, traded breath we pull in and then release.

I'm not sure what's happening right now, but I'm not going to abandon the indignation and outrage I've wrapped around me like a comfy fall sweater to explore the intrigue that's scratching at the back of my mind—no matter how persistent it might be. No. This witch needs a reality check, we both do. I may have been doing this for less than a day, but I am the next Osseous heir, and none of my ancestors would stand for this shit.

"I think we got off on the wrong foot," Rogan tells me, his husky voice breaking the silence, his eyes searching my face, a hint of contrition in his studying stare.

"You think?" I deadpan, unfisting my hands from his shirt, the soft charcoal-colored fabric now scrunched and creased as though I've left my fury stamped all over it.

He doesn't move away, and his features soften ever so slightly. His shoulders drop almost imperceptibly as though a burden was just heaved squarely on them, and I feel more than see a heaviness settle in his countenance.

"I came here because I needed your grandmother's help finding my brother. She was my last hope." His gaze is earnest, and his tone is softly pleading. "Lennox, will you please help me? I'm running out of time."

His stare is intense, and I suddenly feel like he's too close. His presence is sucking up all the oxygen, and it feels as though this is more of an illusion of choice that's being offered than an actual choice. His long black lashes and green eyes do their best to hypnotize me, but I trace the scar that cuts down part of his face from brow to cheekbone to keep from falling into them.

I need to go through the guidebook I have somewhere in my apartment, and then I need to find the Osseous grimoire and see what it says about tethering. Fixing whatever happened here today is the priority, and then I need to stake my claim on this shop and get established in the magical community. The last thing I need is to get caught up in whatever is haunting this man and his family. Maybe that's callous, but his attempts to force me into helping him haven't earned him any of my sympathy.

I'm about to open my mouth and tell him no, but something happens that has me pausing. A stinging current strikes through my limbs. With a sigh, I'm reminded of the fourth task I was sworn to uphold: take over the shop and guide anyone the magic chooses. As much as I want to deny it, I know that I can't. The zap I just felt was inarguably the magic choosing him.

I have to help.

It's written in the stars with the blood of my ancestors.

And I fucking hate it.

5

Resolve leaks out of me like I'm a sieve. It's as though someone has come along and poked enough holes in my determination that not even my stubbornness can keep the purpose from spilling out. I have to help this self-righteous prick, and it's honestly the last thing I want to do.

Out of nowhere, Mary Poppins's "A Spoonful of Sugar" starts in my mind, but I mentally flip off the perky anthem and press the off switch to my subconscious's efforts to cheer me on. Dancing cartoon penguins and Julie Andrews's silvery voice aren't going to make this fucked up pill any easier to swallow.

I step away from Rogan, my teeth gritted against the capitulation in the move, and run my fingers through my dark-chocolate and cinnamon swirled curls. He watches me carefully like my surrender is suspicious and he's not quite buying it yet. Good. I may have to help him, but I don't have to be nice about it.

"Fix what you did to my magic, and I'll help you," I offer, deciding that he doesn't need to know that my assistance is already, so to speak, a done deal.

"I told you, I don't know how to reverse it, but I know who does. If you help me find my brother, I'll make sure to set things right. I vow it."

I study him for a beat and then nod. "So vow it," I agree, wondering what a vow looks like to a Blood Witch. It better not be that blood brother kind of crap, because science has come too far and taught us too much to go mixing our lifeblood all willy-nilly.

Osteomancers in my line will give away a bone. Usually something small from an animal, but the bone will be infused with the magic of that Osteomancer's promise. When the vow is complete, the bone disintegrates to dust. I hope this doesn't go in the direction of Angelina and Billy Bob. I really don't want to wear a vial of anyone's blood around my neck.

A switchblade once again appears in Rogan's hand. Now that I'm closer, I can see it's not just your run-of-the-mill pocketknife either. It's gold and it appears to have Rogan's family sigil in rubies on the handle. He better be careful flashing that thing around; we're not in a bad part of town, but people have been mugged for less.

Rogan pricks his finger and then draws a line of blood down the front of his throat. He whispers an incantation so quickly I can't make it out, and the next thing I know there's a tickling sensation on my wrist. I look down to see a delicate, ruby-red, lace-like circle with a swooping and elaborate *K* in the center. I stare at the magical tattoo for a moment, sifting through the surprise I feel over having it there.

It's like a demon mark, only demons mark a person's feet when they give or take a vow. I don't know what their obsession is with feet, but I remember my father talking about it when I was younger. I didn't know that some witches could mark others in a similar way.

I look up at Rogan, who watches me as he slips his knife

back into his pocket. His green eyes drop to the mark on the inside of my wrist and then rise to meet my gaze again. I nod at the question I see in his eyes. "Let's get on with it then."

A relieved sigh pours from his lips, and he reaches into his other pocket and pulls out that mysterious plastic sandwich bag again. "Can you read these?" he asks, holding the baggie out to me, his question hopeful and his movements hurried.

I take it from his hands, and the contents look like ash. I look up, perplexed.

"They were in my brother Elon's apartment. They were encircled in a ring of crushed rowanberries, and I think they're what's left of his familiar."

My eyes widen with this information. I know rowanberries have medicinal purposes, but I can't think off the top of my head what ceremonial value they might have. Anger and sadness simmer in my gut at the thought of a familiar being killed in such a brutal way. Maybe it was to weaken the witch, but it seems especially cruel and unusual. I was always told that familiars were off-limits. Then again, a stranger off the street just turned me into one, so what the hell do I even know?

I cradle the bag of ash in my hand and, with heavy, tired limbs, turn and walk through the rubble of the shop in the direction of the reading room. Glass skitters and tinkles across the floor when I accidentally kick it, and I can hear Rogan crunching behind me in my wake. My shop is a mess, and I wonder if he'll help me clean everything up after we discover whatever there is to discover from his brother's familiar's remains.

I sit down in a chair, my legs grateful for the reprieve, and take a deep breath. I've seen my Grammy do this before. I've watched her hold a bone and read it, gleaning whatever she can from its cells. I, on the other hand, have never attempted it. I can only hope it's as easy as it looks.

Rogan sits down next to me, and I can feel the tension pouring off of him and settling into the air all around me. Pressure pecks my skin, and it doesn't take the High Council to tell that there's a lot riding on this for him.

I steel myself, pulling in a fortifying breath, and then I open the bag.

Here goes nothing.

I dump some of the contents into my cupped palm, and my hand starts to warm. I close my eyes and feel the sensation, willing the remains to tell me their secrets. A flash of worry strikes through me as I realize that maybe the remains will have me watch their death. My stomach roils at the thought, and I try not to panic. I don't want to watch someone burning a witch's familiar alive or, worse, experience the sensations the animal did as it perished, but I might not have much choice in the matter.

I'm reminded of all the things I wish I had asked my grandmother when she was alive. I had a well of knowledge and experience at the ready, and I never bothered to tap into it. I know I thought Gwen was a shoo-in for this power, but I suddenly wonder if it made my Grammy sad that I never took more of an interest in her life simply because it was *her* life.

I try to compartmentalize the guilt and sadness that settles on me like frost on unexpectant spring leaves, and focus on the remains cupped in my palms. Nothing happens. I pour more of the ash into my hand and once again wait for magic to somehow show me the way.

Except it doesn't.

I give things a couple more minutes before opening my eyes and releasing a defeated sigh. Frustration immediately taints Rogan's demeanor. "Are you even doing it right?" he demands, pushing out of his chair and beginning to pace again. I've never seen anyone actually do that when they're frustrated, and it could be oddly soothing if he weren't so damn annoying.

I try not to get defensive over the accusation, because, real talk, maybe I'm not doing this right, but I'm not sure what else there is to do. Grammy Ruby would only ever hold the object she was reading. I never saw her mumble an incantation or add an elixir or powder to aid her. She just held the bones and spoke their secrets.

I shrug. "I'm pretty sure reading something just involves tactile connection and then interpreting the things that come to you. Maybe I'm wrong, or maybe these ashes don't have enough bone matter in them for my abilities to work. Did you try your magic on them?"

Rogan shoots me a withering look that makes it clear what he thinks about that question. "Of course I did," he snaps.

"And…"

"And nothing, I couldn't get anything. Maybe they're spelled somehow."

I tip my palm over the opening of the bag and spill the ashes back into the plastic receptacle. He could be right, but I don't sense any traces of magic on the remnants. "Are you sure these belonged to his familiar?" I question, trying to think through why there's no residual information on or in the substance.

Rogan runs his fingers through his luscious and annoyingly healthy looking hair and turns to pace back in my direction. "I can't be sure. Part of her collar and tag were sitting in the pile. It could be her, or it could be some kind of plant or decoy, it's hard to say," he admits, starting another round around the room.

"Okay, so start at the beginning and tell me what makes

you think he was taken and that the same thing happened to the others."

"I will explain, but first is there anything else you can do, any other means to test what that is if it's not the ashes of my brother's cat?"

Out of habit, I wipe the grit from my hand onto my pants and then immediately cringe when I realize what I just did. Disgusted, I hold my hand away from me as though it's contaminated. I just wiped mystery dead crap on my favorite boyfriend jeans. *Nice one, Lennox. Ew.*

"Um, again I'm new at this. I can *read* dead things but not do a reading *for* them, so that rules out tossing the magicked bones on their behalf. Maybe there's something in the grimoire that could work," I propose, pushing out of my chair and trying not to touch myself or anything else with my ash-coated hand. I leave the bag of remains on the black table and fish keys from my pocket.

Rogan stops his pacing to follow me, and I'm tempted to tell him to wait down here while I go up into my grandmother's former home alone. If I thought for two seconds that he'd listen, I would, but I get the distinct impression that he's used to being the one in charge. I don't really want him up there, a stranger in *her* space, or maybe I just don't want him up there to see how much her absence affects me. I'm already tethered to him magically; he doesn't need access to my vulnerabilities and what makes me tick too.

Looking back at him, I pause with the key in the lock. The determination in his gaze has me swallowing down my argument. His face reads *like it or not, I'm coming*, and I just don't have the energy required to knock him out to ensure my privacy. With a resigned exhale, I unlock the door. It swings open to reveal a set of golden oak stairs, and I tamp down the loss that rears up inside of me as I begin to climb them. I get about halfway up and realize that my presence never tripped the ward I know my Grammy had on the doorway.

She had residual magic encasing the entrance that would make you feel scared and have you either backing away or running up the flight to avoid the monster that you just knew was right on your heels. Maybe I'm immune to it now that the same magic runs through my veins. But when I look back at Rogan, there's no hint of panic, no sweat on his brow that would indicate he's fighting the terror he should be fighting by tripping that ward. He just looks at me curiously.

Maybe the necros cleared it when they came to smudge and retrieve Grammy's body? Cautiously, I turn forward and continue slowly up the stairs. I crest the landing that leads into the large studio-style apartment, and inhale the scents of my childhood. An updated kitchen sits in the right-hand corner with a large eat-in island and stools.

To the left is the wall-less bedroom. She put waist-high open-backed bookshelves around it to delineate the space, and a queen bed is set in the middle of it all, the white painted brick of the apartment serving as a headboard. Hanging plants above the overflowing bookshelves contain her favorite potions ingredients. And the table next to the bed is overflowing with candles, wax drippings covering the shafts and pooling on the cedarwood finish.

I expect to see the bed mussed from use, but instead I'm greeted by a smooth quilt, throw pillows, and extra blanket folded at the foot of the bed. I move in that direction, my Converse thumping against the wood floor, the noise matching the speed of my heart, beat for beat. Yesterday, my grandmother lay down for a nap, never to wake up again. I blink back the emotion that wells in my eyes and try to breathe through my sorrow.

The faint hint of necromancer herbs tickles my nose,

and I wonder how many of them came to retrieve the body and how long the ceremonies they do to cleanse and honor it will take.

Should we have a funeral? What rituals would she want at a burial? Or would she rather be cremated and ride the winds for the rest of time? I'll have to call Aunt Hillen and see what she thinks.

Rogan is silent behind me. I get the impression that he's trying to be as unimposing as possible, and as much as I don't like him, I appreciate the reverence with which he moves through my grandmother's home.

It's my home now, but I can't quite wrap my mind around that. I'm also still not comfortable with living where my grandmother just died. The family will tell me to gut it, redo the entire inside so that it doesn't feel like the same space or carry any remnants of death and sadness, but I'm not there yet. The shop makes sense, because it's what we're destined to do, sell our wares and offer readings and guidance as needed, but living in this apartment is a choice, and I'm not ready to commit to it yet.

I search for the small skeleton key that I know fits into the lock of the drawer on the bedside table. With a click, I pull it open, holding my breath as I wait for the grimoire to come into view. Puzzlement flashes through me as I fully open the drawer.

"It's not here," I mutter, shocked, turning to Rogan. "The grimoire isn't here."

His steps clomp closer to me as he moves to survey the empty velvet-lined drawer that I'm gesturing to like some vacant-eyed game show model.

"Are you sure it should be here? Is there somewhere else she would have put it?"

"No, she was always very careful with it." I look around the room as though the answers to the missing magical book will be there. My gaze stops on the made bed, just as Rogan holds up a long strand of red hair. I narrow my eyes at the sight and let out an irritated growl. "I know who took it," I announce, and then I stomp out of the room and head right for the stairs.

If those bitches think I won't curse them to the ends of this earth just because they're family, then they're dumber than I thought. Looks like it's finally time to play a much anticipated game of whack-a-snob.

6

The tires of my ancient Nissan Pathfinder squeal in objection as I take a turn just a little too fast. I probably just scraped the last of the remaining tread off of them, but it's for a worthy cause. Rogan reaches up for the *oh shit* handle to steady himself, and the hand he has wrapped around Hoot in his lap tightens. Wisely, he keeps his mouth shut as I rage-drive us over to my aunt's house.

I turn my attention back to the road, but I don't miss the tic of irritation in his jaw. He's not a fan of this detour. If it were my brother missing, I wouldn't be either, but without the grimoire, I'm not going to be much help, and Rogan made it clear that I'm his last hope. Or Grammy Ruby was. I'd feel bad, but I just can't find it in me right now, I'm too pissed.

I'm pissed at the bones and at my entitled family for stealing something that they have no business touching. I'm pissed at Rogan, and most irritating of all...I'm pissed at myself. I never took any of this seriously, and now here I am, chillin' in a pot of water like a frog that doesn't know it's about to be boiled to death. I don't like feeling stupid, and what's worse is *I'm* the one making myself look stupid.

I pick up my phone and open my contacts, I hit the speaker button as I take another sharp turn, and a shrill ringing fills the car.

"Hey, Lennard, you at the shop? Ma and I were thinking of bringing some lunch over," Tad tells me distractedly, the sounds of him starting his dryer in the background.

"Osseous family beatdown commencing in T minus ten minutes," I inform him on a growl, slamming my brakes as the light in front of me blinks from green to yellow to red much too quickly for me to safely shoot through it.

"Oooh, what did they do now?" he asks, eagerly.

"They stole the grimoire."

"Those rat-faced... Maaaaa! Get in the car, we gotta go!"

I hang up before Tad can say anything else.

"You," I snap, turning to eye Rogan in the passenger seat. "Tell me what I need to know about your brother and whatever you think happened."

He holds Hoot a little tighter. "I'll tell you everything, just watch the road while I do!" he orders, panic ringing in his voice.

I change lanes to pass a slow-moving car and wait for Rogan to get to it.

"It started when Elon didn't show up for a standing monthly appointment we have with a client. He doesn't do that...ever, so I knew something was wrong. We talk every day. I had spoken to him the night before to have him bring me some things from his garden, and I knew if something had come up that morning, he would have called me.

"I finished up with the appointment as best I could without him and then drove straight to his house. I called, but his phone went right to voicemail every time. When I got there, I punched in his code to the garage, and his car was still there, cold. Clearly, it had been parked there for a while. But when I went inside, things were...wrong."

"How so?" I ask, flicking my turn signal on and waiting for the green arrow to light up and grant me passage.

"It was subtle at first, a soda can on the counter next to a crumb speckled plate. The TV on and playing some twenty-four-hour football highlight channel. And then I noticed the bones he always warded his windows and doorways with were missing from where they'd always been. I wasn't sure what to think at first. Elon doesn't drink soda, he always says it's bad for your bones. He's a health nut and cringes at the mere mention of white bread, but that was the loaf that was open on the counter. The only sport Elon thinks is worth watching is hockey or soccer. He couldn't care less about football."

I slow as we get closer to a gated community entrance. This one isn't manned. It only requires a keycard to be swiped in order to have the gate swinging wide open to grant entry. Little does my aunt know that I have a client who lives in the same community. She used to come into my work twice a month, but when her MS started acting up, she asked if I could do house calls, and I've been scanning that keycard to get in twice a month ever since.

"When I went to walk past Elon's living room to check upstairs, that's when I saw the circle of crushed rowanberries and the pile of ash. It was still smoking. I called for him and checked everywhere, but he was just...gone."

"Did you call the Order?"

A disdainful scoff bursts out of Rogan. "They wouldn't help my family. The Order only cares about things that serve them. They're all about politics and power plays, not truth and justice."

I keep my thoughts to myself. I was under the impression that they were tasked with keeping the magical community in line, but what do I really know. Grammy Ruby never seemed too keen on interacting with them. She never said why, and I always figured it was a typical *cops make people nervous* kind of thing. A person could be the epitome of innocent and law abiding, but if a cop pulls up behind them, the anxiety and panic hits. I thought the Order were the witch police, but from what Rogan is saying, I might not have a full grasp on how they work—or don't, according to him.

"So what makes you think this is some big conspiracy instead of some messed up prank? Maybe your brother is shacked up with a girl he met, and the ashes are from the cleaner's vacuum exploding?"

An uneasy feeling churns in my stomach, and it's as though my instincts are setting off a *you're wrong* buzzer like I'm a game show contestant who just guessed an incorrect answer. Rogan shoots me an unimpressed look that has me questioning my own intelligence for a second.

"Elon wouldn't leave without telling me, and the entire situation was off. When I started looking into things, reaching out and speaking with trusted friends, that's when I discovered that there were others. Three Osteomancers and a Soul Witch."

"What could the kidnappers want with fertility magic?" I ask, the Soul Witch part throwing me for a loop.

"What do they want with any of them?" Rogan counters. "They're all alive, I know that much at least, but depending on why they've been taken, that could be a good or a bad thing."

The agony in Rogan's statement makes my chest hurt. I focus on the asshole side of the family that I'm headed to deal with so that my mind doesn't wander to dark places that play out scenarios of all the bad things that happen to people who are taken against their will.

"And how can you be sure that they're all alive?"

Rogan looks at me again like I'm an idiot, and I'm starting to get really tired of seeing that particular look on his face.

"If they were dead, their magic would choose the next in line, just like Ruby's did with you," he points out evenly.

"Oh, right."

Okay, maybe I earned that last scathing look fair and square.

"Magic hasn't transferred to anyone else in any of the missing witch cases, so whatever it is that someone wants them for, they have to be alive. I'm terrified *that* could change at any moment though."

I tear my attention away from the tic in his jaw and the sheen of pain that wells up in his clover-hued eyes. We both fall silent for a moment as the weight of his words settles all around us. "How much longer until we get to wherever it is that we're going?" he asks impatiently, and I suddenly feel like there's some hourglass of doom looming over us, each grain of sand counting down the milliseconds until everything shatters. I have no idea how I'm going to help him, but I know I have to, and I sure as hell know I need the grimoire if I hope to have any chance of doing it.

My SUV threatens to tip as I take a sharp left and force it to charge over a steep hill. "We're almost there."

I turn down a ridiculously long driveway that's lined with tall majestic trees that are just on the cusp of shedding all their green for a myriad of oranges, plums, and yellows. I hate my aunt, but the beauty of her property can't be denied. What can be denied, however, is her claim to own all of it. These eighteen acres originally belonged to the family in its entirety, but somehow through sketchy wheeling and dealing, they ended up in just one sister's name several generations ago, the Harridans. The property was then passed down to only her line instead of belonging to all the Osseous clan like it was originally intended to be.

The whole situation is fuel for feuds. Some of the family has given up on trying to change things, but it doesn't keep the rest of us from giving them the stink eye and cursing their every move. While I was growing up, Grammy Ruby tried to pull the tattered branches of the family tree back together, but now that she's gone—and with the stunt Magda and Gwen Harridan just pulled—there will no longer be any hope of that happening.

The dense line of trees thins as I speed down the lane. Up ahead, the driveway loops around a gaudy and ostentatious fountain spewing water from various statues' orifices. There's a mansion that was built on top of the skeletons of old colonial style homes that our ancestors built, and the monstrosity that now sits before me can't make up its mind between being some kind of English-inspired castle or a Craftsman on steroids.

We screech to a halt in front of the large entrance, and I turn in my seat. "Hoot, I want you to go in there and pee on anything and everything you can find, do you hear me, buddy? Now's your chance to say *fuck the patriarchy, I'll go where I want to go!*"

With that, I shove my door open, the hinges squealing in outrage, and jump out of the car. Rogan meets me as I come around the side and speed walk to the front doors. I'm not sure if they know that I'm here. I didn't go through the front gate where a guard would have called them to ask if I was authorized, but they probably have cameras somewhere that alert them to what's happening on the property.

I reach for the brass knob, and the door opens without the slightest hint of objection. "Of course the stupid elitist pricks didn't lock the door," I grumble as I let myself in.

Surprisingly, no one comes running to intercept me. I

call out *hello* a couple of times and give it a minute, but nothing happens. Well, that's anticlimactic. Even if Magda and Gwen are somehow not here, they usually have a whole staff of maids and cooks running about. I look around, not sure what to do. As much as I'd love to tear through this entire house to find the grimoire, Rogan's made it clear that we don't have a ton of time. If only I were a Sanderson sister and could call the book with an enticing sing-song voice. Shit would be a hell of a lot easier if it would come floating out to me from wherever they've decided to hide it.

A round mahogany and glass table sits in the center of the foyer. I stroll over to it and grab the large vase of flowers from its middle. I double-check that Rogan still has Hoot in his arms, and then I chuck what is probably a Ming vase—that costs more than everything I own combined—at a gargantuan brocade mirror that's hung on the wall of the entryway.

The sound of shattering glass slices through the quiet house like a knife. Shards of the vase and mirror crash to the marble tile below. Chunks of flowers and filler plop to the ground in a staccato of splats. And hurried footsteps pound in our direction.

"Well, that's one way to get their attention," Rogan observes behind me. He's looking around at the house, but he doesn't seem impressed or intimidated by the opulence; he just looks, surprise surprise, impatient.

"Theresa, what in the name of the equinox is going on in here?" my aunt demands as she rounds the corner, her lips pursed and her brows dipped with irritation. Her angry gaze lands on me, and she freezes mid-step. "How did you get in here?" she demands, her voice pinched and a little higher pitched. Her dreary gray-blue eyes widen with shock and a tinge of fear, and satisfaction warms me.

"You should really start locking your front door. Wealth

doesn't make you impervious to crime," I tell her, just as a slight woman in a crisp blue dress and apron comes rushing into the foyer. She takes one look at the mess, then at me, crosses herself and then promptly leaves. I'm not sure if she's making a break for it or just going to fetch a broom and a mop.

"You are not welcome here, leave," my aunt growls, steeling her spine, but the panic in her gaze gives her away.

"Oh come on, Aunt Magda, aren't you going to congratulate me?" I taunt, stepping closer to her. Glass crunches under my sneakers as I close the distance between us, and her whole body tenses.

"Mother, what is going on? I told you I need to study, but how am I supposed to do that if the maids can't keep from destroying the house while they're cleaning it?" a whiny shrill voice demands, and right on cue, my cousin Gwen rounds the corner.

Unlike her mother, she doesn't seem to notice that she has an audience. Her petulant stare is fixed only on Magda, as though she's solely responsible and needs to be taken to task. It isn't until my aunt trains her anxious gaze on her daughter, that Gwen takes a moment to assess the scene. Bright blue eyes turn and take me in, but instead of fear, rage flashes in Gwen's doe eyes.

"How dare you show your face here," she seethes, stepping in my direction, her hands balling into fists at her sides. I'm uncertain if she's about to throw a temper tantrum or a fist.

Rogan moves protectively closer to me, and both Magda and Gwen seem to notice him for the first time. Gwen stops, as though his presence has glamoured her and she's forgotten what she was just about to do. Her mouth drops a little with surprise, but she recovers quickly and delicately presses her lips together in an annoyingly enticing way.

I want to look over at Rogan to see if he's captivated and trapped by her obvious attraction, but I internally slap myself for caring. Gwen *is* beautiful. She's all long red hair, legs for days, and the D cups that her mom bought her for graduation. But she's a vapid, selfish, little twit, and if that gets Rogan the Ridiculous all hot and bothered, then more power to him, why should I care?

"Who are you?" Gwen asks, her voice breathy and missing all the acerbic bite that was just there for me.

I roll my eyes.

"Rogan Kendrick, and you are?" he asks, his tone dripping with manners he's never bothered to use on me.

Outrage hammers through me, and I turn an offended look on him. "Are you serious?" I demand. "I get magic whammied, and she gets Southern charm?"

Gwen and Magda both refocus on me, and it's like that mirror wipe challenge I've seen on some clock app: wipe, moony eyes and flirty smiles; wipe, vicious bitches with dagger-filled stares.

"Excuse the trailer trash, she's practically feral," Gwen tells Rogan with a sneer that morphs into an inviting smile when her eyes move from me to him.

"All these years, and trailer trash is still the best that you can come up with?" I taunt, unaffected.

"Listen here, you little mongrel," my Aunt Magda snaps, stepping even with her daughter. "Either you leave now or I'll call the authorities."

I gasp, forcing my eyes wide with fear, and throw a hand over my mouth. Rogan stiffens with concern just behind me. "Oh no, not the authorities," I plead overdramatically, bringing the back of my hand to my forehead and wobbling like I'm about to swoon. *Nailed that Scarlett O'Hara impression.* "And which authorities would that be, Magda, the Lessers or the Order? Pretty sure when either finds out that you've burgled a dead woman's house before her bones even had enough time to grow cold, and then stole things that don't belong to you, they won't be too fussed with me," I point out as I straighten up.

"Things that don't belong to us? They *only* belong to us. Gwen is the rightful heir, and every scrap of our magical lineage belongs to her," she snarls at me, outrage flaring in her nostrils and her dim blue eyes.

Gwen adds a haughty nod and crosses her arms over her chest. "Rogan Kendrick, now why does that name sound familiar?" she queries flirtatiously, snapping seamlessly out of her irritation with me and right into her interest for him. If I weren't so pissed off, I'd be impressed with her ability to multitask.

"Oh shit, my bad," I announce, popping myself in the forehead in a universal *duh* gesture. "Gwen is the rightful heir? I had no idea. Guess you won't mind showing me the bones then," I deadpan, dropping all the theatrics and leveling my aunt with a baleful stare.

She stammers, her gaze bouncing around the room as her brain struggles to form another delusional argument that we both know has no merit.

"We don't have the bones yet, but it won't be long," Gwen sneers, and with that obvious threat, I'm done fucking around.

I step closer to her, my patience for this situation tapped. Options pop up in my mind, as though I've just opened a closet full of magic and now I need to decide what to wear. I'm reminded of how I felt when I sealed the bones to me and more abilities than I could comprehend wove themselves into my very essence. It's as though, in response to my anger, some of those abilities are asking to be called on now.

Let's see what we're working with then.

The ground below my feet begins to quake. It's slight at

first, but with each steady step I take, the movement grows. The glass on the floor plinks and scrapes as it's jostled, and both Magda and Gwen shriek and reach out for each other as they try to steady themselves, their terrified gazes landing on me as I close the distance between us.

It may look like I'm controlling the elements, a power that an Osteomancer shouldn't have, but what Gwen and Magda don't know is that this house has been built on top of the graves of some of our ancestors who used to live here ages ago. Their bones have long since disintegrated, but their essence and power still remain in the very soil. *That* is what I have domain over, but these assholes don't need to know that. Let them think that I'm some meta witch, maybe then they'll think twice about fucking with things they shouldn't in the future.

"Stop!" Magda screams as pictures fall from the walls and a crack moves up the grand marble stairs to the right. "Please stop!" she begs.

"Where is *my* book?" I snarl, my tone not to be trifled with.

"We don't have it!" she squeals, but she can't seriously think that I'll believe that.

They thought they were big and untouchable when they stole the grimoire, but as the ground quakes beneath them and cracks climb up the walls of this eye-sore of a house, reality is dawning. Magda wants to argue, I can see it in her eyes, but she knows the longer this goes on, the more I will destroy. Right here in this moment, my wrath, my claim, is undeniable.

The power I feel coursing through me is heady. My heart is pounding with excitement as I connect to the essence of those who came before me. The magic inside of me feels eager and ready, like it wants to play and test its limits, but I'm not trying to get myself buried in the rubble of this house. I just want the grimoire and to never see my aunt and my cousin again. Their torturous reign of supremacy and entitlement is over. The bones have chosen, and they're no more special than any other average human. They're the Lessers they always mocked and held themselves above.

Out of nowhere, Theresa the maid comes running back into the room, a large chestnut leather-bound book clutched in her arms. Her gait is unsteady as the ground trembles beneath her, but she staggers toward me, determination etched in her features. I release my hold on the bones that are part of the very fabric of this land, and she hands me the tome. With it, she also passes over my grandmother's scrying board, her onyx pendulum, and a long silver chain with a pendant that has my family's sigil on it.

"How dare you!" Magda shrieks, stomping over easily now that the tremors have subsided. She raises a hand as if to slap the frail middle-aged woman, and without a thought or even an uttered incantation, I lift my hand and stop Magda's bones from carrying out the loathsome action. I'm a little taken aback by the ease in which I just wielded a lot of serious power, but I hide my surprise away and embrace the pride and exhilaration that bloom in my chest.

This whole magic thing is so much more than I could have ever imagined, and I can't deny, boss bitch looks good on me. Magda becomes a statue, her ability to move taken from her as easily as blinking. She can still make noise, but the screech emanating from her is nonsensical without her ability to move her mouth and form words. It all happens so fast that Theresa flinches back, expecting a hit that will never come.

"What the hell did you do to my mother?" Gwen cries out, pulling on Magda's raised arm. It doesn't budge.

She wails and tries to move her mother, to snap her out of the state that I just put her in, but she's more likely to snap her arm if she keeps it up. I have a hold of her bones, and she's not moving until this woman is safely out of here and I have some answers. "Did you think I wouldn't come looking for this?" I irritably ask my frozen aunt. "What was the point of stealing it in the first place?" I'm about to release my aunt's jaw so she can talk, but Theresa's next words stop me.

"They were going to burn it," she tells me quietly, and my mouth drops open in shock. "Gwen was going to read everything in it, and then they were going to destroy it."

Theresa's declaration leaves me speechless. How could anyone be so selfish, so reckless, so completely corrupt? Hate that I have the bones all you want, but the grimoire isn't just for me, it's for every Bone Witch that will come after. They would have maimed our line of magic, and for what?

Disgust fills me. I know the grimoire has protections, but I need to make sure that nothing like this can ever happen again. It's too valuable to allow anyone to get this close to potentially destroying it and crippling our magic forever.

"Thank you for protecting these things," I tell Theresa, my voice hollow with shock. Ignoring Gwen's peals of panic, I pull out my phone and slip a card from the back of my phone case. "I'm incredibly grateful that you did the right thing. I know it wasn't easy, and I know what it'll cost you," I tell her as I hand her my card. "Call me in a couple of days, and I'll help you find a *better* job."

"Thank you, sorceress, you are very kind. I'm so sorry that you were dishonored at the start of your reign. May those who stand against the rightful Osteomancer crumble like pillars of dust," she declares, reaching up and forming the sign of the cross on my forehead.

Surprise flickers through me like a sputtering candle, and I'm taken aback by her respectful greeting and unexpected knowledge of what's happening. I thought she was just a maid, but as she offers me her regard, I can feel that there's so much more there. Magic is wrapped around her like armor, and I can sense that it belonged to my Grammy Ruby. I can feel her blessing all over this woman. The distinct sense that she guided her here, for this moment, washes through me. I stare at Theresa, floored by what I suddenly know about her. She's from a line of coven disciples. I didn't even know they existed anymore, but I can feel Theresa's unwavering devotion to whomever the bones find worthy.

I'm flabbergasted by my grandmother's foresight, and shocked to know that devotees of magic still exist. I stare into Theresa's adoring brown eyes, and it's as though I can feel my Grammy's love and the plans she laid out for me. I know in this moment, without a shadow of doubt, that she knew it would be *me* all along. She set things in motion to help me, and I can only wonder what else she foresaw that I'd be up against.

I look over at Rogan, quizzically. Did Grammy Ruby connect us on purpose too? Did she know what was happening to the other Osteomancers? Is there more to all of this that I have yet to see?

I focus back on Theresa as she steps away to leave. I'm not sure what exactly comes over me then. A warmth breezes around me like it's a summer day, and heat caresses slowly down my spine. I'm hit by a similar feeling that percolated through me when I knew I needed to help Rogan. A calm and clearness sharpens my mind, and I know instinctively exactly what I need to do. I reach out to Theresa and rest my hand on her upper arm. Awe sparks in her gaze, and she holds her breath as I start to speak.

"May your line walk with the honor and steadfastness that you showed here today. And as long as they do, the magic of this line will guide and protect them from their first breath to their last. May this blessing and promise be woven into your very bones, and with it, feel my unending gratitude and regard."

Magic drips down her person from the top of her head to the soles of her feet. It's colorless, but palpable. A captivating shimmer that sparkles all around her as I stare reverently at the magic-laced blessing that moves to cloak her. I've never seen anything like it, and I'm completely floored by just how beautiful and utterly powerful it is.

Theresa's eyes fill with watery gratitude, and a wonder-struck smile spreads across her face. I look down at my hands, astonished. Did I really just do all that?

"I'm honored, sorceress, beyond honored. If you ever need anything, anything at all, please call on any Palliano. That's my family name, and my line will serve you like we've served all the Osteomancers that came before."

"Thank you," I offer and then cringe as Gwen's screaming reaches a whole new pitch.

Theresa leaves without another word, and I'm yanked from the calm of our exchange back into the harsh reality of screams and shrill demands to fix my aunt. I turn back to Magda and Gwen, who is now ruddy and splotchy from her efforts to de-statue her mother.

"Lennox, let her go!" Gwen shrieks once again, pulling at her mother's extended hand. Magda's face is frozen with malicious intent, her narrowed eyes and venomous grimace are the perfect encapsulation of the kind of person she is.

"Stop yanking on her like that, or you're going to break something," I warn Gwen as I open the camera on my phone and snap a couple of pictures of my aunt in all her heinous glory. This year's family Christmas card is going to be epic.

"Fuck you, bitch. If you think you're going to get away with this..." Gwen pulls on her mother again like she thinks there's a hidden lever that will release her, only this time when she does, a resounding crack fills the air, and Magda's arm from the middle of her forearm down, hangs at an angle.

"Oh shit," Rogan mutters, horrified, his fist in front of his mouth like it will trap the shock from spilling out.

"Oh god!" Gwen wails when she realizes what she's done.

I cringe and shake my head. I did tell her to stop doing that.

"You broke her!" Gwen yowls, her gaze murderous.

"Technically, *you* did that," I retort, pointing at my aunt and drawing an air circle around the broken arm she just acquired.

"Let her go right now!" she screams, sounding more like a whistling teapot than a human.

"That might be a bad idea..." I start, but Gwen cuts me off with a scream.

"Now!"

I release a resigned sigh. Fine, if she doesn't want to listen, that's on her. With a flick of my hand, I free Magda from the magic holding her in place. An agonized wail rips through the battered foyer, and she crumples to the ground, cradling her broken arm. Gwen drops with her, reaching for her injured hand.

"You stupid idiot," Magda snarls at Gwen, pulling her hand out of her daughter's reach. She looks up at me, pain and rage alight in her gaze. "Fix this," she orders, holding her arm up to me, the break now hanging at a complete right angle. "Fix this, or so help me I'll make sure those bones don't stay yours for long."

"Are you threatening her...again?" Rogan asks smoothly,

stepping past me and moving his body just in front of mine in an oddly protective way.

"She broke my arm!" Magda accuses, her scream rivaling that of a feral pig.

"*She* did nothing other than stop you from assaulting someone. Your obstinate and careless daughter did that to you."

Gwen's face scrunches in outrage, but Magda cuts off whatever vitriol she's about to spew at Rogan. Bet she's regretting all that drool she left on the floor when she first laid eyes on him. Must be a talent of his.

"You bring some Lesser into my home, attack me and my daughter, and now you let him talk to your blood like that?" she demands, and I snort out a laugh.

"Oh, we're blood now?" I ask, feigning shock. I could point out that Rogan is no more Lesser than I am, but it doesn't matter. She's either trying to offend him by using the slang witches use for those without magic or she's too dense to realize what he is. Either way, dealing with Magda is a waste of time. I got what I came here for, and I'm over being near such vile people. I'll need to cleanse myself and probably burn these clothes just to get rid of their evil eye and shitty vibes.

"Let's go."

Rogan nods and turns to leave. Hoot is completely passed out in his arms, like everything that just happened is the perfect napping soundtrack. The sight makes me smile. Such a weird ass dog. At least the butt trumpeting has stopped for the time being.

"You can't leave. You need to fix this, Lennox!" Magda screams after me, her fury bouncing impotently around the walls and marble floor.

I keep walking.

"Osteomancer! I order you to fix the damage that you've done!" she roars.

I shake my head, baffled by this woman's audacity. I stop and turn back to her, holding up the ancient grimoire that she stole and planned to destroy. "I would love to help you, but some asshole stole my book, and I wasn't able to learn how. Maybe put some Windex on it, I've heard it's a good cure-all, or..." I tilt my head, mimicking the gruesome angle of her arm. "Yeah, you should probably call an ambulance, see what the Lesser doctors can do for you. Good luck!" I call out sweetly over my shoulder as I turn to leave.

We clear the mess I made with the vase and mirror when suddenly Hoot wakes up and starts wiggling around in Rogan's arms like he's been possessed by one of those inflatable air dancers that businesses put outside to draw people's attention as they drive by. Rogan rushes to put him down so he doesn't make a jump for it and hurt himself.

I get ready for the *tater tot* to bolt, but surprisingly, he stops in the middle of the entryway and does what Hoot does best, he stinks up the place via one large pile of shit. The smell is like a jab by a heavyweight to my olfactory receptors. If I weren't trying to keep from throwing up, I'd be impressed with just how much the little guy had in him.

Rogan looks at Hoot with utter shock, like something that cute shouldn't be capable of something so vile. I would laugh except that would require breathing right now, and there's no way in hell I'm sucking those cloying fumes into these precious lungs.

Hoot finishes his gift and then trots to the door, me and Rogan tight on his heels. We hurry out, my aunt and cousin's rage-filled screams chasing after us as we go. I ignore the threats and promises of retribution, mostly because I'm running out of air and need to get outside with a quickness.

I'm sure they'll come for me again someday, but for

Magda, that'll be after a couple of surgeries and some pretty intense physical therapy. They may try to find another Bone Witch to fix her, but unless Rogan and I uncover the mystery of where the others have gone, I'm the only one left on this side of the globe.

I shut the front doors behind me, and the demon screams all but disappear. I take a deep, relieved breath and then another as Rogan scoops Hoot back up and looks at him like he's seeing him for the first time. I reach over and rub behind Hoot's ears. Guess my pep talk in the car really sunk in; he took that shit to the next level, literally.

A lightness creeps into my chest, and I can't help the smile that slinks across my face as I head for my car. I guess all those memes were right, victory really is sweet. I mean, I don't know that I'd say that it's better than any dessert I've ever had, but it's nice to come out on top for once. A girl could get used to this.

7

Screeching tires and the smell of burnt rubber assault me as a Prius comes tearing up the road, rounds the ostentatious fountain, and skids to a stop a few feet away from where Rogan and I are standing in front of the mansion that's now seen better days. Out of nowhere, a barred arm slams against my chest, pushing me back. I shout out an objection, but Rogan is already in front of me, an incantation pouring from his lips, as he throws a vial of some kind of potion at the ground. A thin veil of red shoots up in front of us, separating us from the car.

I grab onto Rogan's shoulder, but before I can tell him everything is fine, he cuts me off.

"Get back, I'll protect us!"

I roll my eyes and turn to find Hoot sitting on the stone walkway, watching, his expression bored. I motion with my thumb toward Rogan in a distinct *can you believe this guy* kind of way, but Hoot just blinks and then lifts a leg and pees on a planter that has a trimmed boxwood growing in it. He's really taking our chat to heart.

"What the fuck?" Tad yelps in alarm as he shoves his car

door open and stumbles out to take in the sudden magical wall of protection.

"Watch your language!" Aunt Hillen warns as she hops out of the passenger side of the car. "I swear if I have to tell you that one more time, Thaddeus Tristan Osseus, I'm going to wash that filthy mouth out with soap!"

I snicker at Tad getting three-named, and Rogan turns to me, confused.

"Thank you, king caveman, for your protection against my cousin and aunt. Whatever would I have done without you?" I deadpan, rubbing at my chest where he just arm barred me.

"I practically save your life, and sarcastic barbs are all the thanks I get?" he deadpans back.

"Saved my life?" I gesture toward Tad and Hillen. "We're not in danger, Will Robinson. I mean, it's a Prius, for heaven's sake, what kind of menace are you really expecting to pour out of *those* four doors?"

"With witches being taken, you can't be too careful," he argues, pulling his switchblade out and slicing a small line in his finger, all in one deft motion. He touches the barrier with a drop of his blood, and the claret wall dissolves like it was made of nothing more than vapor. I step out from behind my unsolicited bodyguard and wave at Tad and Hillen.

"I know I just met you, Rogan Kendrick, but I can already see that you have a tendency to shoot first and ask questions later," I point out.

He scoffs indignantly, clearly not possessing even a single ounce of self-awareness.

"Oh, you don't believe *me*, the girl you sneak attacked and forced to become a familiar? Or maybe we should ask the two innocent people you just tried to magically turn into bacon?" This only earns me an eye roll from him.

"Excuse me, hi," Tad coos as he waves at us frantically until Rogan and I both look over. "As much as I could watch this tête-à-tête that's just oozing all kinds of raw sexual tension all day, we have an ass kicking to get to."

"As if," I counter, apparently going full Valley girl with my denial even though I live on the wrong coast.

"Riiight," Tad snarks back and then points at the front door of Magda and Gwen's house in a *let's get on with it* kind of way. His mahogany-colored gaze is filled with such excitement I almost feel bad that I didn't wait for them.

I adopt an apologetic mien. "You're too late. The smackdown already occurred. In fact, there's probably an ambulance and some cops headed this way as we speak, so we should get the hell out of here."

"Dammit, I knew it!" Tad huffs out. "Stupid school bus, making us miss this. I'm going to track down that driver and fight her if it's the last thing I do," he declares, stomping back toward his car, and I laugh.

"She was like eighty. Give the old lady a break," his mom scolds, and I laugh even harder.

"Oh don't you start, Ma, you were just as excited as I was," Tad volleys.

"You called her a ninny when you finally passed her, isn't that enough?" Aunt Hillen asks as she opens up her car door.

I shoot an amused yet judgmental look at my cousin and mouth, *ninny?*

"She was," he defends. "And when your mother is the swearword-police, sometimes you need to get creative with shit."

"Language!" Hillen snaps.

Exasperated, Tad gestures to his mother while staring at me, his movements declaring, *See! I rest my case.*

I crack up and, with an amused head shake, move to

my car. "Don't worry, I got some pictures. Meet at my house, and we can all laugh about them until our faces and stomachs hurt. I promise to tell you every single detail."

Tad presses his palms together and tilts his head back to declare *thank you* to the heavens. "Good, and when we're done laughing at their expense, you can tell me who the hell tall, dark, and dreamy is and why he's out here instead of chained to your bed."

I can't even get a word in before he's closing his door and quietly starting his car.

Rogan shakes his head, but there's a hint of a smile on his face, and it's clear he's not opposed to a good compliment being thrown his way. With a roll of my eyes, I round my car, placing the grimoire and the other items that Theresa rescued in the back seat, then I jump into my rust bucket of a vehicle and fire her up. Rogan and Hoot slide in next to me, and Hoot's peeing on the boxwood gives me an idea. While Rogan buckles up and gets Hoot situated on his lap, I reach out with my newfound ability and see if there's enough ancestor essence in the hedges and trees around here to do what I'm hoping I can do. Sure enough, I find what I need, and with a snap, I add a little magical cherry on today's sundae of events.

Sirens sound in the distance, and adrenaline spikes through me as I hit the gas a little too hard and pull away. I giggle, and Rogan looks over, his brow crinkling with puzzlement for a moment before he finally sees my handiwork. "Did you just make all her hedges look like dicks?" Rogan asks me, and I can't tell if he's judging me or impressed.

I shrug. "Just a little something to remember me by."

He barks out a laugh, and Hoot lies down across his thighs. Instead of perving out over how muscular they look in the jeans he's wearing, I focus my thoughts on what the heck I'm going to do with Hoot.

He's not my familiar anymore, but I can't just take him back to the shelter. He was on death row there. Aside from the ass napalm, he's not so bad. I know I can't keep him right now, not when we're about to go searching for missing witches and the people or person who's taking them. It's not like I can strap him into a baby carrier and take him along for the ride, even if his gas can be weaponized. When things settle down, he's got a home with me, but what am I going to do with him for now?

A horn blares, making me jump. My thoughts are yanked from Hoot's plight to Tad's tan Prius as he pulls alongside me. He rolls down his passenger window, and I'm forced to crank the old handle that allows my window to descend.

"Last one there is a rotten egg!" Tad yells, and then the engine on his Prius whirrs as he pulls in front of me and begins the race.

"You ninny!" I shout at him, a wide smile on my face, and then I press the pedal to the metal.

"So I see *maniac* runs in the family," Rogan observes dryly, giving the *oh shit* handle on his side of the car more action than it's ever seen in its life.

"Well, if you can't handle it, Mr. Kendrick, you're more than welcome to just undo everything you've done to insert yourself in *my* life and be on your way," I tell him, my tone saccharine.

"Tell me something," Rogan starts, the look on his face assessing. "I thought you were new to this whole magic thing—"

"I am," I interrupt, not sure where he's going with this.

"Then how did you manage all that back there? No incantations, no herbs, no magnifiers or anything else that I could see helping you manage your newfound magic with such finesse. You didn't even need to tap into my magic to make it all happen."

I look over at him, a flicker of surprise moving through me. I could almost take that as a compliment. Almost.

"So if you're so new and underprepared like you said, how did all of that just happen back at your aunt's house?"

There's a hint of mistrust in his tone that I don't like, but instead of addressing *that*, I decide instead to answer his question, mostly because I think if I do, I might get answers to some of my own queries too.

"I'm not sure how selection works for Hemamancers," I start, pulling my eyes away from him so I can weave my way through this gated community and beat Tad's ass home. "But when I sealed myself to the bones, it felt like it unlocked this vault inside of my head. Suddenly I just knew things, knew I now had power, but not exactly how it would manifest.

"When I walked into Magda's house, I just felt so mad. It was like my emotions opened that same vault again, and suddenly I had options for how I wanted to use that power. I could have cursed them, tortured them, destroyed everything they had quickly or slowly. There were so many choices, so many different things my magic could do in that moment, all laid out before me like a catalog. I could sense the osteo matter in the ground, and that's just what I went for. It was as though I put it in my shopping cart and checked out. Then the next thing I know, it was happening. Was it not like that for you? For your brother?"

"No," he answers simply.

I wait for him to elaborate, but he doesn't. Uneasiness seeps into my thoughts, and I'm not sure what to think of that. Is what happened to me not normal? Is it different for each family or each stream of magic?

I commit right then and there to spend the rest of the night reading and studying. Grammy tried to teach us about *our* line and some general witch info, but there's clearly a lot that I missed. I knew there was magic, a little about how it worked and the things that my grandmother did. But my disinterest in knowing more beyond that has clearly crippled me here and I need to rectify that as soon as possible.

"So how *did* it work for you then?" I press, having no intention of letting this go. I assumed how things worked in my family was how it would work for any selection in any family, but Rogan's resounding no has me second-guessing and extremely curious.

"The magic in my line works like it used to when magic first joined with mortals and the first witches were born."

I raise my eyebrows at the very *once upon a time* vibe to his tale, but I keep quiet because it feels like I'm just starting a *Lord of the Rings* book or something.

"We're not selected later in life by chance, we're born with a spark of magic that identifies us as heirs. When we were old enough, Elon and I were sent off to study with the Hemamancer and Osteomancer of our line. We grew up with them, in this world, practicing everything we would need to know for when it was our time."

He explains all of this in a very matter-of-fact way, but I can't help but feel like the way he grew up must have been very cold and lonely. "How did your parents feel about having to send you away?" I ask. Even though I know I'm prying and it's none of my business, I just can't seem to help myself.

Rogan shrugs and runs his hand from the crown of Hoot's head to his rump, the motion steady and I suspect comforting. "My parents were matched because it was magically advantageous. That's how things work with the House of Kendrick. It all comes down to being the best, the strongest, the most powerful. My parents knew what would be expected of them if their children were heirs."

"Are there a lot of families that do things like yours?" I ask, surprised by what seems like an archaic set of traditions.

"Not as many as there used to be, but many founding magical houses are still there, and this is how they've always done things.

"It all seems so stuffy compared to how I grew up, so stifling. Are you sure your brother wasn't running from that?"

Rogan studies me for a moment, and I can't tell if he's thinking about the questions or looking for something in the planes of my face. "Maybe," he finally answers. "I don't think so, but I'd be dumb not to consider every possibility. But even if that's the case, how do you explain the other disappearances?"

"Are the other witches also from *founding houses*?" I ask in my best aristocratic voice as I mime holding a teacup, pinky out, of course. I honk at some asshole who cuts me off going half the speed limit, and angrily change lanes to speed past them. "Learn how to merge, you numpty!" I shout out my still open window, and then I feel like a prick when they give an apology wave. *Oops*, guess I'll just reel my road rage right back in. I return the wave as though we're now road besties and promptly putter away.

"One is," Rogan answers, ignoring my driving faux pas. "But the others are from newer lines."

I grew up in Massachusetts, so the whole *Old Money* versus *New Money* thing isn't new to me, but I'm a little shocked to see it's like that with magic too. I probably shouldn't be; I know enough history to see a pattern of this when it comes to most things. Religion, land, money, magic, politics, the list really is endless, and regardless of which option, there's always a group that wants to be on top, with people at the bottom hoping someday their lot in life will change.

"So what about you?" Rogan asks me as I take a sharp right and barrel down the street that leads to my apartment complex.

"What about me? You know how I got my magic."

"No, what's your sad childhood story?"

"Sad, what makes you think it was sad?"

"Everyone has a sad childhood story," he answers simply, and it makes me pause.

Maybe he's right. Mine's not ideal. I never really thought of it as sad, but an outsider could.

"My mother died giving birth to me," I offer. "It devastated a lot of people. She was pretty incredible, but it left me and my dad to pick up the pieces. My Aunt Hillen helped, and Tad is more brother than cousin, but as sad stories go, mine's a little lame," I joke as I tear into my parking lot and gun it for my building at the back of the complex.

What I don't tell Rogan is that growing up in my family was pretty great until I hit about sixteen. That's when my dad got cancer. I had the typical bad moments as a kid, getting teased for living in a trailer or not wearing the newest clothes and trends, but it wasn't until my dad got sick that I really learned what hurt felt like. And when he died, that's when I felt my first sting of betrayal.

I squeal into my assigned parking spot as though I'm a professional stunt car driver. I activate the e-brake and get ready to celebrate my victory, but when I look up, I see Tad and Hillen in all their gloaty glory standing just outside my apartment door.

My jaw drops in surprise, and Tad's smile grows even wider. I look over at the visitor parking spot to check that his Prius hasn't somehow morphed into a time bending

DeLorean or one of those rocket cars designed to break land speed records, but it's still just a Prius.

"How in the hell..." I ask as I climb out of my car. I had almost a perfect run over here, minus the road rage incident.

Tad reaches up and searches for the hide-a-key that I don't keep hidden very well at the top of the trim around my door.

A loud, mean dog bark sounds off next to me, and I turn to see who let a hellhound run loose in the complex. All I find is Hoot once again wiggling in Rogan's arms. Maybe he's not the cuddler that Rogan seems to want him to be. The bark sounds off again, and I'm stunned to hear that the menacing sound is coming from the tater tot. Shockingly, this pint-sized pup has a Michael Clarke Duncan kind of bark. If James Earl Jones were a dog, his bark wouldn't even be as deep or scary sounding as Hoot's.

Rogan struggles to keep Hoot in his arms, and he quickly bends to put him down.

"He probably just has to crap again. It's a good thing we're outside, but I'm going to go stand upwind until he's done," I announce.

But as soon as Hoot's paws touch the pavement, he takes off in the direction of my apartment. Someone's excited to be home, or at least one would think that if it weren't for the angry barking and snarling he's doing.

"What the hell?" I ask as I take off after him. Hillen will kill me if my former familiar takes a chunk out of her or Tad. Luckily, they seem to be oblivious to what's happening right now as Tad pulls my key down and goes to fit it in the lock.

"Stop!" Rogan shouts, and I snort in annoyance. Does he really think that's going to work on Hoot?

"Don't touch it!" he bellows again, and this time I'm confused by the instruction and the panic in his voice.

Hoot starts to scramble up the stairs like a pocket-sized Cujo, and I turn to ask Rogan what the hell is going on. Tad turns the key in my lock while simultaneously looking back to see what all the commotion is about. And that's when I see what the hell has Rogan so freaked out.

A white charge of power explodes out from my apartment door. It's like a magical bomb just went off, but instead of sending debris and missiles out into the air, the force of the explosion slams directly into Tad. His hand is frozen on the key he's holding in the doorknob as his body bends backward from the impact of the explosion. Tad's face and mouth are contorted in a silent scream that I know will haunt my nightmares for the rest of my life.

Horror jackhammers through me as, helplessly, I watch it all happen entirely too fast for me to stop. I scream and pump my legs even harder. Hillen's face collapses in confusion, and she turns to see the source of the terror written all over my face. I'm halfway up the stairs, practically climbing over Rogan when my aunt's keening wail slams into me like a nuclear pulse. The horrible sound sears my insides, promising that it will be a sound that I never forget.

Hoot reaches the top of the landing first, but instead of going for Hillen or Tad like I originally thought he was trying to do, he charges the front door and starts biting and pulling at something that looks oddly like a shadow. It's like there's a film on the door, and I didn't notice it until Hoot tried to peel it away.

"Oh god, what's happening to him?" Hillen shrieks, the raw pain in her voice like daggers to my heart. Rogan gets to them first, and he quickly pulls Hillen back from the door. Thankfully, she doesn't fight him but allows him to move her so we have the space that we need.

A horrible gurgling is coming from Tad, and there's no question that whatever is happening is fucking painful. My catalog of magical options pops up in my head just like it did at Magda's house, but before I can put anything in my cart and check out, Rogan has his knife in one hand and a deep slice down the palm of his other.

Expertly, he uses his blood to draw symbols against the film that's torturing my cousin. I recognize symbols for protection and banishment, and what he's doing sinks in. An image of a knife pops into my head, and immediately I know it belongs to my ancestors and is made from dragon bone. Need strikes through me, and out of thin air, the purple pouch of bones appears in my hand. I stare at them for a moment, not sure how they got into my palm or why, but I get the distinct feeling that I need to reach inside the bag.

Not willing to waste time questioning that driving instinct, I loosen the top of the bag, reach into it, and pull a hand-sized knife out. Shock rockets through me when I look down to discover that the dragon bone knife I was just imagining is now clutched in my hand. As mysteriously as it appeared, the velvet pouch disappears, and I'm left reeling and stunned.

My Aunt Hillen's crying pulls me from my stupefied inaction, and I shake away my bewilderment. I step up on Tad's other side, ready to get to work, but I don't cut my hand and bleed onto the attacking magic like Rogan does. Instead, I once again trust the push of my magic and use the bone knife to start directly carving my own symbols into the attacking magic itself. Image after image pops into my mind, and I trace each line with the blade into the hex that's been placed on my apartment. The shadow looks soft and malleable from the way Hoot is biting at it, but for me, it feels like I'm trying to cut through a diamond.

The muscles in my arm are screaming by the time I finish three symbols, but I can feel that what we're doing is working. Rogan is repeating an incantation quietly, but it's barely even a whisper, and I can't make out what it is. No incantation comes to me, so instead I lace each slice of the bone knife into the hex with my demand that it leaves, with my plea that Tad won't be hurt, and with my promise to fuck up whoever did this.

Tad's eyes are panicked and terrified as he struggles against the magical force slamming into him. His body is bent back unnaturally, his hand still clutching the key in the knob like it's some kind of lifeline. Pain radiates from every tense muscle in his body, and I want to scream in frustration at the torture I can see he's going through. I channel my aggravation into moving faster and working harder to free him.

Rogan has to slice into his hand three more times before I feel the hex start to really weaken. I've never dealt with a hex before, so I don't know if this is normal, but this fucker feels insanely strong. I call on all my strength and renew my efforts, slamming my blade into the vile magic.

I feel it sink through.

"Got it," I shout out, not sure what I've even got, but my body and the knife seem to be moving of their own accord, and Rogan backs up while I cut my cousin away from the harmful magic. I hear glass break behind me, and Rogan consoling Hillen, explaining that whatever potion he just broke will keep us hidden from anyone who might be watching.

Stupidly, I want to demand where the hell he's keeping all these potions, because with the way his jeans fit, I just don't see where they're coming from. But I've almost got Tad free, and once again the fiend in my brain is being annoyingly inappropriate given what we're dealing with.

Tad gasps as he falls away from the door and is finally able to release the key in the lock. I hold on to him, expecting him to stumble and groan until he's back with us, but instead, he collapses on the concrete, and it's all I can do to keep him from smashing his head as he does.

Rogan dives to help me, and we get Tad turned on his back, where I can see he's gasping for air. "He's choking!" I shout, but Rogan stops me when I move to try and clear Tad's airway.

"No, it's a residual jinx. Did your grandmother teach you how to do a cleanse?" he hurriedly asks, and my heart drops.

Shit, did she?

Tad's mouth opens and closes like a hooked fish that's just begging to be put back in the water. I can't think as he starts to turn purple, and the reality that he's dying right in front of my eyes clobbers me.

"Lennox!" Aunt Hillen screams, the sound a demand that falls on me like a ton of bricks. "Help him!" she begs, her plea so raw and broken that my vision immediately blurs as emotion overwhelms me. Rogan has to push her back with a snarled warning not to touch her son, and I feel something in me shatter.

"Lennox, did she?" Rogan demands, and the tears in my terrified eyes spill over as I look up at him.

"I don't know, I don't remember!"

I drop my gaze to Tad, tears dripping down my cheeks as my best friend's struggle for air grows weaker and weaker. He's going to die, and it's going to be all my fault.

8

"Lennox! Look at me," Rogan orders as panic climbs up my throat, threatening to close my airway.

My eyes snap to his, and the hard unforgiving glint I find in his gaze is exactly what I need to help me get my shit together.

"I'll walk you through it," he tells me, reaching under his shirt and yanking at whatever he seems to have hidden there.

A silky red pouch comes away in his hand, the straps that kept it hidden under his shirt frayed and damaged from being ripped off. He opens the pouch and pulls out a handful of loose herbs, sprinkling them around Tad, who has now stopped struggling, his body jerking with weak spasms as the jinx works to steal the last of his fight.

"*Adhaint*," Rogan commands, and the herbs immediately light and then go out, leaving a ring of scented smoke in their wake.

The smell of sage hits me, and the scent helps to calm my splintering nerves as I watch Rogan sprinkle liquid on Tad.

"Give me your hands."

I reach out immediately, placing my palms in his, and as soon as I do, I feel him activate the familiar bond and start tugging at my magic. I gasp, and he studies my face for a beat before saying, "Your turn."

I close my eyes and open myself up entirely, desperately searching for the connection between Rogan and me, like I did with Hoot when I first checked to make sure our familiar bond was in place. I find it easily, warm and strong and coiled around what feels like my essence...my soul. Surprise flickers through me, but I dismiss it. I'm not a Soul Witch, so I could be wrong, and now isn't the time to dive into what the hell Rogan's magic is doing there.

I yank on the connection, and a small grunt from Rogan confirms that he felt it. I look over at him, and I don't miss the same uneasiness in his features that *I* feel over giving someone access to something that should only be mine. It's as though he's tagged his name all over my insides, and all I want to do is scrub it away. I shove all my concerns and feelings on that matter aside, forcing myself to concentrate solely on saving Tad.

"Repeat after me," Rogan directs, and then slowly he speaks an incantation. He finishes and then immediately repeats it. I listen until he starts again and then add my own voice to the cleansing words. The smoke from the loose sage thickens around us, and the smell of a warm day at the lake billows out from the liquid Rogan sprinkled all over my cousin.

I close my eyes as the incantation spills from my lips. I shove all the magic I can into my words and picture it moving over Tad, clearing away the vicious magic that's clinging to him. I pour out my magic, begging it to save him, demanding that the powers that be make this right. Tears stream steadily down my cheeks as I release all my hope out into the world and pray that it's enough. I chant with all that

I am, terrified that I'll open my eyes and see that it's not working.

My hands squeeze Rogan's as fear and despair taunt me. His grip tightens against mine, and then something strange happens. A coolness trickles over me, not the frigid uncomfortable kind that I experienced when I sealed the bones to me, it's more like a welcome relief that's chasing away the heat and misery. It moves through me, tickling my senses, and then suddenly it feels like I'm not the only one inhabiting my body.

Another awareness is pressed tightly against me, and it sends all my nerve endings firing with all kinds of sensations. A tingling feeling begins to build at my core, but I can't concentrate on what the hell it is as image after image begins to flash in my mind. They move so fast that it's hard to make them out. Sometimes I catch what I think is me as a kid, sometimes there are other children who I don't recognize.

I catch an image of me on Christmas morning opening a toy horse set that I'd wanted for years. A boy cuddling a fat orange tabby. Me crying after my first mean girl experience in middle school. Two boys sneaking out of the house in the middle of the night to go fishing. A man screaming, his face contorted with rage. A pouch of bones that aren't mine. My first kiss. A fistfight between the same boys who snuck out to go fishing, but they're older now, and I can recognize Rogan in one of the teenager's faces.

I see my dad hugging me the day he told me he was sick. Bloody hands that are heavy with despair. Me, sitting in the bathtub, staring dead-eyed at the tiled wall the day I found my dad's note. A beautiful woman writhing in ecstasy as Rogan works himself in and out of her. My last boyfriend dropping to his knees and slowly pulling my underwear down.

Shock ricochets through me, and I try to pull away from the reel of our lives that's flashing in front of me, but before I can do anything, I feel the magic that's blooming in my chest intensify and grow blindingly brighter. It's as though someone just detonated a small atom bomb behind my sternum, and a pulse of light and power explodes out of Rogan and me.

It rips all traces of punishing magic from Tad and throws my Aunt Hillen against the balcony railing when it slams into her. The windows of my apartment rattle, and the door to the empty apartment next to mine cracks up the middle. I pant as waves of emotion and sensation power through me. Confusion, need, loss, interest, frustration, it's hard to think through everything that's bombarding me, demanding my immediate attention.

My hands are still in Rogan's, but both of us have stopped chanting. I look down to find Tad's healthy pallor is back, and he's pulling in deep long pulls of air. I try to reach for him, but my hands are trapped in a steely grip. My gaze snaps up, and green eyes are fixed on mine. Rogan stares at me intensely, his own breathing hard and his cheeks flushed.

Did he just see everything I did?

I stare at him for a beat, as though I could read the answer to that question in his gaze, but when Tad gasps and sits up, Rogan releases my hands, and whatever was just happening between us pops like a fragile balloon.

I wrap Tad up in a bone-crushing hug, and Aunt Hillen tackles us both with a sob. "Thank you, thank you, thank you," she murmurs over and over again as she checks both of us until she's satisfied that we're okay. Tears drip down all of our faces, and we hug and cry and take a moment to just be with each other again.

"Are you okay?" I ask Tad as he separates from our strangleholds. He rubs his hands down his face and musses up his light brown hair.

"Yeah, I think so," he declares, sounding a bit in shock. "I have a headache, and I feel like I was just struck by nine thousand bolts of lightning, but other than that..." Tad shrugs and gives a small chuckle, and I'm so relieved and overwhelmed by everything that just happened that my waterworks kick in double time. I don't miss the slight tremor in Tad's hands as he drops them to his side.

That was close. Way too fucking close.

"I'm so sorry—" I offer, but Hillen shushes me.

"It wasn't your fault, Leni. I don't know who did that, but when I find them, I'm going to rip their heart right out of their chest, like they just tried to do to me. Stupid bastards."

"Aunt Hillen, such language!" I tease quietly as I wipe my face free of tears. She pinches me playfully and pulls me and Tad back into a tight hug. "What would I do without my babies?" she asks rhetorically, and I sink into the embrace for a moment, needing an extra dose of comfort after what just happened.

My heart is still hammering away against my ribs, and I feel wired with adrenaline. I want to hunt whoever just tried to kill my cousin down and make them suffer. I don't know what I would have done if Rogan hadn't been here.

I look up to find him leaning against the side of the apartment, quietly watching our reunion and giving us space to console one another. Hoot is sitting at his feet, leaning against his leg like some drunkard who's three sheets to the wind but won't admit it.

"Thank you," I tell him, my eyes welling up again and my voice thick with gratitude.

"That was meant for you," he declares simply.

"I know," I admit, not sure how to process that someone just tried to kill me, and Tad was caught in the crossfire.

"Does Magda know anyone powerful enough to create a hex like that?" I ask Hillen.

She shakes her head but looks over at the door thoughtfully. "I'd be shocked if she did. She thinks she's a big deal in our family, but outside of *us*, she has no power, holds no sway. She's inconsequential to the magical community; I don't think anyone powerful enough to hex like that would pay her or Gwen any mind."

What she's saying makes sense, but it does nothing to make me feel better. If not Magda and Gwen, then who?

"It wasn't designed to kill you," Rogan states, his green gaze also studying my front door. "It was designed to keep you here, to slow you down. If it had been you, and you were able to break free from the hex, the jinx would have moved slower. *Your* magic would have naturally put up a fight to keep it from taking over," he tells me pointedly. "But your cousin doesn't have any magic at all. His inability to fight off or slow down the jinx turned it lethal. Other than your aunt and cousin, any other enemies?" he asks, fixing a worried look back on me.

A tic in Rogan's jaw begins, and it's clear that he's distressed. He looks as though he didn't see this coming either. I can only imagine that he's also thinking of his brother, of what this means for him. I'm sure he didn't expect for whoever took Elon to find me so fast. Well, that makes two of us. I didn't think the magical community would have any idea that Ruby had even passed yet, not unless the necromancers are a bunch of gossips.

"Aside from a hairdresser that I gave a bad review to once, I don't think I have any mortal enemies. She technically never threatened to kill me, just said I would rot in hell for telling people the truth about the yellow highlights she gave me and whatever it was she did to my hair that made it frizzy for a month. But that was a long time ago, and she was definitely a Lesser."

Hillen gets to her feet, and Rogan is wrapped up in a tight hug before I can even blink. He pats my aunt's back awkwardly as she showers him with praise and admiration. She starts to tell him something, but a tap on my elbow pulls my attention away.

"So...want to fill me in on who the knight in nicely fitting jeans is?" Tad asks, nudging my shoulder with his.

Relief escapes me in the form of a giggle. I pull Tad in for another hug, so overwhelmingly relieved that he's okay. I could have never forgiven myself if something would have happened to him. Tad hugs me back, and we stay like that for a minute, wrapped up in the moment where everything is once again okay.

"*That* is Rogan Kendrick," I start as I pull myself together and reluctantly let him go. "Grammy was supposed to help him with something, which means now I'm helping him with something," I explain as I push my curls out of my face. Why does this day feel like it's lasted for years?

I need a nap.

I purposely leave out all the details about Rogan making me his familiar and then knocking me out. I figure he's earned a bit of hero worship for what he just did for Tad. I'll have to burst their bubble about him another day.

"Rogan Kendrick," Tad repeats quietly, his cadence saucy and a little awed. "I hope when you say *helping him*, it's to your bed, because if not, then you, Leni, are a wasteful girl, and you know how Grammy Ruby felt about that."

An incredulous snort sneaks out of me, and I roll my eyes. "Grammy Ruby was talking about us eating our vegetables, not getting freaky with every pretty face that crosses our paths."

"Was she though?" Tad counters with a wag of his eyebrows.

"Trust me, he's not my type," I argue.

"What? You're not into drop-dead gorgeous half-giants with a hero complex and lips that could steal your soul? Unless...does he play for my team? I wasn't picking up any vibes... Oh fuck, did the hex destroy my gaydar?" he asks, panicked, which of course just makes me laugh. Stress and guilt roll off my shoulders as the mood lightens and relief works its way back into me.

"Language!" Aunt Hillen scolds, interrupting whatever conversation she and Rogan are caught up in. I don't even know how she heard her son's potty mouth over their talking. I smile.

Tad rolls his eyes and decides it's time to get back on his feet. He reaches behind me and plucks the bone knife I used to cut him free, from where it must have fallen, and hands it to me. "I don't know when you started arming yourself, but I'm glad you had this on you. That hex hurt like a bitch."

A jolt of guilt strikes through me as we stand up, and Tad reaches out and pulls me into his side. "Don't do that, Len. Ma's right, this isn't your fault. Don't go getting ideas about distancing yourself for our safety. You'll get better with the whole magic thing, and shi—I mean, crap—like this won't be a big deal."

I nod, but in my gut, I can't help but feel responsible and seriously uneasy. This happened to him because of me. I push the guilt aside, knowing I'll have to come to terms with it later. I stare down at the knife in my hand, my curiosity about it once again piqued.

"The knife was in the pouch," I explain. "I have no idea how it got there. I swear there were only bones in the bag before."

"You conjured it," Rogan's deep voice supplies.

"Say what now?" I ask, as my eyebrows shoot up with surprise, and I look from the knife up to Rogan.

"You...conjured it. We can all do it. We can think of something we need, and as long as you have some kind of connection to the item, you can magic it to you. You also magic it away by putting it back into the pouch."

"Like that sack that Hermione had in...crap, I can't remember which book it was?" Tad queries excitedly.

"No, not like in some kids' books. It's not magicked to hold whatever we want, it's more complicated than that," Rogan declares, a bite of arrogant irritation to the claim.

"Totally would have been a Death Eater," Tad proclaims randomly, pointing a thumb in Rogan's direction.

I chuckle, giving Rogan a scrutinizing once over before leaning toward Tad and whispering, "Called it."

"It's always the pretty ones," he retorts.

"Just like your mama has always said."

"Hate when she's right."

"Amen," I agree without missing a beat.

Rogan just shakes his head, like Tad and I are too much for him. "We need to go," he grumps. "Like I said before, whoever hexed this place wasn't trying to kill you, which means they planned on coming back for you. We should go before that happens."

"I think a better plan is to wait for them. And when they show up, we pounce and fuck 'em up," I argue.

"Langua—" Hillen starts.

"They almost killed Tad, Aunt Hillen, I think we can let a couple f-words slide when it comes to whoever did it," I insert before she can finish the admonishment.

She releases a deep, weary sigh. "Fair enough," she concedes, and Tad's mouth drops open in complete shock.

"What? She becomes the bones' pet and suddenly gets a pass?"

Aunt Hillen playfully slaps Tad upside the head, and Rogan and I both snort out a laugh.

"Hey," Tad objects.

"If you knew more about how to protect yourself," Rogan starts, "and your vulnerable, magicless aunt and cousin weren't here, then I would agree that waiting to see who did this would be a good idea, but that's not the situation we find ourselves in," he points out, and Tad rubs the back of his head.

I look over at my aunt and then at Tad and realize he's right. I can't let anything happen to them. "Is it okay for me to go inside? I need to pack a bag at least for...where are we going?" I press, realizing that I have no idea what the plan is.

"Blackbriar, Tennessee."

"Well, that sounds ominous," Tad observes, and I can't say that I disagree. "What's in Blackbriar, Tennessee?" he asks me.

"I'll explain later, but Rogan is right, you and your mom should go. It's clearly not safe here, and just in case anything else goes down, I don't want the two of you getting caught in the middle of it."

"What's going on, Leni? Why would anyone want to hurt you?" Aunt Hillen questions, her brown eyes apprehensive.

"I'm not sure. That's what Rogan and I are going to try and figure out. You two go, I'll call and check in, explain everything when we get to where we're going."

She studies me for a moment, her gaze moving from me to Tad and back again. I can see that she's torn about getting them to safety versus staying here to try and protect me.

"I'll be okay," I reassure her. "I'm not completely defenseless," I tell her, referring to the magic I now have running through my veins, but she looks at Rogan for a moment before relenting.

"I hate leaving you, kiddo," she states, her voice

wobbling with emotion. "I know we'll just get in the way, which is why I'm going to listen, but I hate the thought of you dealing with any of this on your own."

I open my arms, and my aunt steps into them, quickly wrapping me up in a strong hug. A second later, I feel Tad encircle us both and squeeze. "I'm not alone, and I promise I'll just be a phone call away. I'll keep you updated about everything that's happening. Hopefully, this will all be over soon."

The words spill easily from my lips, and it isn't until after they're out that I realize that they taste a lot like a lie. Truth is, I have no idea how long this will take. Yes, Rogan is here, and he did help save Tad, but that doesn't exactly make up for what he did to *me*. I'm nowhere close to thinking I can trust him. If I account for that and add in the scary taste I just got of how dangerous this all might be, I know without a shadow of doubt I'm in way over my head.

Aunt Hillen kisses me on the cheek and wipes at her eyes. "Call us as soon as you can."

I nod and squeeze her arm before giving Tad one last hug. "I'm so glad you're okay. I'm so sorry you got caught up in all of this," I offer, shuddering at the image that pops into my mind of him turning blue as his body started to spasm and then relax into impending death. I'm terrified that this will be all I'm able to see every time I close my eyes now.

"You saved me, that's all that matters. Just be careful though, I don't know what I would do without you."

"Same," I confess, and with one more squeeze, Tad steps back and wraps his arm around his mother's shoulders. They offer a sad wave and then start down the stairs. Rogan scans our surroundings, and I hold my breath until they're back in Tad's Prius and driving out of the complex. I quickly open my phone and forward the pictures of Magda and

Gwen to them in hopes it will keep them busy and entertained for a bit instead of worrying about me.

A hollow feeling resonates through me as I watch my family go, and without a word, I turn and open my front door, pulling the hide-a-key from the lock and shoving it in my pocket. Hoot brushes past me, but instead of being offended by his lack of respect, I welcome the intrusion. He somehow picked up on the hex on the door, so if there's anything else going on in here, I have hope that he'll give me fair warning before it's me gasping for air on the ground.

Rogan follows closely behind me, not saying a word, and I can feel the tension rolling off of him in waves. My heart is racing, and I can't help but look at my apartment differently. This has always been my space, my refuge, but now it feels tainted. Someone tampered with my home, I don't know what they've touched or what could suddenly pose a threat. I hate that I feel anxious here instead of calm and peaceful like I always felt before.

Hoot sniffs around, and I move slowly into the apartment behind him. He doesn't bark or growl at anything, and now that I know to look, I don't pick up on any anomalies either. There are no threatening shadows or bad vibes coming from anything inside this place.

I hurry through my room and into my closet, grabbing a duffel bag and unzipping it.

"You'll need short-sleeve shirts and pants. It gets cooler this time of year in the evening, so maybe a light jacket or something too," Rogan calls from the living room, as though he could suddenly sense my rushed *what do I wear* dilemma.

I open a drawer and pull out some jeans, grabbing a pair of shorts and a skirt while I'm at it. Then I start pulling things from hangers, rolling them up and stuffing them in my bag.

"Did you take these?" Rogan asks, as though I can see what he's talking about.

"Take what?" I answer, confused, as I pull my underwear drawer open and pretty much dump its contents into the bag. One can never have too many undergarments on a mystery trip to who knows where to hunt god knows what. It's also possible that I might be a bit of an over-packer on my best day. If asked, I would deny that emphatically, but as I shove a couple sundresses into the duffel, as well as some shoe and bootie options, there's no hiding the truth from myself.

"These pictures in your living room, did you take them?" Rogan clarifies.

"Uh, yeah, why?" I answer distractedly as I continue to pack.

"No, reason, just wondering," he replies dismissively, and I hear his carpet-muffled footsteps as he walks from the living room into my room.

I grab the leather-bound instruction manual that I dug out of my cedar hope chest last night. The manual I forgot I had until I was off hunting for a familiar. I found it buried under movie ticket stubs, old diaries, picture albums, and folded middle school letters that would impress an origami pro. I read through it, and I don't think there's anything that I need, but just in case, better to have it and not need it than need it and not have it.

I walk out of my closet to find Rogan studying my bedroom. It suddenly feels weird to have him in my space, judging my soft cream bedding and the number of throw pillows I make my bed with. I'm reminded that I don't know crap about him, and yet the peek he's now gotten into *my* life today is a little unsettling.

"So what's the plan now?" I ask, reaching over and plucking a picture of me and my dad from Rogan's hands and setting it back down on my bedside table where it belongs. He gives me a curious look, but I ignore it and go stock up on toiletries in the bathroom.

"We'll get back to my place a little too late to do much tonight, but tomorrow I'll take you to Elon's house and some other places to see if you pick up on anything as an Osteomancer that I can't. Hopefully, there will be a lead, and we'll go from there. If you don't pick up on anything, I have a contact in the Order who's been working on these cases, so I'll reach out to him to see if he has anything new to go on."

"I thought you didn't trust the Order?" I question as I pack some toys I bought for Hoot.

"I don't, but I trust Marx, and you know what they say about keeping your enemies close."

I file away his use of the word *enemies* but don't question him about it. I have a feeling that, when it comes to him, I'll learn more from keen observation than trying to grill him, which could inadvertently clue him in on the little things I'm picking up on.

I turn the bathroom light off and find Rogan running a hand down an oversized scarf I left hanging on the back of my door. He jerks his hand away and shoves it in his pocket just as soon as I enter the room, and it feels like I just caught him rifling through my panty drawer. Why is he touching my stuff?

He reaches for the ever-growing duffel bag when I try to walk by him, and before I can so much as object, the strap is firmly on his shoulder. I wait for him to comment about the weight of it and demand to know what I have in there, but he says nothing.

I shrug and head to the kitchen to grab Hoot's food. I was going to leave the little stink bomb with Tad, but after seeing his magic seeing-eye-dog skills, I think I'll be better off keeping him close by. I just hope he doesn't get us kicked off the plane on our way to deal with the clusterfuck I find myself caught in the middle of.

"All set?" Rogan asks.

"I think so. What airport are we headed for? I have a pet carrier for Hoot, but will they let him on the plane?"

"We're not flying," Rogan announces as though I'm crazy for even suggesting it.

"Driving will take forever," I counter. "And I doubt my car would even survive that trip."

Rogan snorts derisively, and I instantly grow defensive of my rust bucket. He scoffs, "I doubt we could even make it to the state line in that thing. No, we'll use a ley line."

I bark out an incredulous laugh at his announcement. "Good one. Should I just grab my broom, and we can zip on over to one?" I tease, but Rogan's face is serious.

I study him for a second, waiting for him to crack a smile and say *got ya,* because ley lines are a thing of the past; they're too dangerous, unstable, and unreliable. No one uses them. My amused smile starts to falter when he gets that *I'm dealing with an idiot* look on his face again.

Well, shit. He wasn't kidding.

9

"Is this going to hurt?" I ask, a little more squawky than I'd like. I stare at the empty park, swings swaying in the cooling evening air, and wonder how I never knew a ley line ran through this place.

Grammy had to have known, but why she never told the rest of us, I don't know. Frustratedly, I shake my head. Why didn't she just pull an *Aunt Hillen* and slap me upside the head, demanding that I listen? Why didn't she make it clear that I'd need to know all of this someday? She could have clued me in, told me why I needed to internalize every lesson she wanted to impart about this world and its inner workings, but she never did. She let me decide that it didn't matter, and I'm not sure how to feel about that.

I know in the grand scheme of things, none of this is her fault, it's mine for not caring more. But I wonder why she never pushed to help me care more. Gwen being gifted made it seem like the selection was a done deal. I never thought that might not be the case.

Yes, I knew there was magic out there in the world, that bloodlines stretching back as far as the beginning of time could do incredible, unimaginable things. I was aware that witches had a world and society of their own, but I convinced myself that I was a Lesser. I refused to covet their abilities or dive into a world I knew, as a teenager, wasn't as advertised.

I never sensed in myself what my grandmother so evidently sensed in me, then again I never wanted to. Now I wish I wouldn't have let my anger blind me. I wish I'd spent more time seeing the truth and less time convincing myself that I'd never be a part of it. I'd categorized myself as a *never going to happen*, but I was wrong.

Guilt stings the back of my eyes as I close them. With a sigh, I take in the electric buzz of the ley lines running through this park, the magical hum washing over me from where we're sitting in the car. I played at this place hundreds of times as a kid, but I never felt anything like the charge I feel here now.

I get the distinct impression of one large line with smaller lines branching off of it. It's a spiderweb of connections all leading to other places just like this one, which is freaky when you think about it, and yet I can't deny that I'm kind of excited at the same time.

I want to be annoyed with myself, with the eager feeling coursing through me, but how can I when this is just so epic? For one, vacations are going to be so much easier if I can just zap myself to the Bahamas instead of hopping on a plane. And a girl could really use some R & R when all this crap Rogan's dragging me into is over.

"It doesn't hurt, it's more of an adrenaline rush than anything else," he answers. "I wouldn't recommend trying to travel them on your own though. You can get lost in them, overwhelmed by them, if you don't know what you're doing."

"How do you know what *you're* doing?" I press as I stare

out at the uninhabited space and try to see the lines that I can only feel.

"Elon and I both learned when we were around twelve," he supplies.

"Oh, right. I guess that's on par with the whole old and extra powerful magical line thing you've got going on," I tease flatly.

"Something like that," he responds just as flatly, and I wonder if that could have been me if I had just let it.

Rogan climbs out of the passenger side of my car, Hoot jumping down after him like the tiny little stalker he is. I don't miss the fact that he doesn't seem to like talking about his family much—well, other than his brother, and pretty much all I know about Elon is that he's an Osteomancer and he's missing.

My car door creaks as I open it, the sound loud and grating in the quiet of the empty parking lot. I'm surprised there aren't more people out here, but I suppose the nights are starting to get colder, making it less inviting for late walks and adventures in the park.

Rogan grabs my duffel from the back seat, and I walk around my elderly SUV to meet him on the other side. A crisp breeze shoves my curls in my face, and I struggle to wrangle them back as the sun dips a little further down, and the shadows stretch out across the park like they're rising from a deep sleep and are readying themselves for some mischief.

It's a good night for magic.

I pause and warily look around me for a moment. Rogan starts walking to the middle of a sod-covered clearing, but I'm trying to figure out who just planted that thought in my head. I mean, how the hell would I know that it's a nice night for magic? Or that the moon tonight is going to be a waxing crescent, with a harvest moon only eleven days away?

I give myself the side-eye.

"You're a Blood Witch, so can you tell if my ancestors got it on with any lycans?" I ask as I hurry to catch up with Rogan. He shoots me a questioning look as I pull up even with him and Hoot.

"Why?" he asks. "You feeling the need to mark your territory or dig a hole and bury something in it?" he deadpans.

"Har har," I mock laugh with a raised *I'm not amused* brow. "No, but the urge to drag my ass on carpet is getting stronger and stronger," I snark, eliciting a quiet rumbling chuckle from Rogan. "I'm asking because I just went all *Rain Man* in my head about the moon, and that seems weird, or maybe I should say weirder than everything else has been so far. Why would witches care about the moon? Seems like it would be more of a Were trait," I observe.

Rogan stops walking and looks at me like he's not sure if I'm serious or not. "Fuck the Crone, you really are clueless," he declares, scorn radiating out of his gaze. "Ruby should be brought up on charges for letting her line stew in such ignorance," he states matter-of-factly, and immediately my hackles go up.

"You know, believe it or not, Rogan, Hemamancer of House Kendrick," I quip, "not everyone gives a shit about the witching world of magic. This life isn't exactly all that it's cracked up to be," I snap defensively.

How dare he come for my grandmother. She would have dropped everything to help him. I've seen and been on the receiving end of it enough to know how seriously she took it all. She doesn't deserve his ridicule. I might, but not her.

"And what would you really know about *this life*? From

everything I've seen, the answer to that is nothing," he retorts dismissively.

"Please," I snap. "I didn't need to have magic to see what it does to the people around you who don't. All the stories my aunts and uncles tell about their mother just up and leaving all the time because someone required her help. The stress and pressure it put on their father to never be able to count on her, to have to raise five children on his own until he keeled over from a heart attack. And don't get me started on the fighting and backbiting this world causes. The way it taints people, makes them desperate to be powerful, to feel special, to want it so badly that they end up divided over it and lost. There's so much collateral damage, look at what just happened to my cousin!"

I stop myself there. I don't reveal any more, I don't spill the other reasons I have that made me stop believing in the magic of *magic*. Rogan and I may be tethered, but it doesn't give him an all-access pass into who I am and what's made me that way.

"Grow up, Lennox," he grumbles, throwing his hands up in exasperation.

I'm completely taken aback by the admonishment.

"This is *life* that you're dealing with, not some fairy tale or wizarding story conjured up in the imagination of a starving artist. Life isn't easy. There's good and bad, just like there is in all things. You want to cherry-pick the bad in order to justify your ignorance, go for it, but you're not doing yourself any favors. Like it or not, this world is yours now, and resenting that doesn't change anything."

An incredulous snort escapes me. "Thank you, oh wise and benevolent one, for your gracious counsel. You think I don't know that? But I didn't grow up the way you did in some revered special house of magic, so cut me a little slack. I fucked up, I get it. I shouldn't have pushed my grandmother away when she tried to teach me, but I did. In case you haven't noticed, she's gone now, and I can't take that back. I'm doing the best I can. Had I known the bones would choose me and then some self-righteous asshole would show up and take over my life, I might have done things differently."

Hoot rips a fart so loud and rumbling it would make a Harley Davidson motor jealous. I scrunch up my face and immediately throw my arm over my nose to protect it from the assault I know is coming. Rogan gets hit by the noxious fumes first, and he scrambles away, a dry heave working its way up his throat. I move as upwind as I possibly can, never more afraid to breathe than I am right now. Hoot looks at me and then Rogan, and with a snort that I'm pretty sure means *my job here is done*, he proceeds to roll around in the grass and dirt, reveling in his own stench.

"I call *not it* on giving the fucker a bath," I announce, my voice more Steve Urkel sounding than normal due to my plugged nose.

"That's just wrong," Rogan states, fanning the air around his face aggressively.

I raise my eyebrows and nod slowly in agreement. And then we just stare at each other for a moment, the rising tension that was building between us stopped by Hoot's ass torpedo, but there's a distinct discomfiture now.

Rogan moves toward me, giving Hoot and his evening roll-about a wide berth. He slings the duffel bag around his chest, moving it to sit behind his back. I'm not sure what he's doing, but as he invades my personal space, I step back instinctively. He reaches out and stops me from retreating, stepping into me until my thoughts go somewhere tantalizing.

This is some *first kiss* kind of shit, and we are so not there. I don't care if my lady bits just fired up like some

NASA rocket that's ready to launch, I don't like Rogan Kendrick. I don't care how kissable his lips might be or why he's staring at me with such intensity. A girl's gotta draw the line somewhere, and I draw it at magical enslavement.

"Wha...what are you doing?" I ask, the question airy and giving away just how flustered I feel right now. He holds me against him, and I'm forced to look up to meet his penetrating gaze.

Do not look at his lips. There will be no accidental leaning in. Get your shit together, Lennox!

Rogan's moss-green eyes flit back and forth between my unsettled toffee-toned stare, and his hands drop from my upper arms, skimming down to my elbows before his touch falls away. "I'm teaching you," he says evenly, quietly, and my mind conjures several meanings, all of which send butterflies fluttering through my abdomen.

"Close your eyes?" he instructs me, his tone assured.

"Why?" I argue as I tell myself to step away from him and whatever the hell he's doing, but my feet stay planted right where they are.

"So I can explain to you how to feel them," he tells me. I feel even more befuddled as my eyes automatically shoot to his pecs, and my fingers twitch with anticipation. "The ley lines, I'm going to teach you how to feel them so that you can use them."

Understanding pours over me like a bucket of ice water, and my eyes bounce up to Rogan's lips for a fraction of a second before settling back on his potent stare. "Right. The ley lines. Gotcha." I internally facepalm, but externally I close my eyes. Mortification curdles in my stomach, and heat moves up my neck and into my cheeks. I would laugh at myself right now if I could feel anything outside of undiluted embarrassment.

I seriously need to get a grip. Yes, it's been a while since a good-looking man got all up in my business, but the fact that my brain just jettisoned off into *oh, you know what would be fun? An orgasm!* territory is just plain pathetic.

"Okay, you *should* be feeling the different frequencies that the individual lines give off," he explains, and with a deep breath, I focus on what he's saying. "It's almost like you're listening to several radio stations at once, some louder than others, and you want to pick the loudest out of all of them."

Using my other senses, I study the different energy sources all around me until I can pinpoint the one that feels the most dominant. Rogan is quiet, patiently giving me time to work through what he's telling me to do.

"I think I've got it."

"Good. Now observe it for a moment. You should be able to instinctually sense it's frequency, and when you do, you should also feel your magic almost responding to it."

I concentrate on the buzz of the ley line and try to recognize a similar hum running through me. It takes me a moment, but I start to feel a vibration moving through me, like I'm a tuning fork or something. I smile but bite back the giggle that annoyingly bubbles up in my throat. I can hear the different pitches, mine versus the ley lines'. Awe settles in me. I concentrate harder on the threads, the pitches clashing and making me want to match them. Offhandedly I wonder what happens if I make my pitch sound exactly like the line's, is that even a thing?

"Shit! No you don't," Rogan exclaims, and strong arms clamp around me, shattering my focus. With a squeal, I'm yanked away from where I was just standing, and my eyes fly open to find Rogan whisking me away from whatever he just perceived as a threat.

"What happened?" I ask confused, my eyes darting around, certain there must be something dangerous headed right for us. Magic swells in my chest, responding to my duress, ready to be called on.

"You almost rode the line. I didn't think you'd catch on that fast," he announces, his tone sounding half surprised and half shaken.

"Isn't that a good thing?" I query, perplexed by the panic I see in his features.

"No. I mean, yes, it will be at some point, but if you don't have a destination, you can trap yourself in the line or apparate somewhere dangerous."

"Oh."

"Yeah, oh," he agrees as he releases a relieved breath. "I feel like my heart just tried to crawl out of my throat," he confesses, pressing a palm to his chest.

I should probably feel bad, but it's not like he told me to be careful or warned me at all that I could get myself sucked into a ley line forever. This is probably why I was under the impression that they were too dangerous to use anymore.

"So how do you figure out where you're going and tell the ley line that?" I query.

"You have to know the frequency of the line you want to travel to, you have to know exactly where you want to stop on that line. Once you connect and are pulled into the ley line, you shift your magic to the frequency of your destination, and abracadabra, you're there."

"Abracadabra? Really?" I tease.

"What would you rather I say? Shazam? Boom shaka laka? Voilà?"

"I mean, a simple *yeet* would have sufficed, but boom shaka laka is a solid choice as well."

"Noted," he deadpans, and I fight a smile.

"So, if I don't know the frequency of where I want to go, I'm screwed. Is that the gist of it?" I reiterate, making sure I understand everything correctly.

"Yep, you got it. You may think you can wing it and just create any frequency to see where it will lead you and learn that way, but if you drop yourself in the middle of the ocean, you're screwed. A current could pull you away from the line...like that." He snaps his fingers, and I blanch. "You wouldn't be able to get back on it, and that's only *one* of the many bad things that could happen. You could apparate to freezing temperatures in the Himalayas or a volcano. The middle of a board meeting, exposing us to Lessers."

"I hear you loud and clear. Don't be stupid and play around," I tell him.

I sigh. So much for the Bahamas.

"So how do you learn the frequencies of where to go, if you're not allowed to figure things out via trial and error?"

"There are recordings you can get. They're like a ley line map. You study them, and then practice with someone who's experienced until you've got it down safely. Once you've got it, there's an app you can download that's a ley line directory."

"Seriously?" I ask, shocked.

"What? Witches can't be technologically savvy?" he teases, a glint of amusement in his eyes.

I realize then that he's still holding me against him, and my heart rate responds to the sudden awareness. My fingertips lightly skim the soft fabric of his shirt, and I can feel his unyielding muscles as they press against me. I have the uninvited urge to reach up and trace the scar that cuts down his one eye with my fingers, finding myself abruptly curious about how he got it. Rogan pushes a wayward curl out of my face, and then it's as though whatever spell we're under bursts. He clears his throat and releases me, stepping back to put space between us.

"We should go," he announces, and I blink myself back into the here and now, nodding my agreement.

"Right, yes. Blackbriar, Tennessee, here we come," I declare awkwardly, feeling the need to run off into the surrounding trees and hide. What the hell is wrong with me? It's as though my hormones are going haywire and misinterpreting everything around me.

Rogan releases a chirpy little whistle, and Hoot comes trotting over. I stare at the little furball, slightly offended that he listens so well to a man who should practically be my enemy. Traitor. Hoot is scooped up, and then next thing I know, Rogan is wrapping his arm around me again.

Right on cue, my insides revert into teenage lust mode, and just when I'm about to scold the shit out of them, Rogan tells me to hold on. Reluctantly I wrap my arms around his waist. I stare off into the trees, trying to think about things like calculus and paying bills so my inner fiend can get the hint and fuck off.

My eyes zero in on a strange movement in the shadows, and trepidation creeps through me. I can barely make out the black silhouette of a person, and they appear to be watching us. But before I can open my mouth to say anything, I'm dissolving into an infinite number of pieces and being siphoned out into the universe. It's as though I'm grains of sand being sucked up into a vacuum. One minute I'm whole, standing in the middle of a park, and the next, I'm nothing, and everything around me is gone.

10

The steady hum of tires against a smoothly paved road serenades me as I languidly rise to the surface of consciousness. My face breaches the dark pool of oblivion as though I'm lazily coming up for air, and I'm all at once aware that I'm strapped in a car with my face pressed against a cool window. There's a seat belt cutting across my chest, and a trickle of drool making its way from the corner of my mouth down my chin.

I sit up, wiping at the evidence of the deep sleep state I was just in, and try to get my bearings. I'm in a car, a nice car if the leather front console and fancy dim lighting are anything to go by. I look to my left. And yep, Rogan's driving. Snoring rises up from the back, and I look behind me to find Hoot, who has made himself at home and is out for the count.

"What happened?" I ask groggily, looking around outside of the sleek car, but it's too dark to really make out much. "Did you knock me out again?" I accuse, my tone too sleepy to communicate the annoyance I feel at that possibility.

"No, you and Hoot passed out when I pulled us out of the line. It's normal. It can take time to get used to fragmenting and coming back together."

My stomach roils at that thought, and I try not to picture my parts scattering to the wind and then getting sucked back together. There are just some things that a person doesn't need to imagine, and this is going on that list. I pat myself just to be sure everything ended up back where it's supposed to be, and breathe out a relieved exhale when it feels like I'm just as I was before. My chest constricts in an uncomfortable way for a moment, and I observe the feeling, dismissing it when nothing worse happens. It'll probably take time to feel all the way normal again.

"Where are we?" I question as we pass a streetlight that's illuminating wild grass and some mystery expanse of land that stretches past the light, far out into the darkness.

"We're about forty minutes from my home," he tells me, and I nod even though I'm unsure how I feel about that. He buckled my unconscious body into his car, and we've been driving for who knows how long. Seems like a weird thing to do. Then again, he's a witch, and I'm discovering that weird is just part and parcel.

"The biggest ley line near me is two hours away in Gallywough. I would have waited for you to wake up, but it was getting late and we would have been vulnerable just sitting there so close to a line," he offers, obviously picking up on my discomfort.

My chest tightens again, and I'm not sure if it's a warning of something or some residual effect of what my body just went through. I rub at my sternum and wince at the strange sensation.

"Do you need some water or something? I have a couple bottles stashed behind the seat."

"No, I'm..." I trail off as we pass another streetlight that's illuminating a sign for an exit that's forty miles away. "I'm fine, I think, I just feel...off," I explain, not sure how to put into words what's happening with me.

"That's normal," Rogan explains as he shoots me a sympathetic look. "Ley lines can act like chargers; you might feel like every cell in your body is lit up with a shit ton of magic for a while."

I take stock of myself. Is that what I'm feeling? Is it adrenaline and a surplus of magic and energy that's creating this anxious undercurrent that's running just below my skin? It's hard to say since I've never ridden a ley line before, and I'm not sure what recovery is supposed to be like, but whatever is happening, I'm not a fan. I feel almost itchy with anticipation, and it sucks.

"So I'm strung out on magic, no biggie," I announce with a shrug, but my voice is pitched higher than normal, meaning this is absolutely a biggie, and I just might be starting to freak out about it.

"Breathe, Lennox," Rogan commands as he shoots me concerned looks while still trying to pay attention to the road.

I can feel panic scratching through my body like it's some terrifying monster that's ready to rip me to shreds. "Distract me," I pant out as I try not to claw at my throat and the seat belt that suddenly seems too tight against my chest. The window next to me rolls down a little, and cool, moisture-heavy air caresses my face and tries to calm me. "Just talk, tell me what a day in the life of a Blood Witch looks like. Or...whatever...just tell me something," I plead, desperate to think about anything else other than how I feel and all of the crazy things that have happened in the last twenty-four hours.

Concern laces his green gaze, but he listens. "Uh, well, my day varies, depending on what clients I have scheduled," he starts, his deep voice filling the car. "Some are sick and need weekly healings or potions delivered regularly to help with various things from ailments to beauty treatments to health regimens.

"I work monthly with a blood donation center to weed out possible issues with donations and apply blessings on what they're delivering. Some doctors refer patients to me if there's a struggle to pinpoint an issue. I also work with a local coven here and there. We like to combine our resources and create more potent brews and talismans.

"It all really just depends. Elon and I work together for some clients, but he runs a separate business as well. We try to do Tincture Tuesday where we get together and sort out what we need to make for the following week," he explains with a quiet chuckle that morphs into a sad sigh, his voice and this information exactly the distraction I needed.

"Hmmm, what else?" he hums, checking on me out of the corner of his eye as the road curves to the right. I lay my head back against the headrest, closing my eyes and reveling in the feel of the cool air from the window. The weird feeling is there still, but it's not nearly as overwhelming as it was.

"There's also clients who hire me specifically for the other side of our abilities..." he goes on, the change in direction intriguing. "You know, curses and things of that nature, or maybe you don't know," he corrects himself.

"I know that magic and what we do as witches isn't all sunshine and rainbows," I tell him as I settle into the steady rhythm of the moving car. "I did just watch my cousin get hexed," I remind him, and he nods in understanding.

"I work by referral only, so new clients have to be vetted, especially if they're requesting help like that. I don't take any of it lightly, so a lot goes into making sure that the darker side of things is done correctly and only on the deserving."

"You talk like you're worried you're going to scare me away," I point out. "Dark magic is just as important as the light. I at least paid attention to that lesson as a kid."

"So then your grandmother did try to teach you?" he presses.

"Of course she did. Like you said, she was one of the best. She would get all of us together for lessons. I bought into all of it until I was eighteen, and then I..." I pause as that constricting feeling in my chest tightens even more. I sit up, opening my eyes, and look around me.

"And you what?" Rogan presses.

An off-ramp is coming up, and an exit sign indicates that we're approaching Sweet Lips, Tennessee. I chuckle at the town's name, but my chest gets even tighter, and I practically choke on it.

"What's wrong?" Rogan asks, reaching out to push curls out of my face.

"I don't know, can you pull off here? I need to get out," I instruct as I clutch at my chest. Am I having a heart attack? It doesn't hurt so much as it's just uncomfortable as hell.

He turns his blinker on and pulls off at the exit, his flashy car slowing smoothly and feeling more like a spaceship than an automobile.

"Go right at the stop sign," I tell him, something inside forcing me to go all backseat driver.

Rogan thankfully doesn't argue, and when he turns right, the vise in my chest loosens just slightly. I pull in a deep breath and call out a series of directions, like Sweet Lips and I go way back. I have no idea how I know where to go, but I do put together what all of this means as the velvet pouch of bones that I tied to my belt loop, the ones now resting against my hip, begin to grow warmer and warmer. It's like some fucked up version of *hot and cold* bones-style, and I have no doubt that I'm going to find someone who needs my help at the end of this skeletal rainbow.

"So this is what it feels like," I state absently. "This is the urge my grandmother was talking about that could hit at any time."

"Are you being summoned?" Rogan asks.

"Yeah, it's so weird." I look down at my arms as though the anticipation crawling under my skin will be visible, but they look the same as they always do. I rub at my chest, wondering how many times this happened to her. Was it like this every time, this physical need to take action, or was it more of how I felt when I knew I needed to help Rogan? That was more of an instinctual feel, this...well, this feels so much more urgent.

We round a corner onto a well-lit street, passing closed shops, a few open restaurants, and a smattering of people walking around. My heart hammers in my chest as I spot a bar with a few trucks and motorcycles parked outside.

"Here," I point out, and Rogan pulls his too-fancy, out-of-place car into an open parking spot.

"The Eagle Fang?" he questions, reading the lit sign hung above the peeling stucco of the building.

"Actually, I think it's called the Beagle Fang," I point out, gesturing to the rusty-looking unlit *B*.

"Yeah, that doesn't sound any better," he deadpans as he scans our surroundings, looking like he's been asked to touch something he finds gross. "This doesn't look very safe," he observes, and I just breathe and stare blankly at the front door.

"Would you say the same thing to your brother if he were the one who was summoned here?" I ask, unable to really disagree with his assessment. It looks like some run-down biker bar, not a place strangers would stop in to check out as they passed by, but what can I do? The bones are most definitely calling me here.

"I would," Rogan answers as he looks off into the surrounding shadows as though he can see into their depths.

"Well, better get on with it," I declare on a sigh, reaching for the door handle and stepping out of the car.

Rogan gets out on the other side. "What are you doing?" I ask, confused as to why he's following me. His brother is an Osteomancer, he knows the deal. It's the Bone Witches and Corium Witches that I learned about when I was younger who have to deal with this whole magical call to aid those around us. I heard my grandmother talk about it many times. Some call it a gift, others a curse, but either way, there's no getting around it.

"I'm not going to leave you alone in a place like this," he tells me as though that should be obvious.

"Did you ever think that maybe your hulking ass might be what gets me into trouble in a place like this?" I ask, gesturing to the front door. "I doubt anyone in there would care about some woman stopping in for a drink, but you...well, you just look like someone who wouldn't mind creating a good ruckus or two."

Rogan rolls his eyes. "I'm sure any old woman would have a hard time from at least one person in a place like this, but someone like you...here...that's what's going to cause a ruckus."

"What does *that* mean?" I demand. "I know I'm new to all of this, and aside from you, this will be my first summoning, but despite what you think, I can do this. I can also take care of myself, thank you very much," I huff as I round the front of the car.

Rogan reaches out for my arm, using my momentum against me and swinging me around until I'm facing him instead of stomping toward the door. I didn't even see him move from where he was standing next to the driver's side of the car.

"I've seen how you can take care of yourself, and as impressive as your right hook is, I still won in the end," he points out, and indignation fires through me. "I never said you couldn't do this—I don't even think that—I was saying that a beautiful woman walking into a hole like this is bound to create issues."

"Are you seriously using the fact that you attacked me against me?" I question, completely floored and willfully ignoring the *beautiful* comment. Mooning over that is just going to get me nowhere. "First of all, I had no idea you were going to do what you did, and second of all, if you didn't have magic, I would have taken you."

"Oh please, do you really think anyone is going to give you fair warning before they come for you?" he exclaims, his tone astonished and dripping with judgment. "And if I recall correctly, you attacked me first. I didn't get physical until you did, and even then, I was just trying to keep you from hurting yourself."

"You are fucking delusional. You made me your familiar less than two minutes after meeting you. Maybe I threw the first punch, but you most definitely attacked first. And if I didn't have someone in there that needed me, I'd show you just how helpless I'm *not*. So just stay the hell out of my way, or so help me, I will test all the different ways I can break your bones without killing you."

I pull my arm free from his hold and march toward the bar's entrance. Rogan doesn't say anything, and I hope that he'll just stay in the car with Hoot and let me do what I need to do. I'm nervous enough as it is, but now I'm pissed and shaking with adrenaline from the argument I just had. It's not exactly the state of mind one should be in when someone needs help.

I practically stomp into the bar. It's dimly lit, with a pair of pool tables off to the right and neon signs hung up on the walls that announce what brands of beer are sold here. I rein in my irritation over what just happened outside and head for the bar, taking in the dark booths to my left and the high-top tables and stools scattered about.

There aren't a lot of people in here, and surprisingly, I'm not the only woman in this place. There are three men, who I assume belong to the bikes parked outside, playing pool with a woman who most definitely is a bottle redhead and looks as though she takes fashion tips from Peggy Bundy. Two older gentlemen sit at the bar, and there's a man draped in darkness, sitting in the booth farthest from everything else.

The pouch of bones blaze against my hip, and the anxious clenched-feeling in my chest immediately subsides as I lay eyes on the man in the booth. I'm tempted to immediately walk over now that I know he's the one I've been summoned to assist, but I stay on my route to the bar. Nerves scramble inside of me like ants over an abandoned picnic lunch. All at once, I feel like I'm in sixth grade again, standing on a high riser, blinded by a spotlight, and completely forgetting the words to the song I spent months practicing for the choir performance. My mouth grows dry, and I realize I have no idea how to do this.

Do I just walk right up and say *you called*? Does he even know that he summoned me, or is it more like I've been guided here by the universe? I try to think back to what Grammy Ruby used to say about this, but I'm drawing a super helpful blank. Are the people of Sweet Lips, Tennessee, going to burn me at the stake if I walk up to a complete stranger and ask if I can read his bones?

I cringe at the thought. Even if they don't string me up, I sound like a freakin' serial killer with a line like that, or a really bad prostitute. I go over the options in my head for how to approach the lone figure in the booth, without looking like I want to take him home or cut him up into little pieces, but everything I think of makes it seem like I'm going to try and sell him something. He doesn't look like the type who needs lipstick that never wipes off or a pretty new set of earrings, so I abandon that line of thought and start stressing about how to even help him if he lets me. Will it be as simple as a reading? Will there be more to it than that?

"What can I get you to drink, miss?" an older woman with a kind face asks me.

"Oh. Uh...do you have Michelob?" I ask, embarrassingly frazzled.

"I do, hon. That'll be four dollars."

Shit.

I tap my pockets like I'm going to somehow magic money there, but I didn't even think to grab my wallet, and my phone with my emergency credit card isn't tucked anywhere on me.

"I got it," a deep and annoyingly familiar voice announces, his strong arm rubbing against mine seconds later as he presses next to me at the bar.

I release an exasperated breath as I look up into moss-green eyes, and I shake my head in frustration. "Where's Hoot?"

"Asleep in the car. I cracked the windows," he states evenly, ordering something for himself and handing over a twenty. "Keep the change," he tells the obliging bartender, but instead of it making her more endeared to him, a suspicious gleam enters her hazel eyes. I decide I like her right there and then.

She hands me my bottle of beer, and I pull a small sip

from it, enjoying the cool liquid and the light taste in my mouth before I swallow it down. "Well, I hope someone breaks your windows because they think you left a dog in the car to die," I tell him with a tilt of my bottle in a faux cheers, and then I leave him at the bar and approach the man in the booth.

Here goes nothing.

11

I take a deep fortifying breath, and then without working myself up any more than I already have, I slide into the booth on the other side of the man. He looks up at me, confused, and quickly shoves something in his pocket.

"Nice night for a drink," I tell him, taking a sip of my beer and internally wanting to flick myself in the eye.

Really, Lennox? That was the best you could do?

"It is," he agrees awkwardly, looking around for a moment before his gunmetal-blue eyes land back on me.

"How's your night going?" I ask at a loss for how else to approach this. Maybe he'll just come right out with whatever is going on with him.

"Listen, as flattered as I probably should be that someone that looks like you is talking to someone who looks like me, I saw that big guy come in after you," he tells me, gesturing to Rogan at the bar with his sweaty glass of half-drunk beer. "I've been married long enough to recognize a woman who's cheesed off at her man, and I'm not interested in getting in the middle of whatever the two of you have going on," he finishes, taking a quick drink from his mug before setting it down and slowly spinning it, once again appearing to be lost in thought.

"Who? That guy?" I ask, feigning bewilderment as I turn to look at the bar. It doesn't help that Rogan is watching us like a cat watches birds that are playing on the other side of the window it's perched in. "He's just my stalker, you don't have to worry about him," I explain dismissively. "And he's not why I'm here," I add.

The man studies me for a moment, and I take in the dark circles under his eyes, the limp plaid shirt that's hanging from him like he's lost a bit of weight recently. His golden-brown hair is dull, and he keeps spinning the mug in his hands like if he stops the world just might crumble all around him.

I find myself unknowingly reaching out to him with my magic. He's definitely a Lesser, and his bones don't reveal to me any kind of illness or cause of the deterioration I sense, but there's a deep-rooted exhaustion there that makes me want to sing him a lullaby and stand guard over him while he sleeps for a month.

"Then why are you here..."

"Lennox, my name is Lennox, but you can call me Leni," I supply, and he nods once. "I'm here to help you," I tell him simply, and a flash of shock moves through his features before moroseness regains its hold on him, and his face sags with gloom.

"And how do you think you can help me?" he presses, the skepticism bleeding out of his words.

"I'm not sure yet, I just met you..."

"Paul," he provides, and I offer him a kind smile in exchange for his name.

Paul leans back against the cracked pleather of the booth seat, and I can feel that he's sizing me up, trying to figure out what the hell I'm doing here and what he wants to do about it. "Why would you want to help me?" he questions, and there's such raw vulnerability in the question that it makes my heart ache for him. I don't know who he is or what he needs from me, but I can feel that he thinks he's unworthy, I can feel in that moment how painfully broken he thinks he is. It breaks my heart.

"This will probably sound weird, but I felt pulled here. I felt with everything in me that you needed something or maybe someone, and I just couldn't walk away from that feeling. So here I am, a complete stranger, sitting in your booth, here to help you with whatever is going on."

Emotion wells up in Paul's eyes, but he doesn't let it escape. I watch quietly as he wrestles with what he's feeling, and I wonder what has this man feeling so shattered. He looks maybe a handful of years older than me, and although I don't get the impression that life has been easy, I don't sense that it's been overly hard either.

"My Phoebe was like that," he tells me, his voice cracking on the name. "I've never seen a kinder, more compassionate person in all my life, and there are some good people in these parts. She would bend over backward for anyone. It used to drive me nuts, but now..."

It hits me then why Paul is feeling so crushed. He's lost someone.

"But now...you miss it," I provide, filling in the blanks from where he trailed off. He nods solemnly, staring at the mug he keeps twisting in his hands as though it's a lifeline.

"Came home once, and our couch was missing. I thought maybe we'd been robbed, but Phoebe informed me that an elderly woman moved in down the way and she didn't have a lick of furniture. So what did she do? She gave her some of ours. Then she went around to our neighbors to see what they could part with.

"I'd just gotten home from a ten-hour day. I was ready to

shower, put my feet up, and eat some dinner, but just as quick as I walked in, she told me that we needed to trek across town to pick up a mattress for Ms. Briscoe," he tells me with a hollow chuckle and a shake of his head. "I was so mad at her, but she wouldn't hear it. Someone was in need, and that just never happened on Phoebe's watch."

"She sounds like the best of souls," I offer.

"She was," he agrees, and the battle with his emotions starts anew.

I give him time to grieve, silently lending my support in whatever way I can. I don't say anything, not wanting to minimize his suffering with useless phrases like *I'm sorry* or *It'll be okay*. I know how I felt when my dad died, and there wasn't a single thing that anyone could do or say that made it hurt any less.

A flash of me sitting in a bathtub, staring dead-eyed at the wall, pops up in my head. Working with Rogan to undo the jinx on Tad unloosened the memory, and now it wants attention that I don't have the time for. I push the image and thoughts of my father away and focus on the man hurting in front of me as he tries to compose himself.

The velvet pouch of bones warms at my side, and I reach down and untie them from my belt loop. "Paul, can I do a reading for you?" I ask soothingly, tamping down on the nerves that surface as I pull the bag of bones into my lap.

"Like you want to read me a scripture?" he asks, confused and a little testily, and I quickly shake my head.

"No, um...so...it's more..." I stammer, uncertain how he might take what I'm going to say.

A lot of people think things like this are bad. They get it in their head that it's voodoo or the work of the devil. Grammy Ruby had way too many stories of people flinging their vitriol at her and what she did. Unfortunately, there's just no telling where Paul will fall in the spectrum of *fine with it* or *offended*. I know if I offer help and he refuses it, my job here is done, but I'm surprised to feel just how vehemently I'm hoping he'll accept it.

"It may seem a little odd or even unconventional, but I'd like to read my bones for you," I tell him straight up. I've spent a long time resenting magic, of keeping as far away from this world as I could. But it's time I stop avoiding it or thinking of it as a bad thing myself. It's time to own it. Good or bad, I'm a Bone Witch.

I place the purple velvet pouch on the table, and Paul stares at it for a moment before his eyes fill with mistrust. My heart drops a little.

"There's no charge. I don't want anything from you," I hurry to explain. "I know this may seem even stranger than a stranger sitting down across from you, but what do you have to lose? I can see that you're hurting, what if in some small way this can help?" I ask him, gesturing to the waiting bones on the table, my eyes pleading with him to trust me.

His pain-filled blue gaze moves from the purple bag up to me, and after a moment of scrutiny, he sighs and gives me a shrug. "Fine, do whatever."

Elation slams through me, helping to drown out my worry. I have no idea what this reading will tell him, but I know he needs it. I loosen the strings, opening the pouch. "I'll need three things from you, Paul, things that mean something to you. I'll give them back just as soon as I'm done, but it helps me interpret what the bones need you to know."

He hesitates for a moment, his eyes wandering around the room like he's wondering who's watching or what they might think of this whole exchange. I almost think he's about to change his mind and tell me to get lost, but just as I'm about to try and plead my case again, he reaches into his pocket and pulls out a worn-looking penny. Then he pulls a chain from around his neck until a dainty set of rings appears. Carefully he unclasps the chain and pulls the soldered set of rings from it.

I feel tears well up in my eyes at the sight of what I know is his wife's jewelry, the symbol of her commitment to the man in front of me. I work to blink them away. If Paul can keep it together, then I will too. He gives me the penny and Phoebe's rings. And then he looks at his hand for a moment before pulling off his own wedding ring and handing it to me.

Despair pours out of his eyes, and I close my hand around his precious totems, my toffee-colored gaze never leaving his. Silently I try to convey how grateful I am that he's trusting me with these items, with this whole situation in general. Goosebumps crawl up my arms, and I promise Paul with my gaze that whatever happens, I'm here for him. Paul's breaths come a little quicker, and I can see that he's losing the battle with his grief. I give him a reassuring nod, and then I get to work.

I place the rings and the penny in the bag and cinch it shut. I close my eyes and shake the bag, imbuing it with my plea to help Paul with whatever it is that he needs right now. I shake until a sense of peace comes over me, and that's when I know the bones are ready.

I've watched Grammy Ruby do this for me and others probably hundreds of times, but just before I open the bag and pour the bone pieces on the table, I'm hit with an overwhelming feeling of purpose and worthiness, and for a moment, it steals my breath away. This is right. This is what I was made for. Grief and appreciation bloom in my chest, but this is not about me right now. This is for Paul, and it's time to guide his way.

I open the bag and upend the contents. Bone pieces and Paul's items pour out onto the table in front of me. I give them a moment to settle and for Paul's gaze to move from the bones back to me, and then I start.

It takes me a second to get my bearings. I'm not sure what to expect, but just like with the other times I've needed to use magic, it just seems to come to me. The bones have arranged themselves into little groupings, and I take in the symbols that are showing and where they're located in relation to Paul's objects.

Around his wedding ring is every bone that signals death, loss, and emptiness. But the ring itself is sitting on bone that has a rising sun carved into it. I take in the positioning of the grouping and give a little gasp, my eyes shooting up to Paul's.

"You're going to kill yourself," I announce quietly, and his eyes don't even widen with surprise as his head dips into a nod confirming, with no emotion, what I just accused him of. I want to argue with him about why he shouldn't do it, but I feel the bones warm slightly, and I dutifully turn my attention back down to them.

I trace the death runes and move the circle of symbols surrounding them. "You're going to take poison or maybe pills," I tell him. "They won't work right away like you're hoping they will though. You'll be in the hospital for weeks before your family pulls you off life support."

I look up at him as I say this and don't miss that his hand drops to his pocket. He looks troubled by this information, but it's as though I can see him forming another plan instead of being deterred from killing himself all together. I drop my eyes to the bones again. I trace the symbols, and the bones show me flashes of images as I go, helping me to piece the information together.

I move from the bone that has the symbol for hospital on it to the one that represents family and a gathering. All around that bone are bones that represent decision and pain. I look to the right of that grouping and gasp, pulling my hand to my mouth.

"You have a child. A little boy."

Tears breach my lids and spill down my cheeks at the thought of what that little boy will be left to deal with if his father continues down this path. I can't stop myself when the question *why* spills from my lips, and Paul shatters in front of me.

He drops his face into his hands and begins to cry. Loss and agony pour out of him with each sob, his pain so brutal and palpable. I want to reach out and hug him, but I get the distinct impression that if I do, he'll shut down, and he needs to purge as much hopelessness as he can if things for him are going to change. So instead, I helplessly watch and I cry with him.

"She was everything," he keens into his hands, his chest shaking with the sobs wracking through him. "She was the softness, and the compassion, the love, and the gentleness; I'm none of it. How am I going to keep going without her? How will I ever be anything for our son without her?" he begs, shaking his head in his palms. "Everything was better because she was here, and now she's not, and I don't want this world without her. I don't want anything if I can't share it with *her*," he wails, and I pull up the neck of my shirt and use it to wipe my face.

"But how will he know?" I ask, and after a minute, Paul's red and broken gaze meets mine. "How will your son know all these amazing things about his mother if you're not here to teach him? He's young, I can see that, and his memories of everything she was, of the special things she did, will fade. I see that you have family and that you think they'll do a better job than you will raising him, but, Paul, that's not true," I plead with him.

"You were Phoebe's everything." I point down to the

bones that surround Phoebe's rings. "I can see that you met young, and from that moment until long after this one, you were the world, you hung the fucking moon for her. She *was* special, you're absolutely right about that, and that special creature chose you, Paul. You," I tell him assertively. "Who knew her better than you?" I ask, and I wait for him to answer.

"No one," he says on a sob, and he fishes a handkerchief from his back pocket and wipes at his face and his nose.

"Exactly! No one knew her better than you, and that means no one will be able to tell your son, to show him, the kind of woman she was. All that beautiful compassion and kindness, all the ways she cared for those around her, that's now your legacy to pass down. Only yours."

I watch as he considers my words. I can sense as the truth of what I'm saying dawns on him.

"I know you think he'll be better off without you, but he won't, Paul. Because if you go, he'll never know his mother the way he should, and Phoebe deserves better than that. Your son deserves better than that."

"But how? I work long days. I'd barely be home. How can I be enough for Jackson?"

"She had life insurance," I tell him as I trace the symbols her ring is leaning against. "It looks like she took it out a long time ago when she was working for a bank," I explain, the words sounding more like a question than a statement, but the symbol on one of the bones is very faded.

"She kept paying on it after she stopped working, before Jackson came. She didn't think she'd ever need to tell you about it, and soon it just became a bill that got paid every month without more thought than that."

"What?" he asks, his sniffles slowing and growing quieter.

"She had life insurance," I repeat. "I bet if you called the bank, they could tell you what provider they used when she worked there. Or maybe you have a statement somewhere in the house that will give you the details."

"She did everything electronically. I can't figure out the passwords into the accounts. She changed them all the time because she was worried about hackers and all the big companies that are having issues with data breaches. She was fanatical about it," he tells me with a small sad smile.

"Call the bank she used to work for, they should be able to help you," I encourage.

"How do you know this?" he asks as he wipes again at his cheeks, his eyes looking less desolate and more stunned.

"The bones," I tell him, gesturing down at them.

Moisture fills his eyes again, and he silently nods his head. "Every morning when I'd leave for work, she'd always call out that she was sending her guardian angels with me. She'd say she didn't need 'em and she'd rather I have the extra protection." His blue eyes settle on mine, and his gaze grows intense. "It's like she's still looking out for me," he tells me, his voice cracking as more tears spill down his cheeks.

"She always will be, Paul. I know it's not the same, but she will always watch over you and Jackson, never doubt that."

"Thank you," Paul chokes out, and then he scoots to the end of the booth. I pluck his wedding ring, Phoebe's wedding rings, and the penny from the bones and hand them to him. He slips his ring back on his finger, loops the chain back through her wedding set and places it around his neck. The penny goes back in his pocket.

He reaches out a hand, and I place mine in his. He holds it for a moment, overcome with a wave of new emotion. "I owe you," he tells me as he shakes my hand.

"No, you don't. Now go home to Jackson, wake him up

and hold him, and then start living the legacy that Phoebe deserves to have," I order.

He nods, wiping fresh tears from his cheeks, and then he gets up and walks out of the bar.

I don't tell him about the bones his penny landed on, about the woman he'll meet that will help him find love again. About the way she'll care for him and his son, or about the daughter she'll give him. I don't explain how his new wife will ask to call their little girl Phoebe, and how they'll all live beautiful lives honoring all the incredible things that made his late wife the best of souls.

I can feel that he's not ready for that, so I keep it to myself as I bless the bones with my gratitude and, one by one, place them back in the pouch. I used to only see the bad parts of Grammy Ruby being pulled away all the time. I thought being summoned here and there could only ever be something inconvenient, but as I put the bones away and hear a truck firing up in the parking lot, I know I'll never see things the same. This...this is beautiful, and for the first time, I can't wait to see what's next.

12

"That was pretty incredible, what you did back there," Rogan tells me, his compliment breaking the silence we've been driving in for the last thirty minutes.

I look over at him, the shadows in the car caressing his face and darkening his features. "I don't know what future readings will be like, but for a first one, that was a game-changer," I admit. "Do Hemamancers do readings?" I ask, curious. "I know your magic works differently, but I don't know how it all works."

"Blood Witches don't have any relics like your bones, it's just the blood itself for us. We do have a kind of reading that we perform, but the information we get from the blood is very different from how your bones work."

"How so?" I query.

"Well, for starters, it's a lot less detailed. I can tell from someone's blood that they're depressed or that they're suffering from other physical ailments from exhaustion to disease, but the *why* isn't prevalent in the blood itself. If I had read that man, I would have sensed the depression and known it was at an alarming level, but I wouldn't have been able to discern the cause without him telling me," he explains.

"Does your brother get summoned a lot? Do you go with him when he does?" I ask, wondering what the other Bone Witch's life is like. I suspect it would be fun to have a partner in crime, so to speak. To have someone who knows what you're dealing with when it comes to magic and being a witch. My grandfather knew what Grammy Ruby was, but it never sounded like he fully got what it meant or how it felt.

"It happens now and again, but not often. I've never seen him do a reading; he doesn't talk about them much."

"Wait," I exclaim, turning in my seat so I can get a good look at Rogan. "You've never seen your brother do a reading? Like, ever?" I clarify.

"No," he responds with a dismissive shrug.

"But I thought you said that the two of you worked with the same clients. He doesn't do readings for them?"

"He does, sometimes, but I'm never in the room for that. We make potions together, and things like that work for some of the same clients in different capacities, but, yeah, no readings."

"Hasn't he ever done a reading for you?" I ask, completely astonished by this news.

My grandmother did a reading for everyone in the family when they turned sixteen. After that, she'd do them if we asked or if she sensed we were really struggling with something. It seems weird to me that two brothers would keep their abilities so separate.

"We tried to read each other when we were younger, but it never worked. We asked our uncle about it, and he said it didn't always work for people close to you."

"Huh," I mumble, making a note to read Tad when I get back so I can test that theory. "Did your uncle ever read for you?" I ask, assuming that his uncle was the former Osteomancer in the family.

"No, he always said it would be a waste of his magic. He knew where Elon and I would end up, just like him and his brother."

"Well, it sounds like he was the *life of the party*," I snark.

Rogan gives an amused snort. "That would be a massive understatement."

There it is, I think to myself as I catch the slightest tightening around his eyes when he mentions his family. It doesn't take the bones to tell me that there is something there, something massive and painful. The car grows quiet again, and I find myself studying Rogan's face. I'm sure he can feel that I'm just sitting here staring at him, but he lets me do it without saying a word.

He's hurting. I picked up on that almost as soon as I met him, but I figured it had to do with his brother. But there's more there.

"Would you like me to read you?" I ask randomly as I study the angles of his face. I blink and then try to shake some sense into me when I realize I'm perving out a little too much.

Rogan's brow dips, but in the dark, I can't quite make out if it's confusion or concern that's etched into his features.

"Um, sure, I guess, but it'll have to be some other time, because we're here," he declares, and I pivot to face forward as we pull through the trees into a clearing that displays a large well-lit house. I lean forward so I can take it all in. His house is modern, the structure more windows than anything else. There's a dark gray paneling on the parts that aren't glass, and beautiful cedar accents frame the doors and line the underside of the roof.

Soft golden spotlights light up the property from the outside, and there's a similar-colored glow coming from rooms inside that give the appearance that someone is home. It dawns on me then that I have no idea if Rogan is married or lives with a girlfriend or boyfriend. He made it seem like it was just him and his brother, but I never really asked.

He pulls up to a four-car garage, and the frosted-glass door begins to open. There are other cars parked inside, but it's impossible to tell if they belong to Rogan or someone else.

"Your house is beautiful," I declare, still looking around at the details as though I don't know which stunning thing to really focus on first. "Is it just you in this massive place?" I inquire, not at all smoothly.

"Thank you," he replies as he pulls his sleek car into its spot. He looks over at me curiously as he puts it in park. "And yes, it's just me out here," he supplies.

Relief slams through me, and I take a second to side-eye that. *Why do I care?*

"Do you get lonely in a huge place like this?" I ask, and the rude question is out of my mouth before I can stop it.

"Sometimes," he answers evenly, his eyes studying me intensely.

"Sorry, I don't know why I asked that. I get lonely in my little ass apartment all the time. Size doesn't matter," I blurt and then immediately want to facepalm again.

"Good to know," Rogan states, a small smile twitching at the edges of his mouth.

"Not like that, pervert," I accuse.

"Like what?" he asks with faux innocence.

"I'm not talking about your dick."

"I...didn't think you were," he defends.

"Because size *is* important; it's not *everything*," I correct in case he has a little dick and I'm insulting him. "But it's important," I finish, and I can feel the blush creeping into my cheeks.

Do not look at his lap, Lennox.

"Again, good to know where you stand on dick size."

"But I'm not talking about *your* dick," I hurriedly state.

"Got it," he chirps, and I can see the mirth gleaming in his eyes.

"Well, now that I've made this awkward, I'm just going to get out of the car and stand around until you tell me where to go," I announce, and then I do just that.

Rogan's rich chuckle echoes off the walls of the garage as he climbs out of the car and moves to retrieve a still sleeping Hoot from the back. I grab my duffel bag and then shuffle behind him as he leads the way into his house.

He flips on lights as he goes, and unsurprisingly the inside of his house is just as stunning as the outside is. The floors are a light-blond wood, the banisters are black metal, and the walls are stark and white. The furniture is minimal, but what's there is cozy and inviting. I can only catch hints of dark trees through the massive walls of windows all around me, but I imagine the view in the morning will be mind-blowing.

"Are you hungry or anything?" Rogan asks, gesturing in the direction of a dimly lit kitchen.

"Maybe later, but I have a lot of reading to do, and I'd kill for a shower," I declare, and he nods and guides me toward the stairs. He puts Hoot down on a blanket on his sofa, and the little bugger doesn't even stir. If it weren't for the constant snoring reverberating out of him indicating that he's alive and well, I might be concerned over what that ley line did to him.

I follow Rogan up his floating staircase, looking everywhere but at his ass in his nicely fitting jeans. Nope, definitely not interested in that.

"You can stay here, there's an attached bathroom and a balcony that leads down to the main level if you like morning walks or whatever."

I chuckle a little and step into the room Rogan is gesturing toward. He flips the light on, and I'm met with a huge bed, simple but masculine decor, and another wall of windows. It looks comfy enough, but I never sleep well in unfamiliar places. Good thing I have a magic cram session planned.

"My room is down the hall, so if you need anything..." He pauses for a moment as though he wants to say something else, but instead of voicing whatever is on the tip of his tongue, he steps out of the room and closes the door behind him.

With a sigh, I drop my duffel on the trim wood bench at the foot of the bed and thread my hands through my curls as I look around. It's hard to imagine that I've only been a witch for like a day. So much has happened, and I don't even know how to start processing it all.

I dig my phone out of my bag and head into the bathroom. It takes me a minute to figure out how to turn the water on in the shower, and I do a little celebratory dance when I finally figure it out. Steam starts to fill the room, and I quickly strip out of my clothes and then open my phone. I open my contacts and click the call button; it's probably too late to call, but I did say I would when I got here.

"Leonardo DiCaprio, long time no talk!" Tad answers excitedly.

"You're up," I greet back, half surprised and half happy that he answered.

"Well, yeah. I couldn't go to bed without making sure you were okay."

I chuckle, click the speaker button, set the phone on the

counter, and then step into the hot spray of the shower. "Oh please. Who are you really waiting up for?"

"Pierre," he admits without missing a beat. "He's supposed to call me when he gets off work, we have big sexting plans."

"TMI, dude, way too much TMI."

"What are you up to? Did you get where you were going safe and sound?" he asks.

"I'm taking a quick shower, and yep, I'm in Blackbriar, Tennessee, or at least I think I am, I never really confirmed that, now that I think of it."

"Are you showering alone?"

I snort incredulously. "Of course I am, why the hell would I call you if I was with someone?"

"I don't know, because you're a fucking weirdo? I don't question these things about you, Lennon."

I shake my head and pour shampoo into my hands. It smells very manly. "How are you doing? Still feeling okay?" I ask him, a pang of worry settling in my stomach as I start to wash my hair.

"Yeah, I'm good. I ate like the biggest steak ever when I got home and then went back for seconds three times, but other than being bloated, I'm right as rain."

"Is your mom ever going to let you near me again?" I ask, trying to be funny, but it falls flat.

"I mean, I'm pretty sure she's never going to let me out of her sight again, so as long as you're cool with her tagging along to the bars and shit, we should be good," he teases, and I smile, feeling a little lighter.

"That bad, huh?"

"Worse. I tried to go out tonight, just to make sure my gaydar is fully operational, and the woman almost had a conniption. She practically turned purple with outrage. I tried to take a picture, but she attacked too fast. Hey, speaking of pictures, Ma wants to know if you want a calendar, coasters, or just a hoodie of Magda and Gwen getting their comeuppance?"

I crack up. Just the image of Tad trying to take a picture of a pissed off Aunt Hillen and then her finding all the swag to put Magda's picture on is enough to chase my worries away.

"Probably just some coasters, oh and maybe a fridge magnet or, like, a keychain if she can find them," I tell him through a fit of giggles. "Any word about Magda?"

"Only that she was going into surgery, and the rest of the family is dead to her. Pretty sure there was something about her not having earthquake coverage and expensive repairs too, but Ma stopped listening to the voicemail about a minute in, and I have no idea what any of that means. Magda's probably drugged out of her gourd."

I snicker and rinse the suds from my hair. "Probably."

"So, how's your Death Eater?" Tad asks, king of the nonsensical segue.

"First of all, there's no *my* anything, and second of all, that's not happening," I inform him as I start to work conditioner through my hair.

"You're a disgrace, Lennox! You have to ride that for posterity's sake. I mean, even if you don't end up happily ever after, you'll be able to look back on those orgasms with fondness. Treat yo self, Leni!"

I shake my head, but I can't help but laugh at his antics. "I admit that he's hot, fuck, even Helen Keller could see that much. And yes, he's probably packin', not that I've looked," I quickly insert. "But you know how weird I am about trust and intimacy. Like, I at least have to know someone and think they're a good person before I get all up on that dick," I remind him.

"I am aware of your deficiencies," Tad states sweetly.

"So that's where we run into an issue. I don't know if I can trust this guy. And it's not just because he walked into the shop and made me his familiar, there's something else there. I know I need to help him, so I am, but really trust him...yeah, I don't see that happening."

"Wait. He what?" Tad practically shouts into the phone. I stop finger-combing my snarls and look over at the phone on the counter. *Shit.* I forgot I hadn't told him that part yet.

"Yeah, he made me his familiar," I hurriedly repeat. "Don't worry, I did it back to him too, so we're kinda even, but needless to say, we didn't exactly get off on the right foot."

"You two are fucking *tethered*?" Tad screeches out, and my mouth drops open in shock.

"How the hell do you even know what that is?" I demand.

"Fuck, Lennox, how do you not know...never mind, I know how you don't know, but like, this is really messed up, Leni. That's some serious level shit, and you two need to undo that right the fuck now."

"We are. We're supposed to go get it sorted tomorrow after we check out his brother's house. But tell me what you know and how the hell you know it. I didn't find anything about this in the book Grammy gave us growing up."

"It's not in the books. You might find stuff about it in the grimoire, I don't know, but I didn't learn this from Grammy, I learned it in Magics Anonymous."

"Are you for real right now? There's a Magics Anonymous?" I question, completely flabbergasted.

"It has a nerdier name than that, that's just what I call it, but it's for people who know about the magical community but aren't really a part of it. People who are *magical adjacent* if you will," he declares with a posh English accent for emphasis.

"Anyway, there's this girl in there, and she was talking about how her bloodline used to have magic until it got fucked up. Apparently, some distant relatives tethered their magic because of true love or some bullshit. Everything was fine until the missus discovered that her mister had a wandering cock, and she immediately severed the bond.

"Now before you go rooting for her and screaming *fuck the patriarchy*, here's where shit got fucked up. Because their magic was tethered for a really long time, it became dependent on the other person's branch in order to work properly. They no longer had two separate branches of magic, now they had one, and it would only work if they were together."

"Holy shit," I whisper as I stare through the glass doors of the shower at the phone, as though I can stem the flow of words coming out of it and make them untrue.

"Exactly," Tad agrees. "This girl's ancestor refused to tether the magic again, and it destroyed the line. Each generation since has a small amount of ability, but not enough to make them a full-blown witch."

"Rogan and I have only been linked for less than a day, though. That couple was married for a while, right?" I ask him, my tone practically pleading for some sign of hope.

"Right, so I think you should be fine, but the sooner you separate, the better it will be for the both of you."

"Fuck, I'm an idiot," I grumble as I wipe water from my face.

"No, you're not, Len. You didn't know. I don't think a lot of witches do. Everyone in the group that day was stunned. *He's* the idiot for putting you in a position where something like this could even happen. That's on him."

I sigh and press the buttons that make the shower hotter. I hear a chime ring, and I know it means Tad just got a message. "Pierre?" I ask.

"Yeah, but I can talk to him later, don't worry about it."

"No, it's fine, Tad, I have a bunch of reading and catching up to do tonight anyway. I'll call you tomorrow."

"You sure?" he asks, and I can hear the worry in his tone.

"Of course, go chase that O-face," I cheer and then cringe. "That felt wrong."

"Yeah, never say something like that again," he teasingly agrees.

"Love ya, talk to you tomorrow."

"Love ya, Lennard," he coos back, and then the line disconnects.

Quickly, I wash the conditioner from my hair and scrub my body clean. I stare down at my wrist, at the swooping *K* and the lacy circle surrounding it. Tracing the lines of Rogan's vow with my eyes, I once again wonder what the hell I've gotten myself into. I take my time drying my hair and pulling my pajamas on, and then I crawl into the bed and pull the grimoire into my lap. Guess it's high time I find out.

13

"Listen, coffee maker, I know you think you're the shit because you're bougie as hell, but let's keep it real. You have one job—to make coffee—and, bitch, right now you're sucking at it. You should be ashamed. What would all the other coffee makers have to say about your attitude?" I growl as I try for the hundredth time to make this damn machine work.

It once again gives me a bunch of lip and then does fuck all. I stare at the bag of coffee beans, debating the merit of skipping the middleman and just eating them. That'll show this snooty bitch of an espresso maker what's up. She doesn't own me. I will prevail.

"Oh hey, you're up," Rogan greets from somewhere behind me.

I quickly drop my hands from the triumphant pose I was just making and do my best to look normal.

"Morning," I sing-song, retreating from my battle with the maker of lifeblood and casually taking a seat at the island.

"Did you make some coffee?" he asks, taking in the mug cradled in my palms.

"No, because your machine is evil," I tell him plainly.

He chuckles and plays with the fickle bitch for a moment. Sure enough, he has her singing a different tune in no time. In just a few minutes, where I discover that Rogan has some very attractive barista skills, a latte is slid in front of me. I add some of the fancy vanilla syrup I found in the pantry and take a loud sip from the oversized mug.

"Fuck me, that's good," I moan.

Rogan chokes on the sip of coffee he just took. He coughs and hits his chest with a closed fist, and I swirl my java around in the cup in solidarity.

"I thoroughly get why people dog on Starbucks all the time now," I announce when he finally gets a grip. "How am I ever going to leave, knowing that I can't reproduce such greatness? It's not right. I'd take your coffee machine as a parting gift for all the shit you've put me through, but she hates me already," I mock whine, silencing my rant with another blissful sip of heaven.

Rogan shakes his head and looks at me curiously as he once again lifts his mug to his lips. "How'd you sleep?" he asks, and then he takes a quiet, demure sip that I have no respect for.

"Didn't," I reply as I practically unhinge my jaw and swallow my cup of coffee whole.

"You...didn't sleep at all?"

"Nope, but I did get a fuck ton of reading done. Cover to cover. And I would just like to point out that my ancestors were fucking genius. Ask me why," I encourage, with a wide, excited smile.

I know I have exhaustion to blame for the manic gleam in my eye and the weird golden retriever mode I'm stuck in right now, but I've been dying to talk to someone, and the espresso machine is shit at conversation.

Rogan looks hesitant, but he plays along like the nice

guy he might be...maybe...the jury is still out on that one. "Why?" he asks.

"Because they wrote the grimoire in ink that had bone matter in it, and that means that as I read each word in there, the spells, incantations, recipes, and lessons all got carved into here." I point to my brain. "Permanently. Genius!" I declare, giving a chef's kiss of approval.

Rogan chuckles into his mug.

"What? You don't think it's genius? Don't tell me your grimoire is written in blood and you already know this trick?" I plead, disheartened.

"No, it's genius," he concedes, and a smile once again brightens my features. "So, just out of curiosity, when you don't get a lot of sleep, what's your cycle? Obviously, slap-happy is cycle one," he points out, circling his finger in my direction as if that's all the proof he needs.

I think about the question.

"Slap-happy, hangry, impatient, and then cuddle slut is a solid pattern for me," I reply candidly.

"Good to know," he quips on another chuckle, and then he places his now empty cup in the sink. "So, I can see you're dressed and ready to go. We can head out to Elon's place, then feed you and, depending on what we find, go from there?" he asks.

"We need to go see whoever you know that can untether us," I add to today's agenda.

"They don't gather on Mondays, but we can go at dusk tomorrow when they'll be there."

I study him suspiciously for a moment, and he sighs like he's tired of my mistrust.

"I told you I would undo everything just as soon as we found my brother. I won't betray that promise, Lennox," he tells me, gesturing to his vow mark on my wrist.

I let out a sigh of my own. "Fine, but I'd feel a lot better knowing that you actually knew how to do it. I didn't find anything in the grimoire about tethering, but my cousin knows a bit about it, and we shouldn't fuck around with this. I will help you find your brother, but we shouldn't risk damaging our magic over mistrust. I'll vow to help if that's what you need."

"I don't mistrust you, and I'm not lying when I say that the coven we need to speak with doesn't gather on Mondays. Tomorrow evening will be the first chance we get to speak with them."

"Okay, then tomorrow it is," I relent, finishing my cup and pushing up from my stool. I walk over to the sink and place my own mug next to his. I fill them both with water and turn to find Rogan watching me intently.

"Well, let's go then, before my hangry mode kicks in."

"After you," he gallantly offers, and all I can do is roll my eyes.

Yeah right, Rogan Kendrick, you're not fooling me.

Rogan's brother lives about twenty minutes away. From what I can see, Blackbriar is a very rural town with houses spread far apart and plenty of trees and land between them. I'm surprised by how green Tennessee is. I don't really know what I expected, but it's beautiful here and peaceful. I can see the draw of escaping the big cities and living a quiet life in a place like this.

The long driveway that leads to Elon's home isn't paved like Rogan's is, and I get a sense that it's like that on purpose. There's an unwelcome vibe to the property, and I suspect that it's the result of a ward placed around the property. I didn't feel anything like this at Rogan's house, but all I can conclude about that is that it's possible I might not feel any protections he set because our magic is tied together at the moment. His wards might not see me as separate from him, so they're not being triggered like they are here. Images of when he broke through my protective circle at my shop keep popping up in my head, and although I haven't discussed it with him, I think I'm right.

I can feel the house before I ever even see it, feel the booby traps he has placed all around his property. I would be wary if I weren't in such awe. We crest a hill, and there in the middle of a glade, is a two-story house that would be any Queen Anne architecture aficionado's wet dream. The house is a rich navy blue with crisp white trim and gold accents on the gables, turned posts, and spindle work. But as stunning and impressive as the details and size of the house are, it's the bones I feel in the foundation and surrounding every entrance that have me gobsmacked.

This house is a fortress for an Osteomancer. The care and intricacies of the magic and osseous materials woven into the very fabric of the home and the surrounding property are things I would have never thought possible. I'm almost overwhelmed by the feel of this place, which is funny because it truly is a Bone Witch's safe haven.

"What do you think?" Rogan asks me, a sly smile stretched across his too pretty face.

"I think you know what I think," I whisper reverently, turning my attention back to the house as we get closer.

"I thought you might like it," he declares, pride saturating the statement.

"Is your house like this too?" I ask in complete awe. I don't know why I just assumed witches fit into human society, buying human homes and making do with them as best they could. But no, what's in front of me was built by a witch, for a witch, and I'm envious as fuck.

"It is," he confirms. "There's blood soaked into the land

itself. Every material in the home is painted with blood blessings and wards of protection. There's no safer place in the world for me. And the same should have been the case for Elon too."

The SUV that Rogan chose to drive comes to a stop just outside of the three-car garage, and all I can think is *how much did this place cost?* It's on the tip of my tongue to ask, but my manners kick in, and I bite it back. I know that all the Bone Witches before me in my line left me with a sizable nest egg, but even with *that*, a house like this might very well be out of my league.

"Yeah, I don't see anyone getting through here unless they were allowed," I agree, gesturing toward the surrounding land and distant tree line. "So that begs the question, who did he let in, and why did he keep it from you?" I ask, turning to take in Rogan's expression.

He stares up at the house, the bay windows gleaming in the morning light, and shrugs. "I wish I knew."

I open the car door and step out into the cool morning air. There's not a hint of big city laced in the molecules I inhale, and if I didn't know any better, I'd swear I could taste a hint of acorn squash and apples in the wind as it whips my hair around.

Rogan's car door closes, the sound bouncing off the distant trees, and he walks up to the garage and enters a code that makes the door slowly begin to rise. A smaller white SUV sits dormant, and Rogan leads me past it and into the house. A light wood, herringbone-patterned floor guides us into the kitchen. I can see that the interior is updated but still has all the charm and character of the outside.

There's a loaf of opened white bread on the island, next to a plate and a can of soda.

I recall Rogan saying that his brother didn't eat or drink

any of these things, so I go meander by them to see if there's anything I might pick up that Rogan didn't. I get nothing.

Rogan doesn't say much, just waits until I'm done perusing his brother's space, and then leads me to the next living area. I walk through the living room, giving the pile of whatever it is that's surrounded by crushed rowanberries a wide berth. I meander through Elon's office, observing the pictures on his desk and bookshelves. All of them are of him and Rogan.

Elon is shorter, and his green eyes are darker, but there's no mistaking the family resemblance. "Are you two twins?" I ask, even though I'm pretty sure the answer is no. I feel like that would have been an important thing to mention before now if it were the case.

"No, he's older by almost a year," he tells me from where he's leaning against the door that has beautiful stained glass inlays with bone borders.

"So Irish twins then," I observe as I pull a book out that was sticking out more than the others on the shelf, almost like someone put it back in a hurry. The spine and contents are in a language I don't know, but I flip through it just in case something pops out at me. Nothing does.

We do a quick tour of the upstairs, where I discover that Elon sleeps on a bed frame made of bones, and that's where I draw the line with my envy, because that's just weird. I could feel extra protections in his bedroom, including bones under the floorboards, almost like this room could serve as some kind of panic room, or if there was a last stand to be made, this was the place to do it. It was all a bit too much.

Rogan's phone chirps, and he brings it up to his ear and answers it. I debate spying on him for a couple of seconds, but when it seems like the call is businessy and boring, I see myself downstairs. I stand in the middle of Elon's living room and ask the bones to help me figure out what happened in here, but I feel nothing from them. There's no residual panic or pain that they're hanging onto, there's not even a trace of fear, which there most definitely would be if Elon's familiar was burned in here.

I walk over to the kitchen counter and untie my bones from my hip. I grab the plastic pincher thing that's supposed to keep the twisted opening of the bread closed, and then rip the metal tab off the soda can. I drop both items into the purple pouch, close the top, and shake the bones. I ask them to help me read the person who bought these things, and I shake until the bones let me know that they're ready.

I'm not sure what to expect, but when I dump the bones, a sea of blankness is not it. Every symbol on every bone is face down, making it so I can't see them. The metal tab and the bread pincher are off to the side as though the bones have rejected their presence. I stare at the spread for a moment to make sure I don't miss anything.

Well, it was worth a shot.

I pick up the bones one by one and drop them back in the pouch, but when I grasp one particularly large chip, the bone heats in my hand. I flip it over to see the symbol for letters or language, depending on the context and angle of how this particular bone piece lands. I study it, trying to decipher what this could mean, and after a beat, it comes to me.

I set that bone aside and quickly place the others back in the pouch. I look around me, wondering where Elon keeps his scrying tools, and then remember that I don't need his, I can summon my own, just like I did the bone knife that I used to free Tad from the hex. I close the velvet bag and ask it to give me the scrying board and pendulum I rescued from my evil aunt's house. When I open the bag and reach in, it's there, and excitement flashes through me. Magic is fucking cool, and I hum my appreciation as I pull the scrying board and onyx pendulum from my bone pouch. I set them on the table and then place the bone that warmed in my hand back inside the pouch.

I wipe the bone board down with the hem of my shirt, cleaning out the grooves of the center design, which is an elaborate sun with a face that has closed eyes, and a crescent moon that's cupping the sun from below. It's the size of a large pancake, with the word *yes* centered at the top of the board and the word *no* at the bottom. The alphabet is carved, letter by letter, into the right curve of the circular board, and the numbers one through ten on the left side of the circle.

I give the board and pendulum a moment to get acclimated, and then I grab the bronze chain and lift the onyx stone attached on the other end above the board and demand that they spill their secrets. The pure black stone of the pendulum zings so fast to the letter *N*, that I have to fight my reaction to duck and find cover. I'm suddenly so glad that Rogan isn't here to witness this, because I probably look like an idiot, but I recover just in time to see the stone fly to the letter *I*. *K* follows quickly, and then an *S, M, E, L, S, E, R*.

Quickly, with my free hand, I conjure a pad of paper and a pen. It's the fanciest stationery I've ever seen, and the pen is made from a rabbit's leg, but a witch's gotta do what a witch's gotta do. I write down the letters, staring at them for a minute as I try to decipher what they mean.

"Is this another language other than English?" I ask the board.

The pendulum streaks down to the word *no* and then circles it before going still.

Okay. Not another language. Niksmelser. What the hell does that mean in English then?

"Is this a location?"

No is once again circled, squashing that hope.

"Is this word a code? Is there a key needed to decipher it?"

The pendulum doesn't move, and then I remember that the grimoire states to only ask one question at a time. "Is this a code?"

No.

"Is it a name?" I ask, hoping for a long shot.

Excitement sparks in me when the pendulum moves away from *no* and flashes to *yes*. I stare at the scrying board, surprised by that response, and then I look at the paper. I study it for a moment, trying to pull a name from the arranged letters. I draw a slash between the *K* and the *S* of the word to create Nik Smelser.

Holy shit. It *is* a name.

"How do I find Nik Smelser?" I ask the board, figuring one long shot worked, why not a twofer? The pendulum flies to the letter *R*, then to the *U*, and rests lastly on the *N*. My brow furrows in confusion.

"Run? You want me to run?" I query, and then the onyx stone begins to tremor on the board before it shoots into the pouch out of nowhere. I jump back, startled, and that's when something catches my eye. I look through the bay window that shows the land at the back of the house, and see a man slowly stalking toward the back door.

Oh fuck, we gotta go!

14

Fear hammers through me and sends my pulse galloping away as though it's a thoroughbred making a play for the Triple Crown. My throat grows tight, and I have just enough time to realize that we won't make it out of here before whoever that is comes crashing through the back door.

"Rogan!" I shout in warning as I round the island and thrust out my hand.

I have two warring arguments going on inside of me right now. One is pleading for me to hide, and the other wants to fuck shit up. I lift my hand slowly, tapping into the bones buried all around the yard. When I have a hold of what I need, I close my fingers into a fist, and white missiles rip out of the earth to form a cage around the intruder.

Fuck shit up, it is.

I run for the back door and fling it open. It slams against the wood of the house with a loud bang that sends more adrenaline jolting through me. With my other hand, I call on the bone stakes hidden all around the property. A floating ring of femur-sized spears surround the bony cage, and I take in the trapped intruder as I move cautiously closer.

I expand my senses to see if there's anyone else here besides him, but I don't feel another presence. I shove power out into every bone on the property, and a pulse of magic tears out of me in a brutal tidal wave that sends my prisoner crashing against the bones surrounding him and crumpling to the ground. A flash of something pops up in my mind, but I shove it aside so I can magically feel everything around me and assess the threat level. To my surprise, Elon even hung bone chimes in the trees, making it possible to feel an attack coming from above.

I tuck my admiration away, and focus on the man in the cage as he gets back onto his feet and starts to brush himself off. "I just bought this shirt," he grumps, fingering a tear in the sleeve that must have caught on a bone fragment. My ring of bone stakes constricts slightly, and he looks over at the movement with clear annoyance written all over his face. He turns his gaze on me, his eyes widening a fraction, before a cold wall of indifference slams down in their espresso depths.

"You're not Elon," he states evenly, a strange hint of seduction in the obvious observation. "And you're not any of my missing witches..." he goes on.

"*Your* witches?" I question as a thumping noise comes from the house. I turn to see if Rogan is coming, but an overwhelmingly enticing voice catches my attention instead.

"Drop the weapons, Love, and then drop the cage," he commands, but the words are wrapped in something so luscious and delectable that my whole body warms to it regardless of how ridiculous the order is. "Do as you're told, gorgeous, and then we'll have a nice *long* talk afterward," he practically purrs, and it's as though his words are a soft blanket on a chilly day. I want to wrap them all around me, snuggle into them, and let the hidden promises in each syllable melt me from the inside out, in all the most sinful ways.

What the hell?

I take a step toward my prisoner but stop myself as doubt pinballs around in my mind. I study him for a moment, arrogance etched in his square jaw, cocked eyebrow, and the sensual curve of his lips. His hair is combed to the side in a perfect blond wave, and as nice as he is to look at, letting him out makes no sense.

Understanding dawns on me, just as irritation flashes in his dark brown gaze. He's a Vox Witch. I just read last night about the sirens of old. I focus magic in the bones surrounding my ear, and the heady buzz his magic has resonating through me stops like someone just flipped the off switch.

"Very good, Osteomancer," he commends, no more magic dripping from his words.

"Who the hell are you, and why are you here?" I demand, forcing my bone stakes to streak toward him, stopping only inches away from his throat.

He holds his hands up as if to plead for me to stop, and a booming *whoa* sounds off behind me. This time, I don't take my attention away from the witch in the bone cage as Rogan comes running up beside me.

"Took you long enough," I snap, and I don't miss that the Vox Witch's face relaxes slightly when Rogan enters the picture.

"Well, if someone hadn't thrown me off the stairs with their burst of magic, I would have gotten here sooner. What the fuck are you doing?" he snaps at me.

"Exactly what it looks like I'm doing," I snap back. "I'm getting some answers from the lurker I found in the backyard."

"Lennox, this is Marx, the witch from the Order I was telling you about. The one investigating the disappearances. I asked him to meet us here."

I huff out a frustrated breath and turn to him, vexation radiating out of me. "You didn't think that maybe a heads-up would have been good in this situation?" I grumble, flinging my arms back so the bone stakes and parts making up the cage bury themselves deep in the ground again.

"I got tied up, and he got here faster than I thought," Rogan defends, turning his attention to the Order member Marx. "Are you okay?" he asks, stepping toward him and extending his hand.

Marx extends his as well, and they grip each other's forearms in the witch version of a handshake.

"You owe me a shirt," Marx deadpans, and Rogan gives a humorous snort as they separate and look over at me. "And who is this? I haven't received word that any of the missing witches' powers had moved down their line."

"They haven't. This is Ruby's successor."

Marx's head snaps to Rogan, shock replacing his swagger, and there seems to be some kind of odd unspoken conversation between the two as Rogan nods his head once in confirmation. The exchange happens so fast I'm not sure what to make of it. But before I can so much as try to interpret what just happened between them, Marx's eyes are back on mine. He closes the distance between us, his hand extended, and as uncertain as I am, I also don't want to offend the Order in any way.

When he's right in front of me, I take his arm, gripping his forearm hard enough to convey, *you don't want to mess with this*, without downright offering a challenge. He holds my arm a second too long, his fathomless espresso stare studying me intensely.

"I'm sorry to hear about Ruby. She was greatly respected

and will be eternally missed," Marx offers, and the reminder of her loss makes my throat grow tighter with emotion. Marx releases his grip, his fingers running a line down the inside of my forearm as he steps back. Then just before he pulls his hand away, he flips my palm up and runs his gaze over my wrist.

He does it quickly, smoothly, probably hoping his touch alone serves as enough of a distraction that I won't think twice about what he just did. But Rogan's vow mark sits crimson against my skin, and suspicion swells in my gut.

How did he know to look for that?

"What are you doing?" I ask evenly as he casually steps back, an attractive and friendly smile on his face. It's probably meant to disarm me, but all it does is serve to make me even more uneasy.

Marx's brow dips in confusion, but his eyes don't radiate the same emotion. "Getting acquainted with the newest Bone Witch of the revered Osseous line. Why?" he queries innocently.

Rogan moves his weight from one foot to the other, and my eyes narrow.

"What am I missing here?" I press.

"What do you mean?" Rogan counters.

"Don't answer my question with a question, what's going on?"

"Lennox—"

"Don't Lennox me, Rogan. This place is like that bunker the government built inside a mountain in Colorado," I point out, gesturing to the house behind me. "I swear on my ancestors I will walk right in there and make this bitch *impenetrable* if you don't tell me what you two are up to. And don't even think of insulting me by saying nothing. Something else is going on here, I feel it in my fucking bones," I snarl at the two shady witches.

They both just stare at me, silently, and I can feel my rancor rising. I spin on my heel, but Rogan reaches out and catches my arm. With a flick of my wrist, there's a bone spike centimeters away from his throat. He bats it away like the threat means nothing, and it makes me want to scream in frustration. I can't really do any serious damage to him without risking it affecting *our* magic.

"Ooh, this is fun," Marx quips as Rogan and I stare at each other, fuming.

"Three months ago, your grandmother warned the Order that someone wanted to restore the fragmented branches of magic back to one." Rogan stares, his eyes burrowing into mine. "She didn't know more than that, said it came to her in a dream. She tried to dig into who and why, but she told us no matter what she did, she was blocked, that she couldn't see more than the warning itself."

"We, of course, took note of the cautionary message, but with no one else in the community reporting a similar vision, and with Ruby unable to dig any deeper, it was filed away and forgotten," Marx adds.

"And then witches started disappearing," Rogan states quietly.

I pull my arm from his grip and step back, needing distance between us as I reel from what they're saying. "How do you know all of this?"

"I didn't at first, not until Elon disappeared. I hit a dead-end and called Marx, hoping he could help, and that's when he told me about your grandmother and her warning."

"Guess who was tasked with filing the report," Marx states, pointing a thumb at himself.

Anger and bewilderment nest behind my sternum, and I try to piece together why Rogan didn't tell me all of this from the beginning. "So what does all of this have to do with me?"

"I went to see your grandmother, hoping somehow she could shed some light on this. I thought if Elon's disappearance had to do with her warning, maybe now she might be able to pick up on something. Hopefully give us a lead, but when I got there, I found you."

His green eyes shoot to Marx for a millisecond before coming back to me, and my hackles go up in warning.

"When I realized that Ruby was gone, it dawned on me that maybe the reason she couldn't see, read, or sense who might be behind her warning was because the culprit was close to her. So I—"

"You thought I was behind this?" I interrupt, gesturing to his brother's safe haven behind me. "And what, making me your familiar..."

"Was an insurance policy," Rogan finishes. "If you were behind it, I could put you in check. If not, no harm done."

"No. Fucking. Harm. Done?" I seethe.

"I didn't know you were going to tether us," he defends, and rage overcomes me.

"Are you insinuating that this is my fault?" I shriek, and I feel the land beneath my feet and the house behind me quake slightly with my fury.

"Whoa, just calm down," Marx inserts.

"Shove calm up your ass, Siren," I fling back, and his answering chuckle pisses me off even more.

"My grandmother had just died, you discovered that when you walked into the shop that morning. How could I have done any of this? I didn't have any magic before then, what would be the point of kidnapping a bunch of people more powerful than me?"

"You don't have to be a witch to get the drop on other witches. Not having magic doesn't rule you out as a suspect or make you powerless. You were the next in line, it was a fair assumption Kendrick made," Marx points out in Rogan's defense.

"I didn't know I was the next in line," I counter. "And I didn't kidnap anyone. I don't give a shit about the *fragmented branches of magic*. So are we good now? Can I go home and be done with all this bullshit?" I question, hating the betrayal I feel and just how badly it stings. I knew there was more to all of this, but I didn't know *I* was on the suspect list.

"Why am I here?" I ask, my tone hollow. "You knew before now that I wasn't involved."

"I did, but I was hoping you could still help," Rogan admits. "That maybe you could pick up on something I couldn't." He rubs the back of his neck awkwardly, a sheepish look on his face. "There was also the issue of the tether. A coven here is the only one I've ever heard talk about it, so I knew they could fix it."

My eyes jump back and forth between Rogan and Marx as I place all the pieces I just learned in front of me. "If you're the member of the Order, and the one investigating the missing witches, why didn't you come to speak with my grandmother?" I ask Marx, not understanding that part of the puzzle. "Why would you come?" I question Rogan.

Marx's eyes drop to the ground, and he toes some ripped up earth from where a piece of bone buried itself. "Because this isn't an official Order investigation."

"I don't understand," I confess as confusion hammers me so hard I can feel a headache coming on from it.

I need a damn nap.

"It's not an official investigation, because we don't want anyone in the organization to know we're looking into things. That's why *I* didn't go to meet with your grandmother; I can't leave my assigned district unless it's for a case, and technically *this* isn't one," Marx supplies.

"Our theory, before we suspected your grandmother,

and then subsequently you..." Rogan adds, "was that maybe someone high up in the Order was behind this. Which is why we have to be careful."

Understanding crashes down on me like an anvil. I don't like any of it, but I can't pretend that it doesn't all fit together. I just wish I knew how to feel about everything they just purged. I want to tell myself that I shouldn't feel betrayed—I knew Rogan was playing close to the vest—but everything feels tainted with deception now, and it's bothering the shit out of me.

I shake my head and fold my arms over my chest, as though the stance can somehow protect me from any more duplicity and hurt. "Nik Smelser," I offer, my tone thoroughly pissed off.

"Nik Smelser," Rogan parrots.

"I don't know who it is or if they're even involved, but it's the name the bones gave me when I was scrying."

Rogan's head snaps to Marx, who is already writing the name down.

"Did you get anything else?" Marx asks, his dark brown eyes rising from the small magicked notepad in his hands and settling on me.

"No," I declare, deciding to keep the flash I saw when I connected to all the bones on the property to myself. I'm not sure what it means yet, and these guys aren't the only ones who can hold out until they know more.

"That's a lie," Marx declares, with a cocked brow, his tone a dead ringer for Maury Povich's.

Shit.

I forgot Vox Witches could hear that. Stupid walking, talking lie detectors. Rookie move, Lennox. Rogan's face clouds with anger, and for some reason that makes me feel better.

"Don't look at me like that. If I'm holding back, you only

have your own omissions and cagey behavior to blame," I defend and release a resigned exhale. "I'm not sure what it means yet. If I decide it's pertinent, I'll tell you. That's how you two like to roll, isn't it?"

I turn and stride back into the house, dodging Rogan's effort to grab me again and stop me. I duck out the door leading to the garage but get boxed in by the two of them before I can go any further.

"This isn't a game," Rogan growls as he lords over me, backing me into Marx until I'm pinned between them.

"I'm not playing one. This isn't tit for tat. I need to see the other Osteomancers' houses before I know if this is even relevant," I defend.

"Fine, I'll take you to them, but keeping anything to yourself right now is a stupid move. It could mean life or death in the end if it *was* pertinent," he grumbles, his stare both angry and desperate.

I give a derisive snort, hating that he's right. I take a deep breath and slowly let it out. "The pile of ashes inside the rowanberries are from the grill outside. I don't know what purpose the presence of the smashed berry circle serves, but I think its only purpose is to throw anyone looking for Elon off."

"How do you know this?" Marx questions, and I shoot him a glare. He holds his hands up in surrender. "I'm not saying you're lying, it's just a side effect of what I do, I question everything."

"Because when I went into defensive mode, I tapped into every bone that exists on the property. I wasn't picking up on anything unusual inside the house because the bones that had this information aren't inside the house," I explain.

"Your brother's familiar is a corgi right?" I ask Rogan.

"Yeah, her name is Tilda," he confirms.

I nod and continue. "Well, Tilda was chewing on a

venison rib bone when she watched the ashes being moved into the house and the berry circle drawn around them. You'll find a different piece of her burnt collar on the ground around the grill."

"Did she see who did it?" Rogan asks, grabbing my arms as though he's ready to shake the answer out of me at the first sign of resistance.

"That's the thing," I hedge as anxious butterflies riot in my stomach. "It was your brother."

15

"Tell me again what you saw," Rogan grumbles, the engine of his SUV growling ferociously as he stomps on the accelerator.

I try not to roll my eyes at the request or the maniacal driving, but I lose the battle. "I saw your brother dump the ashes from the grill into his living room. I mean, I saw it through Tilda's eyes, but you know what I mean."

Rogan's hands clench around the steering wheel, his knuckles going white, and I grab onto the armrest on the door when he takes a turn a little too fast. Good thing we left Hoot at the house earlier. That furball would be a windshield pancake otherwise.

"Then I saw Elon hooking a halter around Tilda and leading her out the front door. She stopped to drop some deuces on the lawn, and because your brother doesn't pick up after his familiar, I saw in the bone matter she left behind, that he had on a big pack, the kind you use for camping. That's all I got," I repeat...for the third time.

"It just doesn't make sense," he whispers angrily for the thousandth time, and I swallow down an exasperated sigh that wants to punctuate my annoyance.

I should feel bad for Rogan. I know he's going mad worrying about his brother and what happened to him, but I'm finding it hard to reach my soft empathetic side through all the hurt and bitter anger I feel surrounding it.

"Then who the hell is Nik Smelser?" Rogan questions...again.

"Like I said *before*, I don't know. I don't even know if he's relevant to anything. It's just the name the bones gave."

"Fuck!" Rogan snarls, slamming a hand down against the steering wheel. I jump at the unexpected outburst, and my fight or flight instincts get ready to take over the show.

"I get that you're pissed, Rogan, but I don't want to die. So slow down and chill out or pull over so I can safely get us somewhere where you can execute the epic tantrum that's clearly crawling under your skin."

He doesn't say anything, but the car gradually starts to decelerate, and I inhale and then slowly release a relieved breath.

"As I said back at Elon's house, there's no point jumping to any conclusions until we have more information. Marx is looking into things now, and he said he would let us know when it's clear to go look at the other Osteomancers' houses."

"But why would he willingly leave?" Rogan argues, and I run my fingers through my curls in frustration, pleading with my ancestors for patience.

"Dude. Pay. Attention!" I growl, clapping three times to punctuate each word. "We don't know that he did. It's hard as hell to interpret the world through a dog's eyes. I'm literally reading information from bone matter in shit. Maybe Elon left on his own. Maybe he was spelled. Maybe he was coerced some other way. There could be a logical explanation for all of this. Or maybe the Osteomancers are all working together to bring out the cult in occult. We just don't know yet."

A yawn forces me to pause. I need to up my caffeine intake, or I'm about to pass out.

"I need coffee and a massive grilled cheese, oh and pie, or something pumpkiny. But not pumpkin coffee, that shit just tastes like burnt Thanksgiving. If you can get me somewhere that has grilled cheese *and* tomato soup in the next ten minutes, maybe I'll stop being as pissed as I am with you...maybe."

The car accelerates again, but this time, my stomach and I welcome it. I've definitely entered the hangry phase of my exhaustion cycle, and it's not being helped by everything that Rogan and Marx revealed back at Elon's house. I replay the conversation, picking apart things that I feel like I still need answers to. I lean back in my chair and turn to face Rogan as he races to make things up to me.

It dawns on me that I should probably appreciate that he's trying, that he cares enough to attempt to make things right in some small way, but we'll see how I feel after I get done grilling him.

"Why did you and Marx suspect my grandmother?" I ask, ticking off my first question on the list I made in my head.

"What?" Rogan asks, looking over at me for a moment before focusing back on the road.

"You said that when you found out that my grandmother was gone, you thought maybe I had something to do with the disappearances, and that was why Ruby couldn't read or sense anything. But after that, you said that you suspected her too. I want to know why."

"Suspected is probably the wrong word. Marx and I were just trying to look at things from all angles. Ruby was the strongest Osteomancer alive. So it could be argued that if someone was trying to meld the branches, she'd be the only one powerful enough to do it."

"So when you came to see her, if she had been the one in the shop that day, you would have made her your familiar, wouldn't you? It wasn't a last minute Hail Mary decision, it wasn't an insurance plan that kicked in because of me," I clarify.

Rogan studies me for a moment, but I see the answer in his eyes before he voices it.

"Yes. Marx and I thought it was the best and fastest way to gain control over the situation."

I shake my head and turn away from him. "You're lucky it was me that day. She would have ripped you apart," I tell him quietly, hating how alone I suddenly feel.

"Very lucky," he repeats just as softly, but I don't bother trying to interpret what that could mean.

With squealing tires, Rogan slides us into a parking spot dead center in front of a diner. "Seven minutes and counting," he announces with a small hesitant smile.

I unbuckle my seat belt and reach for the door handle. "Impressive," I admit as I climb out of the SUV. "Now I'll daydream about breaking two hundred *five* of your bones and not the full two hundred six that you actually have," I tell him as I stride for the front door.

He beats me to it and pulls it open, sleigh bells tinkling and announcing our arrival to a waitress. I shake my head at him. "I'm still not buying it," I censure.

"Buying what?" he queries.

"That you're a gentleman. So no need to keep up the act on my account."

He doesn't say anything as we're led to a booth and handed menus. I slide into my seat, and I'm reminded of doing the same thing just yesterday, when I sat down to talk to Paul. His face flashes in my mind, and I wonder how he and Jackson are doing today. I close my eyes for a moment and send them warm, hopeful thoughts.

"What can I get you to drink?" the waitress with short salt-and-pepper hair and amiable blue eyes asks.

"May I please have some coffee? And do you have tomato soup here?"

"Yes, and yes," she tells me warmly.

"Two hundred and four bones now," I correct, looking over at Rogan.

I order my wish list, completely over the moon when they have everything I've been craving. Rogan gets some kind of melt and blueberry crumble for dessert, and as soon as he orders it, I start debating if I can be pissed at him but still ask for a bite? I'm thinking yes.

"So how did you and Marx become such good friends?" I ask as the waitress brings over two bowl-sized mugs and pours almost a full carafe of coffee into them.

I start doctoring mine up, waiting for Rogan to answer the question. I can feel his hesitancy, like I can feel the waitress's sore bones as she moves gingerly from table to table, refilling the other patrons' drinks.

"We used to work together," Rogan finally tells me as he shakes a few packets of sugar, tearing them all open at once and dumping them into his mug.

I ponder that answer for a moment, mostly because I practically chug my cup of coffee down, but surprise zings through me when I put things together. "You used to work for the Order?"

He nods solemnly and then demurely samples his brew. "We were on a team together. We were who the Order called when they needed elite magic to deal with something."

"Oh, the best of the best," I mock, and he sighs and fixes me with an unamused stare.

"Anyway, I know about the Order and the rampant

corruption firsthand. Elon and I almost didn't make it out of their ranks alive."

A chill runs up my spine at that revelation, and I randomly have the urge to reach out and offer a comforting touch. I look down at my hands—which are cradling my coffee—and glare at them as though they've betrayed me.

"What's wrong?" Rogan asks, studying me.

"Nothing," I answer a little too quickly. With a swift shake of my head, I dispel the uninvited urge and focus back on what we were discussing. "So that's what's up with all the protective measures?" I ask, placing another vital piece of understanding in the puzzle that is Rogan Kendrick.

"It's good to have protections in place with any home, but yes, Elon and I are overly cautious. We have good reason to be."

"So all the blood protecting your house, is that yours?"

"No, I'd never be able to build up the quantities I needed if I used only my own. Certain wards or blessings required my blood, but the rest was from the blood bank. I take the units that are not transfusion quality and use them for what I need."

"That's smart," I blurt and then wish I could take the compliment back when he gets a cocky grin on his face. "I mean, they probably think you're a vampire or something, but you and the Order are already at odds, so good for you, live your best life."

Rogan chuckles. "There's no exposure risk there for our kind. They think I work for a contracted quality control company. They get a discount on my rate if they allow me to deal with the unusable blood."

"For real? They pay *you*?" I laugh, unable to deny how sneaky and well played that is. It makes me wonder what other witches do to source ingredients and all the witchy things they need.

Our food arrives and we fall into companionable silence as we stuff our faces. I dip my sandwich into my soup and practically orgasm with the first bite. Rogan just shakes his head and tries to fight a smile as I make sweet, sweet love to my lunch without a single ounce of shame.

"Crap, now I have to figure out how to steal your coffee machine and make it like me, while also relocating this diner across the street from my house. That was so good," I purr as I sit back and pat my happy food baby.

"It was *just* a grilled cheese," Rogan points out with a judgmental chuckle.

"Just? *Just* he says. Dude, that was exquisite, that's what that was."

The waitress drops the check off in front of us with a wide smile. She's been sneaking peeks at Rogan the whole time, and she gets this adorable blush when he catches her and gives her a toothy grin. It's a sweet thing to do, but I'm still not falling for his act.

"You know," I start, catching the waitress's attention. "There's an herbal tea that really helps with muscle and joint pain. It's pretty much just willow bark, turmeric, ginger, and some eucalyptus, but I could bring you some if you're interested," I offer. "I can't imagine it feels good to be on your feet for so many hours out of the day," I add so I don't make her feel self-conscious about picking up on her pain.

"It does get harder every year. I'll try anything as long as it's legal, doesn't give me the runs, and keeps my head clear," she announces, and I crack up at her candor.

"Yep, it's all legal herbs, with no fuzzy-head side effects or the Hershey squirts," I reassure her. I don't mention the bone powder that's also in it. What she doesn't know won't hurt her, in fact, it'll have her feeling like she's twenty again.

"I can bring some by for you tomorrow if that's okay. No charge of course."

"Well, aren't you just the sweetest. I'll take all the help I can get at my age," she teases, patting me on the arm gently before going to tend to another table.

I turn to Rogan, a satisfied smile on my face. His gaze drops to my lips for a fraction of a second before they bounce back up to my eyes.

"Is there anything else we need to do today while we're waiting to hear back from Marx?"

"No, but as soon as he gives us the green light to check things out, we'll be headed for a ley line," he tells me.

My stomach sinks a little at the thought of dissolving into molecules and snapping back together so hard that I pass out. What if I don't pass out this time, but actually feel it? A shudder runs through me, and I push those thoughts far...far away.

"Fair enough," I concede with an audible swallow. "In the meantime then, is there anywhere around here that I can get bones? I have a tea to make."

My knee bounces with excitement and nervous anticipation as we fly down a winding hilly road.

"So, is there anything I need to know about meeting a lycan clan?" I ask, lifting my thumb to my mouth so I can anxiously bite my nail. Rogan looks over, his eyes dipping to my lips again, and I drop my hand and scold myself for the nervous habit.

"Um, they're pretty much just like you and me, only their magic gives them four legs and the ability to lick their own balls."

I almost choke on a laugh, not expecting that answer,

and shoot Rogan a sympathetic look. "Are you jealous?" I coo at him. He shakes his head and tries to fight the smile twitching at his lips.

"There's no rules about eye contact or anything like that?" I question, not wanting to do anything that will cause any trouble.

"I mean, I wouldn't go challenging anyone to a staring contest or sniff anyone's ass in greeting. Just be normal, you'll be fine."

"No ass sniffing, got it."

"Elon and I've worked with this clan as far back as I can remember. Our uncles procured through them too. A lot of witches around the country hire them to source things; they won't think anything of us stopping by for some bones. In fact, we've picked a good day to drop in; tomorrow is Fall Equinox, and the full moon isn't too far away. They're probably celebrating already," he tells me with a conspiratorial wag of his eyebrows.

I pull in a deep breath. I don't know which is more concerning, meeting lycans in general or drunk lycans. Guess I'm about to find out.

Rogan slows as he approaches a large iron-barred gate. There's a house-sized security lodge to the right of us, and he maneuvers the car toward it and rolls the window down. A guard inside walks toward the glass slider separating us. He opens it and proceeds to stare into the car.

"Rogan Kendrick and Lennox Osseous to see Riggs and Viv," he states to the guard.

"Do you have an appointment?" the guard asks, his nostrils flaring as though he's scenting us.

"Yes, I called and made one just over an hour ago."

Another guard walks over and hands the first a tablet. The lycan at the window looks it over and then nods at Rogan once. "Please exit your vehicle so it, and you, can be searched," the guard declares, and then he shuts the slider and walks away.

"Well, that's new," Rogan mumbles as he puts his car in park and unbuckles himself. I do the same, stepping out of the car and onto the damp bracken of the forest floor. I'm surrounded by trees taller than buildings. There's the smell of rain on the air, and I suspect we must have just missed the storm. I look around at the endless expanse of forest, and it's exactly what I pictured when Rogan told me where we'd be getting bones.

Two beefy guards tromp out of the lodge and make their way over to us. The one with brown hair and a smattering of freckles on his nose rounds the car toward me. He gives me a Colgate grin as his eyes drop down to my feet and slowly climb back up. "Do you mind if I search you, miss?" he asks politely, and I hold out my arms.

"Go for it," I tell him nonchalantly, and he bends and starts patting around my ankles.

His hands move up one calf and then the other. They skim my thighs and then dip into the top of my jeans, circling the waistband. He runs the back of his hands over my stomach, flipping them over to guide his wide palms up my back, and I notice he's pulling in deep breaths of air as he goes. His long fingers find my scalp and part my wildly curly hair in search of anything that could be used against him. His fingers feel good against my scalp, and I have to actively stop myself from closing my eyes and leaning into the touch.

Playing with my hair is my kryptonite.

He gently tugs on the hair at the base of my skull, and it forces me to tilt my head back. I bite back a moan. I meet bright silver eyes and a salacious smile as the guard frisking me runs his hands over the tops of my shoulders and then drops them down my arms.

"All clear," he states evenly, his intense gaze unmoving from mine. "Welcome to the Bristow Clan, miss."

"Thank you," I respond, just a little breathless.

His grin grows infinitesimally wider. "Sorry for the search, but we can never be too careful."

I shrug and shake my head. "No apology needed, I'm happy to oblige," I reassure him, a flirty smile now cresting my lips. I check him out as he steps back. He's lean and fit and, I suspect, filled with all kinds of stamina.

"Are you staying for the festivities tonight?" he asks as he slowly backs away, his eyes suddenly gleaming as though they're lit from within.

I'm completely captivated by them.

"Um, I don't know," I confess as he rounds the car back toward the security lodge.

"Well, I'll keep an eye out later...just in case," he tells me, a delicious grit to his voice, and then he disappears back into the house.

I stare after him for a moment, and then Rogan clears his throat loudly, snapping me out of my creeper mode. Heat crawls up my neck, and I pull the passenger door open and climb back into the car. I busy myself with getting buckled in and fluffing my curls, and the next thing I know the iron gate is sliding open and granting us entry.

"Well, that was interesting," I observe casually as I work to get a hold of my hormones.

"Mmm," Rogan agrees with an irritated man grunt. "Seems they're very personable these days," he adds, his eyes fixed intensely on the road.

The paved path abruptly turns to packed dirt, and we drive for a couple of miles before coming across a large gathering of lycans. We park and climb out of the SUV, and I'm greeted by happy chatter, laughter, and the smell of BBQ.

We park just outside of an enclosure that has little kids running around in it, chasing after random animals. I watch the excitement for a moment, a smile on my face as peals of childish laughter reach me. A little girl catches a snow-white bunny, and in a move so fast I would have missed it if I blinked, she grows fangs and tears into the neck of the trapped animal. My hand shoots up to my mouth, trapping the gasp I just inhaled, and I watch as all the adults around the enclosure cheer and reach for the little girl, lifting her up in celebration.

I turn wide, stunned eyes on Rogan. "Just like us?" I lob at him, with an arched, incredulous eyebrow.

He just shrugs, a cheeky grin taking over one corner of his lush mouth.

Fucker.

I shoo away my shock, not wanting to offend anyone, and a pair of lycans break away from the crowd and move toward us. A brute of a man with a long easy stride closes the distance. His hair is a rich soil-brown, but his long beard is bright ginger. The obsidian-haired woman next to him could give an Amazon a run for her money, and as they get closer, I look around and realize that lycans have dipped many a toe in the *hot as fuck* gene pool.

Strong, virile, tall bodies are everywhere. Both men and women are a feast for the eyes. I have to stop myself from calling Tad and announcing that I've found the promised land. I mean, screw going to the bars when you can just come party in a place like this. Yes, please.

"Rogan!" the male lycan booms, and in one long stride, Rogan is wrapped up in a bear hug of epic proportions. Rogan is huge, but the ginger-bearded man makes him look dainty as he picks up the Blood Witch and spins him like they're long lost lovers.

The sight makes me so damn happy that I don't even see

the Amazon coming right for me. I squeal in surprise when strong arms pluck me from the ground and wrap me up in the kind of hug I didn't know I needed until right this minute. I tense for all of half a second, and then I abandon all pretense and melt right into the embrace.

"I'm Viv," she tells me, her voice resonating from her chest into mine as we hold onto each other.

"Leni," I exchange, feeling like a little girl again as my feet sway in the air. It's the best.

After a beat, she puts me down, and just when I feel like I want to pout about that, I'm yanked into another perfect hug, the ginger beard-hair in my face a dead giveaway for who has me now. Just like with Viv, I squeeze him back just as hard as I can.

"I'm Riggs," he rumbles. "I'm so sorry about your grandmother. When I saw a different Osseous name on the list, I called my necro buddy, and he confirmed her passing. She was a longtime customer and friend, and we'll really miss her," he tells me, and I can hear the ache and sincerity in what he's saying.

"Me too," I admit, the two simple words summoning so much emotion with them. Riggs just keeps me in his arms as I blink the tears away and get myself back under control. He sets me on my feet as I do and pats my mop of curls, empathy and compassion radiating from his every feature.

"Now," he announces with a thundering clap. "Let's talk business, and then we can have some fun. What can I get for you?"

Rogan immediately looks over at me, and I clear my throat. "I'm in need of some bones."

Riggs chuckles heartily and pulls me in for a side hug. "Of course you are, you wouldn't be here if you weren't," he teases. "What's your poison?"

"I'm not really sure what you have. Caribou would be

ideal, but if you don't have that, then deer or elk will work too," I start, thinking through the recipe that I want to make and what bones the grimoire taught me would be compatible.

"We have caribou," Viv tells me confidently. "Would you prefer male or female bones? And any particular part of the body?" she asks.

I stare at her for a beat, surprised that they're that thorough. She just smiles warmly at me, like she's used to the reaction.

"Um, male, please. And any part of the legs would be great, maybe some vertebrae too if you have them?"

She flips open a tablet and ticks away at it. "Small, medium, or large bundle?"

"Let's do...small to start with," I reply, completely impressed with their business acumen.

"Got it, anything else for you, Leni?"

"If you have any gray wolf, I'll take that too. Ribs or pelvis is fine. Preferably a female who's at least had one litter of pups," I request, thinking of some protective potions that Rogan and all his *never can be too careful* talk has me now wanting to have on hand. Nothing better than a protective base of mama wolf when it comes to those kinds of recipes —or so the grimoire tells me.

Viv just nods and jots it down.

"What else do you have?" I ask, suddenly feeling like a kid in a candy store.

"We can get pretty much everything, even human, but that's a special request and we need at least a month to procure the order. We have a sale running on polar bear bones right now, and I think we have a little bit left of tiger if you're interested?"

"No, I don't have any need for virility potions at the moment, but that's good to know," I answer absently as I do a quick rundown of some potions and powders that could come in handy.

Riggs chuckles and gives Rogan an *atta boy* elbow to the ribs. I ignore the innuendo and think through what I need for some defensive spells and brews.

"If you have any male bison, neck or skull, and any wild boar, any part, I'll take it. Oh, and one polar bear jaw, too, please."

"You got it," Viv chirps. "I'll head down to the warehouse now. It should be ready in about an hour, is that okay?"

"Perfect. Thank you, I'm super excited."

She squeezes my arm affectionately and then lopes off without another word. I spin and take in my surroundings, feeling light and happy. I realize in that moment that it's been a long time since I felt this way. I didn't realize how much I missed it.

"Come on, you two, we'll watch the brawls while we're waiting," Riggs announces, gesturing for us to follow him.

"Do you deliver out of state?" I ask Riggs as we start to weave our way in and out of people to get to wherever the brawls are.

"We do. Internationally too if you need. We do standard shipping on everything, which is included in the cost of whatever you order. We also have ley line delivery options, but those are an additional ten percent of your order cost."

"How'd you get into this business?" I ask, unable to bite back my curiosity. It seems like such an unconventional thing, but they're so good at it, there has to be passion for it somewhere in the foundation of it all.

Riggs tosses me a wide toothy smile over his shoulder. "The business has been passed down from father to son for many generations. It started as a way to build better ties in the community, to be seen less as outcasts and more as valued members of the magical community," he tells me, a kind smile on his face, but I can tell from his words that this lycan clan hasn't always been as carefree and appreciated as it seems to be now.

There's a lot of history I can sense in the tone of his simple explanation, and if it's anything like human history, it was filled with bloodshed and battles.

"It all started with us collecting what we could hunt and grow, but we quickly discovered that there was serious demand for the things we could procure. Next thing you know, we were connecting with other lycan clans all over the world and creating a solid source network that changed witch and lycan relationships forever," he goes on with pride radiating out of his features.

"And it's not just the witches who benefit," he adds. "As a clan, we put fun hunting parties together for the animals that are harder to procure. It keeps our palates refined, our instincts honed, and the clan financially cared for and protected by the community that we serve."

"That's incredible," I tell him, respect and admiration spilling out of my tone. "And you can really get anything?" I question, not even bothered by the fact that I sound like a total fan-girl.

"With enough time, we can get anything. Leprechauns have been on backorder for years now, but they're incredibly hard to catch," he tells me.

My mouth drops open with shock. "Really?" I ask, completely gobsmacked.

Riggs cracks up. "No. Leprechauns aren't real, but I just love seeing a new Osteomancer's face for the second that they think they are.

I let out an indignant huff, but it quickly morphs into laughter. He could have had me believing they were real for years. Hell, I probably would have gone on a waitlist for one.

"You're all so gullible," he chortles, and I can't even try to deny it.

Rogan's deep chuckle sounds just behind me, and a blush crawls into my cheeks. Riggs leads us to a packed crowd gathered around a grassy clearing, and the lycans all part to allow him access to a front row vantage point. Bodies are tightly pressed in against each other as everyone pushes in to see what's happening inside of the verdant arena. Stones are stacked a little higher than my knee and set as a divider between spectator and participant. The field is colorfully lush in patches, but trodden and well-used. It makes me think of this place back home where they hold Highland Games every year.

My thoughts of big Scottish giants throwing logs around are chased away when, in the center of the field, standing on top of a tree stump, is a huge, sweaty, shirtless man. He has feral long auburn hair, matching stubble on his jaw, and predatory, gleaming golden eyes. Another equally massive and shirtless man charges him with a bellow, and just when it looks like Brock O'Hurn's beefier twin is about to be shoved off the stump, he nimbly dodges the attack and sends the other man rolling past him to crash into the dirt.

The crowd erupts with noise. Cheers and boos explode all around me. "What's going on?" I ask Riggs, but it's Rogan's voice in my ear that answers.

I realize with a start that he's the body pressed in behind me. And it sends a keen awareness through every inch of me.

"The goal is to push the big guy off the stump. Each competitor gets one try. If they succeed, they take over the position on the stump. The last man standing on it wins some sort of prize; sometimes it's money, other times it's something else," he explains, bending down so that his lips are close to my ear.

I stifle a shiver that wants to strike through me, worried that he might feel it and get the wrong idea. I'm responding to the intimacy of someone being close to me, not to Rogan specifically, I tell myself, and I don't want to give him reason to ever doubt that either.

"So what's the rarest bone you've ever seen here?" I ask Riggs, desperately needing some kind of distraction as Rogan puts his hands on my hips to steady himself when someone jostles him from behind. His muscles tease my back, his warmth soaking into me. Crap, what was I asking? Bones? Right. Bones.

"We've had a fair bit of priceless and precious bones and herbs come through here, but my personal favorite are what's left of the jackalope bits."

I start to laugh, picturing the fabled animal that looks like a jackrabbit with antlers. "You got me with the leprechauns," I confess. "I'm not falling for the jackalope," I warn him, laughter bubbling out of me freely.

His grin grows even wider, and just when I think he's about to concede *you got me*, he pulls at a chain around his neck. A rabbit's foot and a small antler slip out from underneath his shirt. They dangle from the chain like manifestations of the impossible becoming possible.

"No. Way," I argue, veneration spilling out of every syllable.

Riggs holds them out, like he's daring me to test their authenticity. So of course I extend my hand and grip the small antler between my pointer finger and thumb. I'm hit by the smell of wildflowers, the taste of clover, and the sound of a haunting cackle as the rush of running from a predator fills my veins. My bewildered gaze rises to meet Riggs's, a knowing smirk lighting up his whole face, and I'm at a complete loss for words.

It's real.

"How?" I ask with a reverent whisper.

"They're extinct now, the last one we know about was caught when I was knee-high to a grasshopper. My mother gave these to me to remind me of what happens when we don't treasure and protect the things around us."

"Aw, man, now I can't ask for them, knowing that they have such sentimental value," I whine, and Riggs guffaws.

"The antler is a bit stabby, I could be talked into maybe parting with it," he jokes, and my overzealous ass jumps all over that.

"Really? What would it take to talk you into it?" I blurt, like I'm nothing more than a Gollum staring at the one true ring.

Riggs studies me for a moment as though he's actually considering parting with something so precious. I should probably feel bad, but I want the bone something fierce. I have no idea where this intense need is coming from; it's not rational, but I *need* a jackalope antler in my life. I just had no idea that I did until now.

"Okay, Osteomancer, you can have my jackalope antler," he declares with a mischievous glint in his bright amber eyes.

"What's the catch?" I ask suspiciously even though my insides are celebrating gleefully.

He laughs again and gestures toward the arena. "*If* you can get Saxon off the stump."

I turn just in time to see a lycan leap at the man standing on the hewn tree trunk—Saxon, I'm assuming—and the auburn-haired behemoth flips the advancing lycan over his head like the guy weighs nothing. From the loud thump that fills the enclosed area, and the vibration that moves through the ground when the lycan's body hits, I can attest that the man weighs a whole hell of a lot.

Well, crap, there goes my precious.

16

Dust plumes around the man who was just thrown to the ground. The fine mist of dirt starts to slowly settle around the field as murmurs fill the air like bird song. I watch the plume disappear, and it takes with it my overeager hopes to become the proud new owner of a jackalope antler in the very near future. Riggs's smile is cocky and pleased; he knows exactly what he's just done. I want to sulk *that's not fair*, as I've clearly been duped, but that kind of shit isn't cute at any age, so I tamp it down.

His eyes twinkle mischievously, and I find that I really want to shove his underestimation down his throat. I want to make him eat his words. But as I stare out at the tree-sized man on the stump in the middle of the clearing, I'm at a loss for how to make that happen. Riggs chuckles deeply and pats me hard on the back, making me jerk forward and struggle to keep from tilting over from the contact.

"Come now, Leni, I didn't think an Osteomancer accepted defeat so easily, especially not one from the Osseous line," he teases, and titters sound off from the people around us.

My deep exhale is unamused, but as his words sink in, it

dawns on me. I'm a witch. I have magic. I don't have to muscle Goliath off the stump, I just need to flick my wrist and send his big ass bones flying.

Gah, I'm an idiot. How did I not even think about that until now?

A slow smile curls my lips, and confidence fills my gaze. "Fine, you're on," I chirp, and Riggs's amused stare fills with surprise and then bleeds into suspicion. I step over the knee-high stone wall that separates the gathered crowd from the action before Riggs can change his mind about the terms.

"What are you doing?" Rogan growls as he reaches out to try and stop me, but this time I'm wise to his methods, and I scurry away, just getting out of reach before he can snatch one of my arms and stop me.

"Don't worry, I got this," I tell him over my shoulder, offering him a smug thumbs up.

"Lennox, you can't use magic," he calls after me, and my wide *you'll rue the day* smile falters.

I spin so fast to face Rogan it would make a cyclone jealous. "Um, say what now?" I demand sweetly, like the polite tone itself will make him declare something that doesn't completely fuck me over.

He huffs, annoyed, like *he's* the one who just agreed to body tackle The Mountain. "It's part of the rules. You can't use magic on the stump itself or the person on it. You also can't use magic to throw other people at the person on the stump. Oh, and no biting in any form," he adds as though chomping into Saxon would have been my next plan of action. I look over at the mass of muscle on the stump and cock a brow. In the bedroom maybe...

I swat that thought away and try to figure out what the hell to do now. Riggs is laughing so hard his face now matches the color of his beard. And I'm four paces into having just thrown down my gauntlet. I look around at my feet as though I can physically see a gauntlet just lying about. Maybe if I pick it up and do an Ace Ventura rewind back over the low-set stone wall, no one will think anything of it.

I imagine offering the crowd my best pageant wave as I demurely tell them, *my bad, my gauntlet totally just fell, definitely didn't throw it, nope, that'd be some crazy shit.*

I look around at all the judgmental and eager faces surrounding me. Crap, I don't think there's any getting out of this. Which means I have to make an ass out of myself by trying to tackle the guy, probably injuring myself in the process when I bounce off the wall of muscle that is Saxon whatever the hell his last name is, and then tuck tail and go back to Riggs and Rogan sans any hope of ever owning a jackalope bone.

I square my shoulders, fully aware that after I break them in this stupid attempt to shove Saxon off his stump, I won't be moving them for a while. I hesitantly step further into the clearing. The wild grass is clipped short, and the patches of dirt, peeking out here and there, feel like they're mocking me. Saxon turns at the points and whispers of the surrounding crowd. His golden eyes assess me as I amble closer. It's as though, despite my size and sex, he's taking this seriously, looking at me as though *I* really could be a threat. For some reason, this makes me feel better.

I know I'm not going to be able to move his very large and very attractive ass from where he's standing, but he's taking this seriously and...fuck it, so will I. His gilded gaze tracks me as I make a slow circle around him. I stretch out my neck and my arms as I go, which elicits some chuckles from the spectators watching with mirthful anticipation. I look as though I'm trying and failing at intimidating him, but really I'm trying to reduce the odds of pulling a muscle when I finally make a move.

I complete my perusing circle, but I still have nothing, so I start another one. It's not like the scenery is bad. Saxon isn't even sweating from his exertions so far, which is a shame because I could really go for watching a bead of perspiration work its way down his chiseled abs right about now. You know, something to take the edge off.

I leisurely stroll around him, unabashedly checking him out...for weaknesses, of course. I tilt my head appreciatively and try to think through what the hell I'm going to do. I'm not allowed to use magic on him or the stump, but that doesn't mean I can't use magic at all. Charging him with all my might is pretty laughable given what I've seen him toss around already. So what does that leave me?

My eyes trace the curves and dips of his arms, as I complete circle two, and I bite down on my lower lip in thought. Saxon watches me intently, his stare dropping to where I'm gnawing on my mouth, and I watch his chest expand with a deep inhale.

Is he smelling me?

I should probably be embarrassed by what he might be picking up with that deep pull of air into his lungs. *Do dirty thoughts have a smell?* I contemplate that as a sensual grin lifts his plump lips, and an idea sparks in my mind. Maybe getting physical is the right way to go after all. I lick my bottom lip, hoping it looks hot like it does when other girls do it and not as though I'm impersonating a toad catching its dinner.

The gathering crowd appears to be getting restless. Their chatter is getting louder and more impatient, but I don't let it distract me as I pull in my own deep breath.

Here goes nothing.

I push magic out of me in search of bones. Being that

they have a warehouse full of them not too far away, my search doesn't last long. Magically I search through the options until I find exactly what I need. With a small squeak of excitement, I call the bones to me. This will never get old. It takes a handful of seconds for them to travel from where they're being stored to the clearing I'm standing in, and I silently hope that Riggs won't be annoyed at me using them. I'm not technically breaking any rules, I'm just trying to make things even, literally.

I lift my hand in a come hither motion, raising the traveling missiles so that no one gets taken out by one. Saxon studies the movement, and the crowd instantly grows quiet. All at once, long bones come flying into the clearing, and I point at where I want them to stack themselves. A few gasps ring out around me, but I tune all of that out and focus on what I need to do.

Slowly, bone after stacked bone, a rudimentary set of stairs start to form. I'm careful not to touch the stump or Saxon with anything, stacking the bones until I think there are enough steps for what I need. I step on the first layer of woven camel leg bones, testing it, and when it feels like the structure will hold my weight, I climb the rest of the short flight.

Saxon's uncertain stare moves from the bone tower to me as I crest it, our faces now even with each other. I smile brightly, hoping it helps to disarm him a bit, but I can see he's trying to work out what's happening and what exactly I'm going to do with this stairway to his face.

"Hi," I greet with a small wave.

"Hello," he warily answers back, which makes me smile even wider. He's smart to be untrusting.

"I've obviously bitten off more than I chew here," I confess as his eyes once again drop to the bones I'm standing on. "I was dumb enough to fall for a dare, and as kind as you are to make me think otherwise, we both know there's no way in hell I'm knocking you off this log," I tell him matter-of-factly.

His eyes flick back up to mine, and I see him relax ever so slightly.

"So I thought to myself, *self, if I can't beat him to get what I want, maybe I can get something else just as tempting instead*," I profess, my eyes flitting back and forth between his beautiful golden irises. I wonder if it's the lycan in him that creates such an unusual eye color or if it's regular genetics at play.

"And what would that be?" Saxon asks me, a hint of curiosity swimming in the pool of swagger in his tone.

"Can I kiss you?" I ask plainly.

Saxon's brow furrows slightly with confusion, and his eyes drop to my lips of their own accord before meeting my gaze again. "You want to kiss me?" he clarifies, as though the request makes no sense to him.

"Yes, but only if you're okay with it," I add.

He studies me for a beat, like *the catch* to my request is written somewhere in the depths of my eyes.

"Uh...okay," he answers hesitantly, clearly not seeing the master plan hiding in my eyes.

Before he can change his mind, I lean in and gently press my lips to his. He doesn't really respond at first, which is a little disappointing, but I suppose I *am* a stranger and we do have an audience, so maybe he's shy. Instead of pulling back though, I open my lips slightly and sandwich his top lip between them. I suck on it lightly, inviting this kiss to go from friendly to *more* if he wants it to.

I stand securely on the top step of my bone tower, but I reach out with my hands and wrap them around the back of his neck, threading my fingers into his hair and letting my nails skim his scalp. At the same time, I move my mouth to his bottom lip, nipping at it gently and encouraging him to join in. To my delight, he responds immediately.

Saxon's mouth goes from still and uncertain, to dominating and eager in less time than it takes for me to catapult the word *shy* right out of my brain. His hands wrap around my back, pulling me into him, and an approving little moan sneaks out of me. I flick the tip of my tongue against his, teasing and testing, and his mouth grows even more demanding, the kiss rocketing from flat and unsure to incredibly intense.

He's good, not the best kiss I've ever had, but enjoyable nonetheless. He's a little too loopty loo with the tongue at first, but the more I show him how I like to nip, suck, tease, and swirl, the more he's catching on and doing it back. I tug at his hair lightly as our mouths begin to move in smooth harmony, and he growls into my mouth. We meet in a crescendo of hungry lips and taunting tongues, our bodies pressing even harder against one another, our hands itching to explore and turn up the heat.

Arousal starts to pool low in my belly, and my thoughts morph from my master plan to wondering exactly where Saxon and I might go with this. I thought this would be my best tactical advantage, my best way to catch him off guard, but I could easily get lost in this for a night. Lord knows I could use some serious stress relief. Saxon's hands caress lower on my back, and it helps me rein in my wandering thoughts. As intrigued as I am by our obvious physical compatibility, I really do want that jackalope bone. The question right now is, which do I want more?

Saxon cups my ass with his large hands, squeezing my cheeks suggestively and encouraging me to wrap my legs around his waist. Maybe he'll step off the log on his own to pursue the fire now burning between us, but if he doesn't...

I chase away my reservations, making up my mind once

and for all. A night of potential molten sex could be epic, but jackalope bones trump that at the moment. Pretty sure my ancestors have ruined me. If anyone would have told me a week ago I'd pick a bone over a potential hot as fuck *bone*, I would have laughed my ass off as I hurriedly peeled off my clothes and prepared for that dick.

I lean back a little, my body telling Saxon that things are coming to an end, but I'm sure to mix the signals by kissing him even more feverishly. Saxon presses forward, determined not to let me go, and it's all I can do not to smile at his reaction. I suck his bottom lip into my mouth with a salacious moan, pressing my breasts even harder against him.

I'm on the cusp of making my move. I can see it so clearly in my mind. I'll pull my magic away from the bones under my feet. They'll crumble, and with the help of gravity, I'll start to fall. He'll feel me begin to slip away, and I'll do my best impression of a sandbag and let my weight drop. Saxon, being the teachable good kisser and the gentleman that I hope he is, will do his best to rescue me from the sudden precarious fall. I, of course, will have to sell it and make it seem like I'm about to plummet off a cliff instead of the four feet I would actually drop. But if I can execute this just right, Saxon will abandon his position on the stump to ensure I meet the ground safe and sound.

I tilt back a little more, making sure I set Saxon up to be as off-kilter as possible when I withdraw my magic in three…two…

Out of nowhere, I'm yanked away. My lips are abruptly stolen from Saxon's searing attentions, my hold torn from around his neck. My body is separated from his so fast and so forcefully it takes me a moment to realize what's happening.

What the hell?

A growl sounds off behind me, and it's matched by an

even more menacing snarl coming from Saxon as he fixes his golden gaze on whoever just fucked everything up for me.

"Interference on the play," I shout out in objection as I try to wiggle free from whoever has a hold of me.

I can practically see the coveted jackalope antler slipping from my grasp, and I'm about to lay a serious lycan beatdown on whoever just got in my way. I expect to find a raging, jealous girl or even guy, frothing at the mouth, pissed maybe that I crossed a line. But what I'm not prepared for, when I finally wiggle enough to see who has a vise-like grip on my waist and a possessive snarl in their throat, is…Rogan.

I'm so floored to see him that my brain temporarily freezes, like the scene just doesn't compute and therefore will not be processed by my gray matter. In my shock, I release my hold on the bone stairs, and they tumble down, but the commotion is completely ignored.

"What are you doing?" Saxon barks, stepping down from the stump and menacingly stalking forward as Rogan continues to pull me away.

"Does that count?" I shout out a little too frantically as I point toward the now vacant stump.

No one answers me.

"Witch emergency," Rogan announces, turning and carrying me toward the stone border that surrounds the festivities.

Concern rips through my resentment, and I try to push out of Rogan's hold and enlist the power of my own two feet, but he doesn't let me go.

"Rogan, what the fuck?" I snap at him, my emotions buzzing inside of me like wild angry bees unsure of where to land.

The heat that was just building between Saxon and me

sizzles and smokes dejectedly like someone just threw a bucket of water on the fire. I'm reeling from the want I was just simmering in, from the excitement and anticipation I was feeling as my plan came together. Disappointment pumps through me as everything takes an unexpected turn, but it's trumped by the worry I feel over Rogan's *emergency* announcement. My varying emotions are seasoned with a dash of *pissed off* because I'm still being carried away against my will, like some tantruming toddler at the grocery store.

Rogan doesn't say a word, and his declaration of *witch emergency* has Saxon backing off as frustration-filled eyes watch our exit. We pass Riggs, who has a wide shit-eating grin on his face.

"He's off the stump," I declare pointing behind me, like a pouty child intent on getting someone else in trouble.

"He is, but who can say if you are the cause or if Rogan here is?" Riggs counters with a shrug as he drops the bones back into the neck of his shirt.

I want to scream *noooo* as I watch the antler being hidden away, but then I really will look like a tantruming toddler, so I bite back my objection. Warm tingles move from my center down my arms as I summon my magic and call on one of the camel leg bones that are now sitting in a pile in front of the stump. I'm about to take a page out of Rogan's caveman book and club him with it until he puts me down. The bone shoots up over the crowd and streaks toward me. I hold my arm out, ready to wrap my fingers around the calcified shaft, but at the last minute Rogan's free arm shoots out, and he catches it, keeping the weapon away from me and foiling another of my brilliant plans.

An irritated snarl vibrates up my throat, and more magic pours out of me as I try to rip the bone from his clutches, but oddly, it doesn't so much as twitch in his palm. Abandoning the leg bone now trapped in Rogan's crushing grip, I call on another bone from the stump ring. A mental image of Rogan and I sword fighting with camel bones flashes in my mind, and I suspect that the lycan onlookers will be down for the show.

"Stop messing around, Lennox," Rogan huffs as we weave past the hustle and bustle of the lycan celebrations and move out in the direction of the parked car.

"Then put me down," I snap at him, renewing my efforts to get out of his hold. "What's the emergency anyway? Did Marx call? Did he find Nik Smelser?"

The chirp of a car being unlocked is the only answer I get before Rogan opens a door and practically shoves me into the passenger seat. Wind teases the side of my face just as I furiously right myself. Jarringly, the door slams shut, sealing me inside of the car as Rogan stomps around to the driver's side, climbing in with a slit-eyed glare aimed in my direction. With pursed, irritated lips, he presses the engine start button a little aggressively. His car purrs to life, and we peel away before I can get my tongue wrapped around the demanding questions in my head.

"What the fuck is going on?" I finally manage as we wind away from the festivities like we're being chased. I look behind us, just to be sure that it's not actually the case.

Rogan doesn't answer.

"What about my order?" I object as we speed further and further away.

"It has already been loaded in the back," he grumbles, and I snap my seat belt on and turn to fix him with a steely glare.

"Oh, so you *can* talk," I growl as I do my best to heat the side of his face with the ire in my gaze. "What's the emergency? Why did you just haul me away? You cost me a seriously precious and coveted bone, Rogan! What the hell are you doing?" I snap at him, once again reminded that those are words that would have never come out of my mouth a week ago.

"*I'm* doing?" he incredulously snaps back. "What the hell are *you* doing?"

"I was winning the coolest thing ever to add to the pouch of bones my line uses. I almost literally had it in the bag before you went and fucked it all up."

"Had it in the bag? Is that what you call what you did back there? Because it looked more like a drunken make out than a winning move," he states with rumbling disapproval.

I stare at him for a beat, trying to understand what the hell is going on here. He said it was a witch emergency, but every time I ask what the emergency is, he deflects.

"First of all, Rogan Kendrick, every move I make is a winning move. Secondly, tell me what the emergency is, *right now*, or I will slip ogre bone dust in everything you eat and drink. And before you dismiss that threat, my ancestors have a lovely recipe that will have you smelling to high heaven and parts of you limp as a cheap pickle spear," I warn.

The tic in Rogan's jaw pulses as he considers my threat. The car slows as the gate to leave the lycan's property rolls open. We rush through it just as soon as there's enough clearance to do so, and I have to fight the desire to turn and see if the guard from earlier is still there. Nope. I can come play *catch the lycan with my vagina* some other time. Right now I need to focus on the Blood Witch, who has a nasty habit of *act now, explain later*.

"You can't pull shit like that with lycans, Lennox," Rogan rumbles, pissed off, his eyes fixed on the road in front of us.

"Shit like what? I was just trying to win," I defend.

"I know, but you can't do it like that," he snaps back, not offering any additional clarification.

"Did I break a rule?" I press, getting even more frustrated by his clipped responses that are still all too vague.

"No. But lycans are territorial. They can get fixated on things they feel like they have a claim to."

"It was a kiss, Rogan, not a proposal. Did you forget what century we're in or something? No one's freaking out over a woman showing her ankle anymore. An affectionate act isn't a profession of undying love and devotion," I snark, but Rogan just shakes his head and tightens his grip on the steering wheel.

"Maybe not in the human world, Lennox, but you're treading in territory you know nothing about," he clips.

"I asked you if there was anything I needed to know when it came to interacting with the lycans. You told me to just be normal," I shout, my threshold for frustration beyond full and now spilling over.

"Exactly! What's normal about kissing strangers for a toy-sized antler? How was I supposed to anticipate you'd do something like that?" Rogan shouts back. "What's normal about anything you did?"

"What's normal about any of this to begin with?" I counter, exasperated. "We're witches hanging out with a bunch of handsy lycans. Who really gives a shit? They didn't stop us from leaving. Saxon didn't drop trou and try to piss a circle around me, staking his claim. So what's the real issue here?" I demand with flailing angry hands and narrowed eyes.

The car is silent other than the hum of tires on pavement and the sound of the wind moaning an ominous tune outside the confines of the car. The sun is setting, and in its multi-hued light, I study Rogan's face, the tic in his jaw, the glare he's wearing, the vexation etched in his masculine features. The longer he says nothing, the more it speaks to me.

Is the witch emergency that he's jealous? Is that really what this comes down to?

A jolt of shock slams through me as that conclusion forms in my mind. I watch his profile intently as though the denial of my thoughts will be evident in his frown or the agitated blink of an eye, but it's not there. I don't know why this potential discovery surprises me so much; it's not like I'm hideous or repellant in any way, I just didn't know Rogan had the depth. If he saw me as anything, I'd have thought it was simply as some kind of stepping stone in the path to finding his brother and nothing more.

I open my mouth to say something, to demand to know if envy is really the foundation of his irritation and what that means. But before I say a word, the wind releases a furious howl, and the next thing I know, something slams into the side of us, and we go spinning out of control.

17

It all happens so fast I don't even have time to scream. One second I'm debating if Rogan might like me and how I feel about that, and then suddenly everything is spinning, and squealing, and terrifying.

Rogan shouts, but it's lost to the sound and feel of airbags exploding all around me. We're shoved off the road with what feels like hurricane levels of force. It's as though Mother Nature just lost her shit and swatted us away like some pesky fly. I'm scared and disoriented as the car tilts precariously, and then all at once, we're flipping down an embankment toward a steep line of large trees.

I feel like I'm stuck in some amusement ride from hell, my stomach turning in time with the car as I'm jerked and jostled mercilessly. Glass shatters and falls all over me, and I try to shield my face as I catch a glimpse of the dusk-kissed sky only for it to be ripped away as we continue to tumble, dirt and debris exploding all around me.

Odd keening-like grunts escape my mouth with each terrible revolution of the car. It's as if we're spinning so fast that it's trapped a scream in my throat and won't let it out. Black dances in the corners of my vision, but just as it dares to come closer, we slam—with a sickening thud and the squeals of bending metal—against something and jerk to a stop.

My bones crack and splinter from the impact as the car quivers and settles against what I suspect is a tree trunk or maybe a rock. Pain explodes through me, dulling my senses, and I blink sluggishly, as I slowly realize that I'm hanging upside down. Curls fall all around my face, and warmth trickles from the side of my head, spreading slowly up into my hair. Finally, the torque of our brutal spin releases its hold on my throat, but the scream that was held hostage there dies, and a muddled moan crawls out of my lips in its place.

Ticks and pops sound off all around me as what's left of the car settles. All I can do is breathe.

In and out.

In and out.

I pull air into my chest, ignoring the bite in my ribs, and release it as I try to clear my mind enough to come up with a *now what*. Questions flash through my mind, demanding to know what could have done this and how, but I push them back and focus on what needs immediate attention.

"Rogan?" I squeak pitifully as I reach out and work to clear my line of sight of airbag fabric, hair, and dirt.

My own pained moan accompanies my efforts as I struggle to move, and panic starts to race inside of me when he doesn't answer. It takes me a moment to get my bearings. I feel like I'm in the back seat somehow, but I know I'm still buckled in the passenger seat like I was before what felt like Mother Nature's beatdown.

The dashboard in front of me is a crumpled mess. Soil and grass now press in where the windshield used to be. I turn to look for Rogan, my head pounding furiously in objection as I do. My vision blurs, and I work to blink it back into focus. I bring a hand to my head and feel the telltale warm wetness of blood.

"Rogan?" I call out again, my tone pleading.

I try to shake the fogginess from my head, which only brings more pain. The blur in my vision sharpens with the hurt though, and I'm able to focus on the unmoving form of Rogan hanging from his seat, tethered only by his seat belt. I call out to him again, but he doesn't even so much as flinch.

"Be alive," I start to frantically chant as I try to free myself from the confines of my own constricting seat belt so that I can check on him.

I press with all my waning might against the button that should release me, and with a pop and a surprised squeak, I fall to the ground. It can't be more than a foot from where I was hanging to where I collapse, but it feels like I just survived a fall from a cliff. I breathe through the agony that radiates through me, begging it to subside. A faint vibrating sensation moves like a wave through the dirt and grass where the windshield used to be, and the hair on my arms stands up in warning. I'm not sure what is going on, but my gut is screaming that the worst might not be behind me, or maybe that's just what internal bleeding feels like.

Magic pools inside of my chest of its own accord as though it feels some kind of threat too. I breathe a sigh of relief as I shove it through me and try to repair what I can of the damage that's been done. I bite back a scream as I feel a rib fuse back together inch by splintered inch. Tears stream down my face as it—in what feels like forever—finally fits seamlessly back together. One down, three to go. The thought of having to endure even more anguish as I knit myself back together makes me want to figure out the fastest way to pass out, but I know I can't do that. I *have* to endure this. I have to be ready for whatever might still be coming.

My head is fuzzy with adrenaline, and my mouth salty

with the threat of vomit as I finish the last of my broken ribs. This time, I don't let myself take a break as I move onto healing my fractured metacarpals and then the tibia in my right leg. My skin is clammy from the agony weeping out from my pores.

"Almost done," I growl to myself, partly as a pep talk and partly as a warning that it's not over yet.

There's no biting back the cry that rips out of my throat when my leg bone pops out of the weird angle it's in and straightens. But thankfully, that seems to be the worst of it. Relief floods me when my vertebrae pop happily like they just had a visit to their favorite chiropractor. My headache subsides slightly and my vision clears up, and the steady ache radiating throughout me starts to dull. I'm still bruised badly all over and I'm pretty sure concussed, but I can make do with that until we can get some help.

I shove magic out of me into Rogan, tears stinging my eyes when I feel that he's still alive. Breath rushes out of me in a relieved exhale as I magically fix the things in him that have fractured and fragmented. I pull a broken rib from his lung and coax it back into place, but I can't help the alarm that blares through me at the injuries I subtly feel that I know I can't fix. I won't be able to make his lung reinflate, or stop the bleeding I feel in his chest and stomach. But if I can get him out and awake, maybe he can tackle the internal injuries.

Reluctantly I pull my power back into myself and start scanning this destroyed car for a way to get out. I search for my phone, but I don't see it anywhere. I debate for a moment if I should try to get Rogan down, but I'm worried his dead weight might pin me down and make it harder to get out. The feeling that we're still in danger is hammering through me, and I don't know if that's because it is or if my adrenaline is spazzing out because we were just in an accident. I've never been in one before, and I have no idea what to expect.

I curse myself as I leave Rogan where he unconsciously hangs. I wiggle between our seats toward the shattered rear passenger window behind the driver's seat. Glass cuts into my arms and hands as I go, but it's unavoidable. I can still hear the eerie cry of the wind as I crawl out of the broken back window, and it feels even more like a warning, one I have no idea how to interpret.

I pull my legs free from the car, the night air cooling the blood still spilling from the head wound I have. The sky is a dusky blue now, with the horizon lit up with oranges, yellows, and reds. The sun is almost gone, but there's enough light to see that the car somehow rolled through the trees before slamming to a stop against a large unforgiving trunk.

I can see the tree line and the base of the embankment that I know leads up the road about twenty feet away. If I can't flag down a passing car, maybe I can try to get back to the lycan compound. I don't think we're too far from them. Or maybe I should try to find my phone first and call for help, that'll probably be faster.

I file my options away and focus on Rogan. Surprisingly, the window on his side is still intact, and I consider breaking it, but I don't know if I'll be able to pull Rogan's massive muscled frame through the too small opening. The smell of gas and hot rubber permeates the air around me. Nothing is flaming or smoking right now, but a sense of urgency pulses through me impatiently.

I reach up and pull the handle to his door, but the dented and damaged panel doesn't open. Blood slicks my hands from the cuts I acquired while trying to crawl out, and I search the battered remains of the upside-down SUV for some other way to get Rogan out. There isn't one. My side of the car is practically wrapped around a tree. A shiver runs up my spine as I take in the damage, and I'm stunned that I'm not hurt worse than I am as I take it in. Rogan is still out cold, and I look all around me for anything that can help me get him out.

I spot a pair of horns resting on a mound of dirt that the rolling car must have upturned. I call to them, and with the help of my magic, the large attached skull exhumes itself from the soil and slides over to me. It's the bison skull I ordered from Riggs. It must have flown out of the car during the accident. I call all osteo matter in the area to me, and in a snap, the contents of the order I placed at the lycan compound are piled next to me.

I take in the collection of bones for a moment, sorting through how I might use them to help me. A lightbulb practically goes off in my mind. I instruct the caribou leg bones I planned on using for the waitress's tea, to break into a different more useful shape. The radius and ulna bones do as my magic commands and separate so that one end has a sharp, smooth angle. I order that end of the bone into the seam of the car door, forcing them to wedge themselves and help me leverage the door open.

I grab the handle, and on the count of three, as though I'm instructing a team of helpers instead of just me and my magic, I pull the door with all my might and simultaneously force as much magic as I can into the wedged leg bones. With an angry metallic groan, the door starts to give. I shove every ounce of strength that I have into my arms and hands, and into my magic. A determined and labored screech pours out from my clenched teeth as I fight with the door, refusing to let it win.

I think I hear the sound of dirt trickling down the hill behind me, but I ignore it, focusing all my efforts on creating an opening that I can get Rogan out through. My arms and hands burn from my exertions, and the headache I thought I had dispelled comes back with a vengeance, but I push through, pulling at the smashed door with all my physical and magical might. Pops and the tearing and scraping of metal on metal fill the air all around me, and all at once the door wrenches open.

I fall back, losing my balance as it tears open, but a bruised ass is the least of my worries right now. I get to my hands and knees and quickly scramble into the car as much as I can to try and get Rogan free. Immediately I press my fingers against his neck, checking for a pulse to make sure he's still with me. An unexpected sob almost chokes me when I feel the steady beat of his heart against the pads of my fingers. Tears start to drip steadily down my cheeks as I reach for the buckle to his seat belt, and I think it's safe to say that the shock and numbness I've been feeling are starting to wear off.

That uncomfortable sense of urgency is breathing heavy down the back of my neck, and I snarl a frustrated growl when his buckle doesn't release easily like mine did. I pull at the seat belt locking Rogan in place, but it holds tight, refusing to release him from its protective clutches. I call the polar bear jaw bone to me that I ordered, and try to saw at the seat belt with the teeth that are still intact and attached to the bone. It doesn't work.

I need to move fast, I can feel it in my bones. I stop yanking at the seat belt and start searching Rogan. I pat his pockets and whimper in relief when I feel what I'm looking for. I have to shoulder him back a little so I can get my hand into the front pocket of his jeans.

"Stupid tight ass pants," I grumble as I struggle to get a hand in. "Stupid big ass muscles and too tight pants," I add as I work the bejeweled knife I've seen him use before up his thigh, with one hand, and shove my other deeper into the pocket.

"What are you doing?" Rogan murmurs groggily as I press in harder against him, trying to hurriedly coax the knife out of his pocket.

I gasp and flinch, startled and not at all prepared for him to suddenly be awake. "What does it look like I'm doing?" I huff, and I can just feel the cold metal of the closed knife against my outstretched fingertips.

Just a little more.

"It feels like you're trying to get your hand down my pants," Rogan observes, his statement a little slurred and worrisome.

I snort. "Yep, you caught me, I thought this would be the perfect moment to dazzle you with my hand job skills," I snark. "Got it!" I announce excitedly, wrapping my fingers around the knife and pulling it free.

"What happened?" Rogan asks, his voice gravelly and his confusion feeding into the panic racing through me.

"We wrecked," I tell him, my eyes meeting his. "I fixed what bones I could, but—"

"You're bleeding," he announces, reaching a hand out to my face and wiping at the steady slow trickle I've had since I woke up. His green eyes flash from perplexed to confused and then to angry.

"We both are," I explain, and then I pull my face away from his hand and get back to work.

The blade of the knife pops out with a *shick* sound, and I waste no time positioning it against his lap belt. "Hold on," I instruct as I prepare to saw away at the webbed polyester, but the knife is sharp as hell and cuts through the belt like butter. Rogan half tumbles on top of me before he seems to catch his weight against the frame of the destroyed car.

I crawl back and out of the tight space, pulling him

along with me. I try to ignore the winces and grunts of discomfort as I go, but that same strange rumble moves through the ground I'm kneeling on, and it feels like it's screaming *you're out of time* at me. Just as the sensation passes, Rogan's gaze snaps up and searches all around us. His face fills with anger, but that emotion is quickly replaced by pain. An agonized groan pours from his mouth when I try to help him get all the way free of the car.

"Lennox, run," Rogan grunts out. He suddenly starts to push me away from him.

"What the—" I object as I pull on him even harder, confused.

"Run," he orders more adamantly. "They're trying to surround us."

Panicked, my head snaps up, and I look all around us. "Who is?" I demand when I don't see anything there.

"Circummancers!" he snaps, the word filled with fury and alarm.

Vicinal Witches, my mind supplies, pulling the name from lessons I didn't think mattered as a kid. And then it all dawns on me. The freak wind that shoved us off the road, the strange current I can feel vibrating in the ground, the sense that I'm running out of time. We're being attacked by elemental magic users, and they're about to lock us into a grid.

"Fucking hell!" I grunt, yanking hard on Rogan and freeing him from the car the rest of the way.

The lesson from my early teenage years comes rushing back. I can hear my Grammy's voice explaining to us the history of witch battles and how they were fought. I remember pretending to be as into it as Tad was as she detailed how groups of witches liked to fight.

"One on one, the odds are more even," Grammy agreed when Tad asked why witches didn't duel like they did back in the olden days. "But no one likes to lose, Tadpole, which is why magic users prefer strength in numbers," she explained, as if it were the most riveting story she ever told.

"Witches like to surround and attack, creating a force, a grid, where magic bounces off of other witches. That way the magic becomes stronger and more lethal," she declares as she mimes a sword fight. "In a grid, it doesn't matter if your magical blow or attack misses its mark. The magic bounces around inside the circle until it hits someone, or a partner-witch takes it and combines the force with their attack, until BOOM!" she shouts, and it makes me and all of my cousins jump in surprise.

Her voice fades as our childish giggles fill my mind, and loss constricts around me, so tight that it all at once makes it hard to breathe. I recall her telling us that normally witches can't feed off of each other like that. That our magic is usually only *our* magic, but witches and covens have found ways around that. I learned that day that amulets that protect and temporarily link witches to a partner in a group have been a game-changer when it comes to fighting, and now Rogan and I are about to experience firsthand why you never want to be in the center of a grid.

Fear rushes through me. I feel like cornered prey that needs to frantically look for a way out. Rogan and I aren't completely defenseless, but in order to even the odds and level the playing field, we have to destroy the protective amulets the witches are wearing before our magic will have any kind of impact. When you're being attacked from all sides, shit gets complicated and deadly, fast.

I want to ask who they are and why they're doing this to us, but it doesn't matter right now. Whether they're linked to the kidnappings or a rogue coven that we just happened upon, who and why will be left to sort out *after* we survive.

Now, to keep them from getting into formation.

The starting beats of Beyonce's "Formation" sound off in my mind, but I don't have enough time to high-five my weird sense of humor; I need to come up with some kind of plan.

Rogan reaches over from where we're both sitting in the dirt just outside of the mangled car. His breathing is labored as he places a warm hand on my forearm, and I know that his lung is messed up from the rib bone I pulled out and fixed before he woke up. The distinct tingling sensation of magic being pushed into me spreads throughout my body.

The blood magic seeps into my veins, swirls through my stomach, and clears my head. The throbbing in my temple and behind my eyes disappears, and I pull in a deep, grateful, pain-free breath. The bruises that peppered my body vanish, taking with them even more hurt and stiffness. The slow steady flow of blood that's been trickling down the side of my face ceases. My cheek cools, and it's as though I can feel Rogan putting a stopper in the drain I've been feeling on my energy.

He pulls his magic back when there's nothing more it can do for me right now, our eyes trained on one another intensely as the weight of the situation we now find ourselves in settles heavy in the air all around us. I can practically smell the tang of angry foreign magic on the innocent breeze that's now moving through the trees. I reach up and push some of Rogan's black hair out of his face, reveling in the feel of its softness for a beat, before I push back and stand up.

"Fix yourself up," I instruct, suddenly feeling numb. It's as though I've activated some kind of battle mode I didn't know I had. I assess what I have around me to work with, and try to feel for the attacking witches' positions. They move silently. I can feel at least a dozen of them, and over half are in place, waiting for the others to close the circle around us.

"I'll hold them off until you can help and we can figure out what the hell they want," I whisper confidently.

Rogan studies me for a beat, his green gaze taking me in like he's all at once seeing me differently. He blinks and just like that, the look is gone. Nodding his agreement to my plan, he then closes his eyes and gets to work healing what injuries on himself he can. I'm not sure if he can combat all the damage inside. I know between the two of us, our powers have pretty solid dominion over the inner workings of the body, but we're not immortal or infinite. Things happen. Witches die. In the end, it doesn't matter what kind of magic you have or just how powerful you are, there's no stopping Death when it comes for you.

Trepidation taints my focus, and I do my best to shove it away. He'll be fine, I reassure myself sternly. We'll make it out of this. We're going to be just fine.

A twig snaps in the distance, and the sound works to cement my resolve and stoke my outrage. I don't know who these witches are, but it's time to do everything I can to make them regret picking this fight.

I call the pointed pieces of caribou leg bones I used to wedge the car door open to me. They come flying into my palms, ready and waiting to be used as weapons. I splinter the wild boar bones I ordered into small sharp toothpick-like pieces and scatter them all around Rogan and me. Skeletons of squirrels, rabbits, and other forest creatures speckle the woods all around me, and I command them to crumble into powder.

The last of the witches are moving into place, and I need to act fast but discreetly. I know they'll have protections on them, but they can't protect themselves from all forms of magic in their entirety. Amulets have a tendency to weaken other amulets, and the more you wear, the weaker they all become. Maybe I can work around the outer protections though and buy us a little more time.

I carefully move the bone powder from the skeletons of long dead forest creatures and create a circular border about ten feet out from where Rogan and I are. When the witches try to close in on us, they'll have to walk through the powder. I know there's at least one powerful wind Circummancer, and if they do their thing like I'm hoping they will, I'll make it work to my advantage.

I search my memory banks for any other details about this branch of magic in hopes that it helps to come up with some backup plans, just in case things don't go exactly as I hope. I know that Vicinal Witches are the most common of the magical community. Many have diluted abilities and can barely grasp one element let alone more. *That* definitely works in our favor. Then again, judging by the force of the wind that tried to take Rogan and me out, we're not dealing with an entire untrained coven of Circummancers.

I put out my magical feelers to ensure there aren't any more incoming surprises, but I don't sense any varying tones of magic moving to surround us other than the power the Vicinal Witches are exuding. We'll be up against the elements, which is bad enough, but it won't be a magically multilayered attack. Thank fuck for that at least.

Subtle movement comes from behind me, and I spin ready to magically cut a bitch. Adrenaline hammers through my veins, but when I turn, I only find Rogan. He looks a million times better, but now I want to punch him for scaring the shit out of me. He steps up next to me, not an ounce of apology in his hard moss-green stare for practically sneaking up on a girl.

"You are in violation of the Engagement Act of 1847," Rogan bellows out into the dark, and I jump, not at all prepared for his voice to rip through the stillness of the night. "You've attacked us without provocation or warning, which is a contravention of witch law and a punishable offense."

I scan our surroundings watchfully as Rogan goes full lawyer and vocally objects to what's happening. I'm not sure what good it's going to do since we're now officially surrounded and they obviously mean us harm, but what do I know? I personally thought guerrilla warfare was our best bet, but maybe we can talk this out. I roll my eyes at that thought. These people just shoved us off a road and down an embankment at sixty miles an hour. What is he expecting them to do, shout *my bad* and be on their way?

"If you go straight up Karen and ask to speak to a manager, you're on your own," I irritably whisper to him as I wait for our attackers to ignore his efforts to shame them into giving up, and attack us already.

Surprisingly, nothing happens.

The night quiets once again, the crickets not even brave enough to send their song out into the tense silence. Anticipation thrums through my chest, each rapid beat of my heart like a war drum in my head. I hold my breath, the inhale and exhale feeling too loud and disruptive as I wait for what will come next.

"Punishable offense?" a smooth, confident voice calls back, and then all at once, a ring of witches in golden-yellow hooded cloaks steps out from the obscurity of the dark and into the dim light of the rising crescent moon. "Maybe, but I doubt anyone would *really* take issue with the removal of the Kendrick stain from the fabric of the magical community," the witch declares matter-of-factly.

With a twitch of my hand, the splinters of bones I spread around us earlier slowly rise. I don't attack, knowing that the small projectiles likely won't make it past any protective amulets, but I have other plans for them. A robed figure lifts his hands and pushes back the hood obscuring his face.

Smooth dark skin, a shaved head, and a short tidy black beard dust the witch's square jaw. His full lips tilt up in a taunting smile, his russet-brown eyes fixed on Rogan in a way that immediately tells me they know each other. It also tells me this is *not* a good thing. He reaches out and lazily swipes at nothing with his hand—a gust of powerful wind surges in around Rogan and me, sending my bone splinters crashing back down to the ground. It's less a defensive move and more of a *you don't want to fuck with us* effort at intimidation.

Arrogance wafts off the Circummancer, his cold stare never leaving Rogan's. With zero hesitation, I take advantage of the witch's preoccupation and send a fine, almost imperceptible, mist of bone powder up into the air to join the dust, leaves, and evergreen needles that have been kicked up by the threatening breeze. None of the other surrounding witches speak up or do anything to stop me, and I revel silently in the success of my actions. That couldn't have gone any better than I had hoped, but I don't let the satisfaction or eagerness I feel show anywhere on my face or defensive stance.

"Prek," Rogan grumbles out, and the hoodless Circummancer's smile grows even wider. "When did they make your sniveling ass a commander?" he questions, and a spark of anger flashes in Prek's steely gaze.

"It's been a while, *old friend*," Prek points out, but the bite in his tone and ice in his gaze betray the sentiment of his words.

"I think we both know who the *stain* truly is," Rogan states pointedly. "Still holding onto unfounded grudges, I see," he adds with a dismissive wave, the tension in his body immediately dropping away as though this situation is no longer threatening and he can relax.

I, however, am not so convinced.

Prek chuckles, but there's not an ounce of genuine humor in it. "Typical Rogan," he purrs, his eyes narrowing slightly. "Always thinking he's the star the rest of us simply orbit around."

I try not to snort out a laugh of agreement. Nope. This prick could have killed us; I will not find him amusing or his assessment mildly accurate.

"Believe it or not, this visit isn't about you," Prek states, his tone suddenly bored as his dark gaze turns to me.

His sharp stare takes me in. His eyes drop to the pointed bone shards gripped in each of my hands and languidly make their way back up to mine. Curiosity flashes in his gaze for a brief moment, but it's quickly replaced by jaded resignation.

"Lennox Osseous, you've been summoned to appear before the Order of Magic. This is not a request, but an order. You are to be taken into custody immediately and brought before the High Council."

"Taken into custody?" I ask, bewildered, at the same time Rogan steps forward menacingly and growls, "For what?"

"Rogan Kendrick, this matter doesn't concern you. You will back off and not interfere with the Order's business," Prek warns, but the light in his brown eyes screams that he hopes Rogan will do the exact opposite.

"Am I being arrested?" I demand, ignoring the higher pitch of the question and telling myself there's no need to panic. I haven't done anything arrest worthy, except maybe threaten Marx, but that was before I knew who he was, and Rogan cleared the whole misunderstanding up.

Prek doesn't clarify, he just repeats, "Lennox Osseous,

you've been summoned to appear before the Order of Magic. This is not a request, but an order. You are to be taken into custody immediately and brought before the High Council."

Prek's robot mode stops, and I look to Rogan, confused. Is this normal? If I'm simply supposed to go with them for some *welcome to the magical community* get-together, then why not just say that? Why attack us first? That doesn't seem like something you'd do to facilitate an innocent introduction. It's very possible shoving us off the road was less about me and more about whatever history is between Rogan and this prick, but being deemed sacrificial collateral damage doesn't exactly make me feel any better about the situation.

Rogan turns and takes me in for a moment, as though he too is trying to work out what's going on. It makes my stomach drop even more to see evidence in his gaze that what's happening isn't normal. I shake my head *no* ever so slightly. I don't want to start shit with the Order, but everything inside of me is screaming not to go with them.

"Lennox Osseous, approach any member of my team so that you can be taken into custody," Prek commands coldly.

Rogan steps protectively in front of me. "Yeah, that's not going to happen," he states evenly as though he hadn't a care in the world and the Order doesn't have us trapped in a grid.

Prek's smile brightens, and for the first time since he's revealed himself, he looks genuinely pleased. Alarm bells ring in my mind as the chuckle that bubbles out of him is tinged with pure delight. "Oh, Kendrick, I was *really* hoping you'd say that."

With a movement so fast I don't even have time to register it, all hell breaks loose around us. The earth beneath our feet begins to undulate as though it's really the sea and had us fooled the whole time. I start to fall back, but

Rogan pulls me to him, slamming me into his unforgiving chest so hard that it knocks the wind out of me. Air leaves my lungs in a rush, and then it betrays me even more by turning and trying to pull me from Rogan's hold.

Wind assaults me from every angle, and for something that technically isn't tangible, it feels like a giant fist wrapping around me while bellowing *fee fi fo fum* and promising to crush my bones into paste. I scream, but it's torn away from me by the attacking gale. I hang onto Rogan for all that I'm worth, but suddenly he's choking and coughing up water, desperately working to dispel the liquid from his lungs.

Terror seizes me. I know I have fractions of a second before I'm torn away and might very likely be forced to watch Rogan die. Part of me wants to argue that this isn't right, the Order can't just go around doing this to innocent witches, but I'm not that naive.

Fear swirls in Rogan's eyes as he clutches onto me in a bruising hold with one hand and claws at his throat with the other. Heaves and wet coughs wrack his body, as once again everything goes so wrong so fast. Rage explodes through me, my blood heating with the potent and punishing need for vengeance.

In a flash, I lash out with my magic and snap my tethers to the bone matter all around me taut. Bone matter that this coven of witches has been breathing in while they waited for Prek's next orders. I bypass any protection amulets they might have leaving their bones alone and only calling to the particles of powder I sneakily introduced to their systems. I wrap the tethers of magic connecting me to each of the Vicinal Witches surrounding me, around my fist, and all at once shut each of them down.

Thoughts of mercy flee my mind as I direct the bone powder to close their airways. The assaulting wind around me stops, and Rogan falls to his knees, coughing, and finally able to try and breathe. Witches around me wheeze and choke, their gurgles slowly growing silent as their wide panicked eyes turn terrified.

I should feel bad as I pull air deep into my lungs and watch unconsciousness—and I know eventually death—creep into the visages of the witches all around me. But my compassion and sympathy have fled. There's no doubt in my mind that each and every one of them would gladly kill Rogan, kill me, and I've done nothing to deserve it.

Fury scalds me as one witch drops to her knees, her hood flung back to reveal carrot-orange hair and a purple hue to her oxygen-starved skin. Her eyes plead for me to stop, but where was her mercy, her pardon, when I was in a car flipping down the embankment, or when Rogan was being drowned from the inside out?

Other witches fall to their knees, weak and clasping at their impotent throats, but I ignore them and move closer to Prek. I want to see his face as karma bitch-slaps him across it. I want him to look into my eyes as his vision speckles with blackness, so that he knows without a shadow of doubt that *his* vicious actions are what sealed not only his fate, but the fate of everyone on his team.

Fear swims in his gaze as he looks up at me from where he's fallen to the now still ground. He blinks, and then something weird happens. A trail of crimson trickles out of the corner of his eyes. I watch it move down his cheeks slowly, and then see another line of blood drip down from his nose. He's bleeding.

"Leni, stop!" Rogan croaks, and then he's overcome with coughs, the sound of them thankfully dry, indicating that he's dispelled all the water from the abused organs.

I ignore him, too captivated by the trail of blood now seeping out of Prek's ears. I've never watched anyone being strangled to death; maybe the blood is normal. Something niggles at the back of my mind, screaming at me that this isn't normal. That I shouldn't be so calm about something so wrong, so utterly horrifying like watching someone die. But it's as if any ability to care was stripped from me.

Maybe I'm in shock or suffering from some kind of traumatic brain injury. Or maybe I've just had enough of other magic users thinking they can do whatever they want to me with no repercussions. Whatever it is, I'm far past the point of caring.

"Leni, Love, what are you doing?" a luscious and silky voice coos at me.

I pull my gaze from the lines of blood paving their way down Prek's face and look over to find Marx. Surprise flashes through me, quickly replaced by suspicion. What is he doing here? As though he can read the question in my eyes, his lips tilt up in a carefree smile, but it doesn't match the worry in his espresso-colored eyes.

"Rogan called me, beautiful, told me that a coven from the Order was out here messing with him."

I look from Marx to Rogan, who's struggling to get on his feet. Marx quickly moves to help him.

"I sent him a message just after I healed myself," Rogan confirms, his voice pure gravel, and he reaches into his pocket and produces his phone as if I need the extra proof.

"Lennox, you have to stop," Rogan orders once again, but it's as though there's nowhere for his words to settle in my swirling mind.

"Stop?" I ask, confused by the vehemence in his order.

Marx steps in front of Rogan. "You're killing them, Leni, and I promise you that's not a road you want to go down," Marx tells me, his comforting voice warm and cozy. I swallow his words down like I just took a bite from a chocolate chip cookie fresh out of the oven. They feel gooey and delicious, and all I suddenly want is another bite.

I look over at Prek, whose arms are now limp by his sides. Small twitches work their way through his failing body, and all I can suddenly feel is a cold and hollow anger. My eyes find Marx's again, and I feel a tear fall down my cheek.

"They were going to kill us," I tell him in defense, my mind now feeling clouded with wrath and Marx's tempting magic. There's something else there too, something terrifyingly strong and overwhelming, but Marx's warm cookie voice pulls my attention away.

"Let me take care of them, Leni," Marx purrs, imbuing his words with even more power.

I close my eyes and float in it for a moment.

"Lennox," Rogan starts, but Marx cuts him off.

"I think you'll set her off again, Ro, just let me," Marx tells him, and my brow furrows in question.

Does Rogan set me off?

"Leni, please," Marx pleads, and I open my eyes and take him in, the appeal breaking through whatever is going on with me and resonating to the core of who I am.

"Okay," I concede, my voice breaking a little. I release my hold on the Order's Circummancers all around me, suddenly feeling spent and exhausted.

Coughs and labored gasps fill the night all around me, and in two steps, Rogan has me wrapped up in his strong hold as though he knows I'm completely depleted.

"Is the Order allowing unsanctioned attacks on innocent witches now?" Rogan growls, but all I want to do is curl up and go to sleep. I don't have enough energy to feel angry anymore. Maybe in the morning.

"It wasn't unsanctioned, Rogan," Marx clips back as he bends to check on a yellow-robed witch who's not moving.

Relief fills his face when he finds a pulse and moves on to check on the next.

"What the fuck are you talking about?" Rogan snarls.

"You need to go," Marx interjects, cutting Rogan off when he opens his mouth to argue. "I'll come by and explain after I get this shit show cleaned up, but you two need to get out of here now! Take my car," he instructs, tossing Rogan a set of keys, his tone brooking no argument.

Rogan smoothly plucks the keys from the air and, surprisingly without another word, turns and moves us away from the downed Order witches and his friend, who frantically flits from witch to witch and pulls out his phone to make a call. I get lost in the steady sure movement of Rogan as he holds me to him, silently and effortlessly climbing up the steep embankment to the road where a sleek sports car is parked.

I say nothing as he buckles me into the seat, a weird sense of déjà vu running through me. Fear sends my heart galloping, and I suddenly come to the conclusion that I'm not ready to be in a car again. Not after what just happened in the last one.

"It's okay, Lennox. I won't let anything like that happen again. I need to get us home as quickly as possible; we'll be safe there. I wish we had a ley line closer, but this will do," he tells me, motioning to the car, with reassurance bleeding out of his gaze.

Emotions flood me, and it's as though everything I should have been feeling during the near-death encounter comes surging in at me. My breaths get shorter and more panicked, and Rogan's face moves closer until it's a hair's breadth away.

"You're safe now. I've got you. You're drained, and this is your body reacting to that vulnerability. This is normal. You just need to rest," he reassures me, brushing matted curls back from my face.

I absorb his words, comparing them to the trepidation that I feel as though I just might drown in, and recognize that he's right. I feel empty, like I can't protect myself, and it's feeding the anxiety that I can feel crashing through me right now.

"Do you want me to help you rest?" Rogan asks after a beat.

I focus back on his moss-green gaze and nod my head. I don't know if I can calm myself down on my own. Understanding alights in his soothing stare, and the back of his fingers gently stroke my cheek. I don't miss the small warm streak left in their wake. I don't know how I know, but I'm certain it's blood, and for some reason it doesn't bother me.

"Thank you, Lennox," he whispers, his eyes brimming with appreciation and respect as his breath teases my lips, his mouth so incredibly close to mine. "Thank you for saving my life," he adds, the tip of his nose skimming mine intimately.

Heat unfurls deep in my core, my body responding to his closeness like some sun-starved plant. I breathe him in, desire pooling between my thighs as he gently runs his thumb across my bottom lip. A gasp of exquisite anticipation almost escapes me as his mouth just barely skims mine, our eyes locked on each other and brimming with complicated layers of emotion. But instead of closing the distance between our lips and stoking the flickering need now blazing to life inside of me, he whispers *Seno* against my parted mouth. Then all at once, I collapse against him as everything in and around me bleeds black.

18

A loud snore wakes me up with a start, and I open my eyes and stare at the unfamiliar ceiling for a moment. Another snore fills the stillness of the room, and I'm not sure if it was my snore or Hoot's that woke me up. It takes me a moment to get my bearings, but as I sit up, I recognize the guest room that Rogan assigned me. He's not in here, not that I would expect him to be, but disappointment flashes through me, and I give it the side-eye for a moment until another jarring snore has me looking around the room for Hoot.

I find him conked out on the bench that sits at the foot of the bed, snuggled up on the extra blanket I draped there. It takes me a moment to blink him into focus in the dark of the room, but as I do, I realize that Hoot's shacked up with a fluffy black and white cat. This must be Rogan's familiar.

I run my fingers through my hair, but they get stuck in the nest of tangles I'm sporting, so I leave Hoot to his cuddle party of two and make my way to the bathroom so I can get cleaned up. My phone is still MIA, and there's not a clock anywhere in the room or attached bathroom, so I have no idea what time it is. It's still dark though, and when I peek out the bathroom window, the moon is on the descending side of its apex, so I can't have been asleep for that long.

I find my wide-toothed comb and start working on my mane as I turn on the water to the shower, waiting for it to heat up. Flashes of what happened the night before strobe through my mind, and I have a hard time figuring out how I feel about everything. The lycans, the Order, Rogan, Marx, it's all so convoluted and overwhelming. I'm not sure what to think about any of it. I have so many questions, but the leading one at the moment has me looking in the mirror for answers.

I almost killed people yesterday.

Witches, I correct myself, as though that changes things. But the *who* of it isn't really the issue I'm trying to sort through as I stare into my tired toffee-hued eyes. No, the who of it almost feels inconsequential, what's really fucking with me right now is that *I* was ready to end them all. *I* almost killed them.

I look for the guilt that should be bubbling up in my chest at that thought. I try to find the sick feeling that should accompany the realization that I almost ended someone's life, multiple someones, but it's not there. *That* almost concerns me more than my actions do. Not only did I almost kill over a dozen Order members, but I don't even feel bad about it.

That can't be normal, can it?

I abandon my remorseless eyes in the mirror and step under the spray of the shower. What is happening to me? I feel like I'm losing who I am, but as I think that, it doesn't resonate in my soul as being true. The thought that maybe I'm *finally* finding who I really am pops into my mind, and with it comes a feeling of validation, of knowing that *this* is the heart of it. I don't feel like some hardened killer, I just feel like someone who's done taking shit. I feel like someone who operates by the code that you give what you get.

I wash my hair thoroughly, plucking pieces of windshield from my curls and letting my thoughts wander to Rogan as I finger comb half a bottle of conditioner through the rest of my tangles. How he looked when he was unconscious and vulnerable in the car. The relief I felt when I discovered he was still alive. The way he stepped in front of me against the Order. His lips almost against mine.

Excitement flutters through me, but it can't breach the confusion I feel about it all. Why am I going full middle-school-girl-crush on him? Yes, he's gorgeous, but he's also arrogant, cagey, myopic when it comes to his brother, and selfish. These are not qualities that I look for in a man. So what is it about *him* that's encouraging me to ignore good sense? Is it the dark mysterious vibe? The take control attitude? His body?

I snort out a laugh at that thought. Maybe I have to admit that I'm shallower than I thought, and this simply comes down to the physical side of things, but that feels like bullshit too. I wash my body, taking note that there isn't a bruise or a mark on me. Other than the occasional pieces of glass washing down the shower drain, it's almost as though the accident was just a dream. I know Rogan and I didn't exactly escape injury, but thanks to our magic, we walked away from all of this without a scratch.

Bowing my head in awe of that fact, I send out a quiet *thank you* to my ancestors. So far, this whole magic thing hasn't proven to be without its issues, but there's no ignoring how grateful I now feel to have it, to be alive and injury-free now because of it.

I rinse off and dry my hair, my thoughts wandering to the Order and what they could possibly want with me. I wrap a towel around my body and head back into the room to track down some clothes. Hoot looks up as a sliver of light from the bathroom cuts through the dark and falls on his snuggle session. His cat friend looks over at me with a yawn, but the two white stripes painted down its back give me pause.

I tilt my head as I take the little guy in. Its markings are strange for a cat, and yet I can't help feeling like I recognize them from somewhere. It flicks its fluffy tail once as it settles in once more against Hoot, and that's when it clicks. That isn't a cat, it's a damn skunk. Panic shoots through me, but I'm frozen in the bathroom doorway, not sure what to do. Did Hoot somehow invite the walking stink bomb into the house?

Shit. Rogan is going to kill me. He seems anal about his house being clean, and now my deficient ex-familiar has gone and booed up with this foul-smelling vermin.

"Hoot, come," I call out, snapping my fingers and pointing to the ground next to me as though I expect the little rebel to actually listen to anything I tell him to do. He, of course, does nothing. "Hoot, come here right now!" I whisper growl, not wanting the skunk to get any negative vibes that may make it want to pick out fun things to spray.

Hoot just blinks at me.

"You know what? You're ungrateful. Anyone ever tell you that?" I lob at him as I inch away from the bathroom doorway, deciding he can fend for himself.

Like some overprotective girlfriend, the skunk lifts its head and, I swear, shoots an unappreciative look my way. Immediately I freeze, throwing my hands up like the skunk just barked, *you're under arrest.* I watch petrified as it gets up, arches its back with a stretch, and then levels a cold obsidian stare on me. If I didn't know better, I'd think it was offended on behalf of Hoot. It watches me, and I watch it right back for what seems like forever. I feel like an ant under a magnifying lens just waiting for it to find the right angle and singe my ass with the sun's brutal rays.

I gather up my courage and move to the side slowly, non-threateningly, and then stop in my tracks when the skunk's tail twitches in response.

"You're okay," I coo silkily at it. "I'm just trying to leave so you and Hoot can get back to your cuddle party," I add, trying for another step.

The skunk's weaponized ass starts to angle in my direction. I look at Hoot, stupidly expecting him to tell his little friend to simmer the fuck down and behave, but he just yawns. Yep, it's official, it's every man for himself up in this bitch.

"You don't want to do that," I declare confidently to the skunk as it turns even more. But apparently it really does, because it's armed and loaded butt is pointed at me before I can even finish my sentence. "Mother fuck—" I scream and dive to try and get out of the way of any noxious projectiles the little beast can send my way.

A loud thump fills the room as I land hard. It knocks my grimoire off the dresser, and next thing I know, it's plummeting down toward me. Unable to roll away in time, I take a book spine to the ribs. I swallow down a yelp that could very well give my position away to the enemy, and start to army crawl toward the window. That bastard skunk probably thinks I'll make a run for the door, but I'm one step ahead. Unagi all the way.

Ross would be so proud.

The door to my room slams open with a loud boom like it was just kicked in by SWAT. My head snaps toward it just in time to see Rogan stomp in, his green eyes furious and searching.

Fuck, he's directly in the line of fire!

I push off from the ground, my towel abandoning me in

my haste. My head is on a swivel as I look from the skunk to Rogan, who's just standing in prime spraying range. I leap for him, screaming for him to get down like some crazed banshee. Rogan's eyes widen as I tackle him, his arms wrapping around me as we both go down like felled trees.

He hits the ground first with an *oomph*, and I bounce against him from the impact. I squeeze my eyes shut, knowing that the skunk is going to release its deluge at any moment. Hopefully, I get the worst of it and Rogan is somewhat spared.

"What is going on?" he growls, making my eyes pop open to find his green gaze going from me to the room as though he's still searching for the threat.

"Hoot let a skunk in the house. Close your mouth, we're going to be sprayed any second now," I bark at him, once again squeezing my eyes shut and taking my own advice and clamping my mouth closed too.

Rogan doesn't say anything, proving his self-preservation instincts are firing on all cylinders. I wait, every muscle tense, for a malodorous mist to cascade down upon me, but nothing happens. I wait a little longer and then a little more. Nothing. I risk cracking one eye open to take in what's happening. Maybe the skunk wanted a better angle.

I look over to find the little menace just sitting and watching us, Hoot right at its side, like Rogan and I are their entertainment for the evening. I turn my perplexed gaze to Rogan, who doesn't look nearly as worried or pissed as I thought he would, and the gears in my head start turning.

"You know this skunk, don't you?" I ask on a whisper, just in case my voice sets the little striped demon into a spraying frenzy.

"Lennox, meet Gibson. He was my familiar before..."

I let out a huff and try not to roll my eyes. Of course he had a skunk for a familiar, why wouldn't that be completely normal? And here I was thinking a ferret would have been bad.

"Um, he won't hurt you," Rogan supplies, like it should be obvious and he's trying to figure out why I'm acting like a mental case. "He was de-scented as a baby," he adds casually, and I feel a blush crawling up my neck and into my cheeks.

"He can't spray?" I ask warily, because that skunk was ass out and ready, which makes no sense if it can't actually use said ass as a weapon.

"Not at all," Rogan confirms.

"Why the hell didn't you tell me you had a skunk for a familiar?" I demand, pushing up from his chest so I can stare down at him annoyed.

He ignores the weight of my irritated glare and moves into a sitting position, which has me straddling his lap, and us chest to chest. I'm painfully aware that I'm naked, but I'm hoping if I don't draw attention to it that he won't notice. This plan is getting less and less feasible as I feel my skin morph into a lovely shade of scarlet, but it's all I have to work with at the moment.

"There's been a lot going on. I guess I forgot," he offers lamely, but I don't know that I'm buying it one bit. Maybe he didn't anticipate a naked tackle, but I could totally see him getting a rise out of freaking people out.

"Oh, you simply forgot," I snark, my tone making it clear just how much I believe that crap.

"Why on earth did you tackle me?" he defends, turning this around on me. Typical.

"I was *saving* you," I point out incredulously.

"From a skunk that can't even spray?" he counters ungratefully.

"I didn't know that at the time, you ass. It twerked in my

direction, and I got the fuck out of the way. I didn't stop and examine its equipment."

"Gibson does not twerk."

"Hate to break it to you, Rogan, but he sure as hell does."

"Why are you naked?" he asks, and my mouth flops open wordlessly.

So much for his not noticing. His thumb paints an arc on the skin of my hip, and I all at once can't help but notice how his body feels against mine. I clear my throat, brushing aside the way his soft T-shirt teases my now peaked breasts. Or the way the rough texture of his jeans feels between my thighs. I ignore how close his face is to mine, or just how intimate our current position is.

"Because your towel abandoned me in my time of need," I defend, suddenly feeling a little breathless. "You should really get towels made of sturdier stuff."

"I'll get right on that," he answers without missing a beat, his eyes fixed on mine and unreadable.

I know I should tell him to close his eyes while I get out of his lap. I know I shouldn't feel any amount of satisfaction as he hardens beneath me. Excitement shouldn't light up my insides simply because his breaths are coming a little quicker. His response to me shouldn't matter. *He* shouldn't matter. But as his eyes dip down to my lips, and his fingertips warm my hips, there's no denying that *something* is here...and it matters.

My heart picks up its pace, and I'm not sure what I should do. I feel like I'm on the cusp of something, but I'm not sure exactly what. Will he lean in? Do *I* want to kiss him? Is it wise to add this potential complication to an already messed up situation? His eyes flick back up to mine, and I can practically see the same questions swirling in his gaze. We stare at each other, one second flowing into another. We don't advance. We don't retreat.

We just sit in indecision until doubt starts to bloom in my chest.

We have more important things to worry about right now. This is silly and rash and the last thing we need to add to our plates. I could be reading him wrong, and really he's just waiting for me to get my naked ass off him.

"We should, uh…" I start, shattering the weighted silence. I'm not sure if I'm putting a stop to things or offering one last opening and waiting to see if he'll seize it.

"Right," Rogan agrees, snapping out of his transfixed state.

I push up from him, and his hands at my waist help lift me as I go. It's not until I stand up that I realize what a bad idea this was. Because now my crotch is staring him right in his face. He clears his throat softly, and I scramble away from him. I hurry to pluck my towel from the ground and wrap it around me. I hope like hell it serves as a tourniquet and stops the embarrassment bleeding out of me all over the place.

I probably look like some desperate thot who just keeps throwing myself at him. My face is on fire with mortification. Rogan gets to his feet, but I can't bring myself to look at him. I don't want to see what might be written all over his face. Or worse, look and see that he doesn't give a shit at all.

"I'll, uh…I'll be in the kitchen…when you're ready," he declares, and then just like that, he's gone. It's like he couldn't get out of here fast enough. I plop onto the edge of the bed and let my face fall into my hands.

What am I doing?

I look up to find Hoot and Gibson are gone. Seems like the show is over, or maybe all of this was too much for them, not that I can blame them. It's too much for me too…or maybe the issue is that it's not enough? I growl into my hands in exasperation and get up to get dressed.

"Stupid, stupid, stupid, Leni. What are you thinking? You want to fuck him, but you don't trust him. You want to get lost in the feel of him, but at what cost?" I ask myself as I step into my underwear and wiggle into a pair of jeans.

How can I so easily forgive what's happened between us, what brought me here in the first place? Gibson is his ex-familiar because he made me his against my will. He tethered us together with no thought as to how I would feel about it. He can claim it's all for the greater good, and maybe it was, but it doesn't make it right. It doesn't excuse the violation. And now, I what...think we're somehow going to find *happily ever after* in missing witches, Order attacks, secrecy, and lies?

I shake my head as I hook my bra together behind my back. No. It doesn't matter that sex with him would probably be epic. It's a distraction that we don't have time for. I pull a shirt on, fluffing my disgruntled curls as I search for my shoes. Nope. Just going to pretend like this never happened. So he saw me naked, who cares? I love what I'm working with, so no shame there. Yes, he took a bush to the face. It's unfortunate, but there's no getting around it now. I'm sure we can both behave like civilized adults and just never talk about it again.

Yep. Solid plan.

My stomach growls, and I know there's no avoiding the kitchen. Crap. Please don't let me turn beet red as soon as I see him, I plead with myself, pulling on my big girl panties and heading down to the kitchen. I take the stairs a little louder than usual, announcing to Rogan that I'm coming and it's time to prepare for his role in Operation Avoidance.

"Hey," I offer casually as I pass the kitchen island, making a beeline for the fancy coffee machine. Dammit. I still don't know how to make it submit.

"Hey," he offers back, taking the large mug from my

hand without missing a beat and getting to work making me a delicious cup of decadent brew.

I give him room to sweet talk the machine and grab a seat at the island. I look around the kitchen to try and figure out what time it is, but there isn't a clock anywhere. Note to self, get Rogan a clock.

"How long was I out?" I ask, taking in his jeans and T-shirt. It's definitely the middle of the night, but he's dressed and ready to go, which is a little odd.

"It's just past four in the morning," he tells me as the coffee machine starts gurgling and making noises that tell me a hot cup of joe is not too far away.

"Oh, I feel like I've been asleep forever, but I'll take a handful of hours," I note with a shrug.

"No, it's four in the morning on *Wednesday*. You've been asleep for more than a day," he reveals casually as he opens the fridge and pulls out those fancy syrups and things that I used to think people could only get at a legit coffee shop. I wonder if Riggs is his supplier. I'll have to get in on that if he is.

"Wait. What?" I squeak out in surprise as what he says registers. How did I crash for that long? "What about the meeting with the coven? Did Marx come tell us what the hell is going on? Did I miss anything else?" I fire at him, not even stopping to reload the air in my lungs as worry sends my pulse galloping.

Rogan hands me a large cup filled with liquid salvation, but I'm too shocked and worried to dunk my face in it like I normally would.

"I rescheduled the meeting with the coven for this afternoon. Marx hasn't come by yet; he got tied up with the attack, and it took longer to square up than he thought. I got a message from him just before you naked tackled me. He said he'd drop by in a couple of hours to fill us in on what's happening."

I narrow my eyes at him—mentioning the thing we're not supposed to be mentioning is not part of the plan. Then again, maybe if I clued Rogan into the plan, he might follow it better. But that means I'd have to bring up the thing that I don't want to bring up, so I'll just shoot him a warning glare and hope he picks up what I'm putting down.

"The only other thing you missed was this..." Rogan continues as though my warning shot fell on deaf ears. He walks out of the kitchen, and I debate for a moment if I was supposed to follow him. Before I can make up my mind one way or the other, he comes back with a massive white box. He sets it on the island next to me and hands me an envelope. I open it, pulling out a card that has a neat but masculine scrawl on it.

Lennox,
When we heard what happened, Alpha Riggs insisted on sending you this. I, of course, then insisted on playing delivery boy. When you're well and rested, call me. I'd like to take you to dinner sometime, maybe even find a stump and see where the night takes us.
Saxon.

He drew a winky face just before his number and a heart just before his name. I trace the angle of Saxon's handwriting as I read the note again, and a small smile works to claim my mouth. I set the note and envelope down and reach for the lid of the huge box. Sadly, it's too big to be a jackalope antler, but who knows, maybe this is one of those *present inside a present* tricks that are fun to do to people, but annoying when you're the one opening fifty boxes just to find a lame-ass cuddle coupon. Rogan plucks the note from the counter, reading it and grunting with annoyance before tossing it aside. I pull the top off and find a stack of various bones. I study them for a quick second and realize it's a duplicate of the bone order that I lost in the accident.

My smile grows even wider. Looks like I've got some spelling to do.

"Told you that you'd have a problem on your hands with that one," Rogan grumbles, jutting his chin in the direction of the tossed aside note.

I snort out a laugh. "Oh yeah, a dinner invitation and the drop of the digits is stage five clinger status. Alert the authorities," I gasp in faux outrage. "Oh wait, they tried to kill us," I point out snarkily, adding an eye roll for effect.

He shakes his head but doesn't say anything else. I take a sip of my coffee, and it forces me to close my eyes and revel in the explosion of flavors on my tongue. I welcome the heat that pours down my throat as I swallow, and I swear this cup of coffee is a better lover than a fair percentage of my past dalliances.

"I want to have your babies," I state matter-of-factly, opening my blissed-out gaze and leveling an arduous look on the coffee machine. Rogan barks out a laugh.

"Should I leave the two of you alone?" he teases.

"Please don't, you know she only puts out for me because you tell her to," I plead, and he laughs even harder.

It's a nice sound. He looks so carefree and relaxed with his head tilted back and a chuckle bouncing around the kitchen. It warms something in me to see him not bogged down by stress and worry, even if only for a moment. I drop-kick that marshmallow of a thought as far away as I can. Not today, Satan. Not. Today.

"Alright, Rogan Kendrick," I announce, taking another sip of my delicious mocha to help fortify my resolve. "I'm going to whip up some potions and protections, and while I do, *you* are going to sit here and tell me, once and for all, what the fuck is going on. Enough is enough, it's time to get it all out of the cauldron. And before you even think about holding out on me, you should know that I have a recipe for a potion that will leave you unsatisfied by anything you taste, do, or fuck until the antidote is given. So if I were you, I'd have a seat and spill it."

Rogan's green gaze looks more interested than cowed as it dips down my body and then floats back up. "We wouldn't want that, now would we," he practically purrs, and his deep irreverent tone lights up my lady bits like it's accelerant and a struck match all in one.

Well, crap. I just handed over my king on that one. My vagina screams at me *that's checkmate, bitch*, and then practically squeals with excitement, ready to be plundered. I wrangle the wayward direction of my thoughts and focus back on Rogan, who is now wearing a knowing grin.

Stick with the plan, Leni. Stick with the damn plan.

I toss him an unimpressed smile, hoping he can't see the new pink tinge of my cheeks. Note to self: no more sex threats. I don't think the plan can take it.

19

I find the pelvic bone of the female wolf and lift it out of the box. Closing my eyes, I thank the spirit of the wolf for its offering and then move back over to the large mortar and pestle that Rogan supplied me with. It worked out for me that Rogan's brother often does spell work here; I've been able to find everything I need and more.

Rogan watches me work, the worry and tension back in his eyes, and it has nothing to do with my promises to make him spill all his secrets. I know he's picturing the last time his brother was here, prepping spell work like I am now. Rogan's fear and sadness are almost palpable, and I wish we had new news in the search for Elon and the other missing witches. I find myself wondering where he might be, if he's okay, and how he might feel about me messing with his things.

I reduce the pelvic bone into a fine powder in the bowl and then add some raw amber and sandalwood to the mix. Two spelled splashes of frankincense oil join the potion, and then I go about crushing and grinding everything together with the pestle. Rogan's eyes watch the rhythm of my movements as I work the potion into the consistency that I need. I wait patiently for his green gaze to find my expectant one.

"You can start now," I tell him, when he finally looks up at my face. I'm done asking him to source equipment and the ingredients that I need for today's work, and we can get on with the gab sesh.

He leans back in his stool and releases a resigned sigh, running a hand down his tired face. "What do you want to know?" he asks after a beat, and I flip open my mental list of observations and questions that I've been tabulating since he first showed up in my shop.

"What are you keeping from me?" I start, tackling the biggest issue and concern I have when it comes to Rogan Kendrick and the mystery of the missing Osteomancers. "And before you do me the disservice of saying *it's nothing* or asking me *what I'm talking about*, I want you to think through the consequences of doing that. I'm here, trying to help you, trying to trust you. Please don't taint that with omissions and lies," I tell him, my gaze pleading with him to trust me, to arm me with what I need to know about him, his brother, and what's happening.

He studies me for a moment, his gaze intense and searching as it bounces back and forth between my resolute stare. He blinks and I can see the conviction of a decision in his eyes. I hope for the sake of whatever we have, or might have, between us that he's going to drop the bullshit and be real with me.

"I'm not purposefully trying to keep things from you, Lennox. It's not personal, I promise you that. It's just that..." He leans forward and rests his elbows on the counter, releasing a weary exhale. "It's just that I'm used to keeping to myself. I'm accustomed to only relying on a very small circle of people. People who have earned my trust."

"And I haven't?" I ask simply as I add mugwort and obsidian tears to the mortar.

"It's not that, you have..." he answers with a shake of his head, his stare trained on his clasped hands. "You have," he repeats as though it's as much a confession to himself as it is to me.

His eyes lift to find mine, and he traces my features with his gaze for a beat. "My mother is Sorrel Adair," he tells me, and it's clear he expects me to know the name.

My brow furrows in thought as I search for why I should know that name. "Adair..." I repeat as though saying it out loud will conjure recognition. "Wait," I exclaim, my eyes growing wider with understanding. "Adair as in High Priestess Adair?"

"The very one," he confirms, and the admission sends me reeling.

His mother is the leader of the Order, she's more or less the Queen of the Witches.

"Holy fuck," I whisper in awe. "But I thought you said your uncles held the magic in your line?"

"No, I said that they were Elon's and my predecessors, *not* that they were the only magic in my line. My mother, as you know, is a fire-wielding Vicinal Witch. My father, the High Priest, is a Soul Witch. And my two uncles on my mother's side are...were...a Blood Witch, and a Bone Witch. They were both Order Summoners, or High Lieutenants as they're called now."

I take in what he's saying as I reach for the green velvet bag that has all the vessel options in it for amulets. I quickly pluck an oval ring from the bag and try it on my hand.

"Okaaay, so you're witch royalty. Should I brush up on my curtsey skills or something?" I tease, a little deflated.

This is the big secret? *This* is what's been setting off my internal *don't trust him* alarms? The ring fits snugly on my middle finger, and I pull it off and look into the bag for a second option. I pull a chain out and then freeze, the bag of jewelry all at once forgotten as a bomb of understanding explodes in my mind.

"Holy shit. You murdered your uncle," I accuse, dropping the chain next to the ring as memories surge through me, and I recall the stories I've heard about the High Priestess and her messed up sons.

I stare at him, completely aghast. I don't pay attention to witch politics at all, but even I heard about the brothers who brutally murdered their uncle in a grab for power. Rogan doesn't say anything, he just watches me like he's waiting for something, and then it hits me in a wave of shock and rage.

"Rogan, you were renounced. You and Elon were cast out," I half shout, half wheeze as panic floods me.

I'm tethered to someone who is cursed and renounced by the Order and therefore supposed to be cursed and renounced by *all* witches. Nausea threatens to climb up my throat. He did something so fucked up that there was no coming back from it, and now I'm here in his kitchen trying to help him find his brother.

I shoved my bush in the face of an evil, renounced witch!

Outrage morphs my features, and I move menacingly toward where he's just sitting and watching me.

"What have you done?" I snarl, fighting the urge to punch him in his too pretty face. "You linked us, knowing it could be a death sentence for me," I yell at him. And when he doesn't respond in any way, it pisses me off even more. "They could purge me just for associating with you! Is that what the whole shit show with Prek was about?" I demand, and something flashes in Rogan's eyes, but he doesn't say a word. "Answer me!" I snap, getting in his face. "If you're going to condemn me to death or shunning, the least you can fucking do is explain why!"

"Breathe," Rogan orders, as though his biggest concern is my potential hyperventilation and not the mess he's dragged me into.

"You breathe," I growl back, internally facepalming at the weak comeback. Is it possible to be so mad that you can't string words together anymore?

"Yes, Elon and I are the reason my uncle is dead, but it's *not* what you think. You can't believe the narrative of the High Priestess or her Council."

"Okay, mommy is a liar, got it. Is that supposed to change anything for me, Rogan?" I demand incredulously. "Are you suddenly not renounced? I'd love for you to explain it to me, because right now all I can see is a man who showed up in my shop, enslaved me, lied to me, and has now condemned me to a seriously fucked up future."

Betrayal settles in my chest as I stare at him, at the thin circle of gold around his pupil. I take in the scar running down one side of his face and tell myself there's more to this. There has to be. Something doesn't add up here, or maybe I'm just hoping that's the case, because as much as I want to punch myself for it, I feel something for him.

Despite my efforts not to…I care.

Rogan huffs out a resigned sigh, pushing up from the stool and raking his fingers through his hair. His gaze floats around the room for a moment before it settles back on me. He studies me for a beat, and then he squares his shoulders.

"Elon and I were born with the spark. We were tested. It was found, and that's how our predecessors knew who the next in line would be," he starts, stepping away from me and leaning against the counter.

"When we were old enough to walk and talk, we were handed off to the person who controlled the branch of magic that we held the spark for. For me, that was my Uncle Kavon, and for Elon, it was our Uncle Oront."

Upon hearing his uncles' names, I try to recall which one ends up murdered in this story, but I can't seem to remember it.

"I saw my parents every couple of months," Rogan goes on. "But other than that, Kavon was all I knew. I was raised in his house, with his family. He wasn't overly warm or paternal, but I wasn't treated badly. It wasn't until Elon was accepted into the Order and assigned to the same division as I was that we were able to spend quality time together. And that's when I discovered how different his childhood was from mine.

"I went to my mother. I told her about Elon's brutal and violent upbringing. I demanded that something be done to Oront and that Elon be kept as far away from him as possible. But she wouldn't listen. Elon's spark meant that Oront was the final authority over him. She wouldn't go against the way things had always been, and because she was weak, Elon continued to suffer. I tried to stop it, but the more I attempted to intervene, the worse it got for my brother."

"Hold on, I'm confused," I interject, swallowing down the sick feeling I have in the pit of my stomach over what happened to his brother. "I don't want to dismiss how fucked up that situation is for you and for Elon, but there's something I don't understand. How are you in the Order if you aren't full witches? I mean, your uncles are still alive at this point in the story, so you and Elon don't have any powers yet, right?" I ask, completely perplexed.

"Death isn't the only way to transfer magic in a line," he tells me simply.

I stare at him for a beat, not registering how that could be true. "Ummm...pardon?" I ask, needing to hear it again.

"*Death* is one way to transfer to the next in line, but it's not the *only* way," he repeats.

"Is this one of those things that's common knowledge to

the witching community, but I ditched the day that lesson was taught and now I'm out of the loop?" I ask, feeling stupid as hell right now.

Rogan cracks a smile, but it's gone just as fast as it came. "No, it's a closely kept secret only certain families know. It's how those families hang onto power generation after generation. Certain families pass magic along to the next in line when they're young and strong and at their peak."

"But what happens to the witch that came before you? Don't people notice that they didn't kick the bucket like they were supposed to?" I question, not seeing how this demon of a secret hasn't gotten out of its salt circle yet.

"They leave," he replies, as if it's all that simple. "They live the rest of their lives as Lessers. They're set up for the rest of their days to revel in the lap of luxury."

"And they're just okay with that?" I press.

"Your potion is starting to dry out," Rogan warns.

I look over at the stone bowl absently and then remember I was supposed to be brewing and spelling *while* I was listening. Rogan's *renounced* bomb completely threw me off my game. I reach for the mortar and give everything a good stir. Then I drop the ring and chain that I picked out earlier into the mixture. With what Rogan is saying, we're going to need these now more than ever.

I lean down and whisper my incantation over the stone bowl. "*Protoro ylius arum forinat cesfrunatice shara vir onyliog ra.*"

With a flash and a pulse of magic, the contents of the mortar weave themselves onto the jewelry. A wide satisfied smile splits my lips as everything works exactly as I'd hoped it would. I did it. I just made my first protection amulets. I pluck the ring from the bowl and slip it onto the middle finger of my right hand. A wave of warmth moves over me, hardening like a candy shell as the spell imprints on me and locks into place. Relief radiates through me, and I already feel a little less fragile or vulnerable to magical attack.

I pull a long chain from the bowl and hand it to Rogan. His eyes widen with surprise.

"You made one for me?" he questions, as though he doesn't understand what I'm doing.

"It was before I knew you'd completely fucked me over," I snark, the sting of truth in my words making him wince. He doesn't move to take the chain from my hands, and I roll my eyes and shake the chain in invitation.

"Just take it, Rogan. I thought a buffer for potential attacks would be a wise idea. That's still true even if you're the reason we're getting attacked."

Instead of taking the long delicate chain from my hands and slipping it on over his head, he leans down so that *I* can do it. I don't move for a beat, surprised by his actions. Indecision battles in me for a moment, but after a beat, I step closer to him, slipping the links over his silky coffee bean-colored hair and settling them around his neck. He straightens up as soon as the amulet is in place, his eyes closed as though he's relishing in the wash of magic that I know is moving through him as the spell imprints.

I watch as my amulet's magic settles all around him. My thoughts and emotions are tangled and conflicted, and I'm not sure what to think about anything. It sounds like there were some seriously fucked up extenuating circumstances surrounding his uncle's death. But even if that's the case, he's still renounced. I sigh and internally shake my head at myself. I've never been into the whole witch thing, so part of me wants to say *who cares*. I never let my dad dictate who I could be friends with, so why should this be any different, but I know this isn't that simple. I may not care about witch politics, but they now affect me whether I like it or not. I have to live and thrive in this community, and associating with a magical pariah blows a huge hole in my ability to do that.

Even if what Rogan did is justified, I don't know that it changes anything. I stare at his closed eyes, the look on his face serene and at odds with the conversation we're having. I can feel the magic of the amulet locking into place, and out of nowhere, I lift my hand, intent on tracing the scar that I've been so curious about since I first laid eyes on him. I have no idea what's come over me, but I can't seem to stop myself regardless of the fact that my internal monologue right now is just an alarm going off in my head, followed by a steady shout of *we've lost thrusters, captain.*

Rogan's breath hitches as my fingers softly touch his face, but he doesn't stop me or ask me what the hell I'm doing. That's probably a good thing, because I don't have the foggiest clue. We both seem to hold our breath as I run my finger through his eyebrow and gently down his lid, his long lashes tickling my finger. I trace the line under his eye, stopping just past his cheekbone.

"How did this happen?" I ask quietly, allowing my thumb the liberty to brush across his cheek just once before I pull my hand away and get a hold of myself.

I'm mad, I remind myself as I step back. I should be kicking his ass, or running, and yet it's the instinct to touch him that overpowers everything else. I'm pretty sure my instincts are malfunctioning. Rogan's eyes open as I move away. He watches me for a moment and then moves toward me before suddenly stopping himself. Maybe his instincts are malfunctioning too.

"Anyway, you were saying," I start, bringing the focus back to where it should be.

He clears his throat and nods. "Right," he agrees, pausing for a second to trace back to where he left off. "Elon and I think it was my transference ceremony that set Oront off," he starts, and for some reason it's as though all the air in the room was just sucked away.

"I'd just come into my full powers, and Elon's transference ceremony was a handful of weeks away. *Finally,* he was going to be free, and Oront would be exiled. We were supposed to become Coven Lieutenants, work our way up the ranks. Get married, breed the next generation, and then one day, one of us just might become High Priest of the Witches. That was the plan anyway. But Oront had other ideas."

Rogan reaches out and plucks one of my curls between his fingers. He rubs the strand, his eyes far away, lost to the memories swirling around in his mind. I'm not even sure if he's aware he's doing it, but I don't say a word or move to reclaim the curl from him.

"Oront tried to kill Elon," he tells me robotically, no emotion in his inflection even though I see it etched in his face. My stomach drops. I saw something like this coming, but it doesn't make it any easier to hear it confirmed. "He was deranged. He had convinced himself that his power wasn't meant to pass on ever. He thought he found a way, some Druid ritual that would seal the magic to him forever and extend his life indefinitely.

"I wouldn't have known until it was too late, but one of the first things I made when I first received my full power was a thread of protection. Elon had tied it around his wrist, and I vowed that I would stop Oront if he tried to beat him again. Oront was so out of his mind when he attacked Elon that night that he cut the thread of protection, and it pulled me right to them." Rogan pauses, taking a moment to collect himself. When he looks up, I'm hammered by the raw emotion I see in his face.

"There was blood everywhere," he tells me, just above a whisper. "Elon was tied to some altar Oront had created, and he had cuts and brands all over him. I thought for sure he was dead. I didn't see how he could have survived what was being done to him. Oront was chanting frantically. He didn't even notice I was there.

"I couldn't move at first. I was too shocked and confused, and then Elon's hand twitched, and it snapped me out of my horror. I shoved as much magic as I could into him to stop the bleeding. I ran for him, but I was only able to cut one arm free before Oront attacked me."

Rogan starts to pace, anger coming off him in waves, and I push myself up to sit on the counter so that he has all the room he needs.

"I was at a massive disadvantage. I didn't have a weapon, and I knew my magic wasn't enough of a defense against my uncle for both me *and* Elon. I was beyond enraged at what this monster had been doing to Elon practically his whole life. The beatings. The torture. The cruelty. And now, after all my brother had survived, Oront was killing him. I lost it. I went for him with all that I had. I didn't care where his knife landed. I didn't count the stab wounds. All I knew was if I was going to die, I was taking him with me."

A tear slips out of his eye. His pain, the agony of living through something so horrible, but also having such evil memories seared into your soul, it calls to me. I can see in his every feature how much this terrorizes him, how much it has scarred him. Agony rips through him as he recalls what happened, and there's no doubt in my mind that what he's saying is true.

"I don't know what I was chanting as I fought to get the knife out of his hands. The words and the magic just flowed out of me as we battled to destroy one another. I should have known the coward would've had backup. But I didn't see his mistress, or the knife coming, until she was slashing at my face," he explains, gesturing to the scar I just asked about.

"I didn't factor her in, but it was probably what saved Elon's and my life. When she attacked me, Oront abandoned our fight and turned back to finish the ritual with Elon. I managed to get the upper hand over Kyat—his mistress—and knocked her out. It was her knife that I used to kill Oront."

I shake my head and stare at him, completely at a loss for what to say. "Your mother renounced you for simply defending yourself and your brother?" I ask, completely revolted by the thought that any mother could do that to them after what they had been through. She failed her sons and then threw them away; I can't even wrap my mind around it.

Rogan releases a weak, humorless chuckle and shakes his head. "No, in the end, Oront's death was an unremarkable blip compared to what happened next," Rogan recounts cryptically, and alarm hammers through me with those words. How the hell does this get worse?

"You see, whatever Oront was trying to do worked," he states hollowly, as though he himself still can't believe it.

"That motherfucker is alive? Your bitch of a mom set you up for a murder you didn't even commit?" I shout, suddenly so pissed that I couldn't stop myself even if I tried. Rogan's eyes snap to mine, and I cover my mouth as though that will help me take shit down a notch and hear what he's trying to say.

Rogan's stare traps me in its intense beam, the gold ring around his pupil more prevalent than it was before. "No, I killed him, and I'd do it again. His attempts backfired. They didn't work for him...but somehow, it worked for Elon and me," he explains quietly, evenly, his eyes searching mine as though he expects disbelief or accusation to immediately float to the surface of my gaze.

Bewilderment rockets through me, but I don't say anything as I try to absorb what the hell that means.

"Kyat woke up," he goes on. "I was in and out of consciousness at that point. I didn't realize what was happening until it was over. Elon and I were both spell weaving, just trying to stay alive, to heal as best we could. Oront was dead, and that meant Elon was hit with the transference. It gave him the extra boost he needed to battle the injuries he'd sustained, but we were both dangerously weak. Kyat had the blade in Elon's throat before either of us could so much as lift a hand to stop her."

I gasp in shock. It wasn't Oront who popped back up like the serial killer in every mainstream horror film, it was his fucked up mistress who survived to wreak havoc.

"Elon pulled the knife out on instinct," Rogan continues, his voice cracking with emotion. "I couldn't work fast enough. He was too hurt, and my magic was fucking useless." He trails off for a beat, his eyes suddenly lost before they refocus on me. "She laughed as he died. I can still hear her deranged cackle as I pulled Elon to me and tried to stop the inevitable. And then she came for me."

I stare at Rogan, heartbroken for him, dumbfounded by what he's saying. He watched his brother die? But then, who the hell did I watch walk off with a hiking pack and Elon's familiar, Tilda? I can feel the truth in Rogan's words, but I can't help the doubt that starts to spread through my chest as I try to make sense of it all. He watches me, and I can see that he's reading the skepticism and uncertainty in my eyes.

I believe him in my heart, but my mind is arguing that I just got epically ghost-storied. It's as though my rational brain was right there along for the ride, enraged, devastated, shocked, and then the story comes to an end, and it's realized that this is all bullshit. Impossible. The storyteller got us. My heart argues to look past what we think we know and see the truth, but I can't deny that I feel torn and suddenly very lost.

"I woke up in a private room three days later," Rogan continues. "Elon was in a bed next to me, which made no sense because I'd watched him die. I thought maybe I imagined it, that my injuries were so severe that it all caused me to hallucinate. It wasn't until my mother, father, and two other High Council members dropped by that I realized what I saw and felt *actually* happened."

"How?" I ask, stunned disbelief spilling out of the simple word.

"Help apparently arrived just after Kyat shoved her knife through my heart. They were able to detain her, but Elon and I were gone. Everything was kept quiet as they tried to piece together what had happened, to make sense of why Oront was dead and what he had been doing. But then everything changed. A day or so later, out of nowhere in the witchery morgue, Elon's heart started to beat. Then mine followed suit. Our injuries began to heal, and no one could make sense of any of it. It should have been impossible, and the High Priestess demanded to know how the hell we had come back.

"Kyat had been questioned while we were out. My mother and her trusted inner circle were able to put together what Oront had been up to. The Druid ritual that Oront was using was known, it had been attempted before and was always documented as a failure. But Elon and I were proof that somehow something we had done made it work. They couldn't suss out what it was though that activated magic long thought dead."

"You're not fucking with me, are you," I realize, my tone hollow and distant. I can see it in his face, feel it in my gut. My head wants to argue, but it'll catch up eventually.

"No," he answers evenly. "Elon and I weren't renounced because we defended ourselves against my unhinged uncle. My mother and the High Council renounced Elon and me because we wouldn't tell them how we did it. We wouldn't tell them the details and sequences of actions that somehow allowed us to cheat death," he growls, his eyes filled with conviction and veracity.

We stare at each other in silence, the word *impossible* teetering on the tips of my lips despite my heart clapping at my mind that it needs to get with the program. Rogan's stare burns into me. And he steps forward until he has me pinned between him and the counter, corded arms boxing me in from the sides.

"I know this sounds crazy. That it shouldn't be possible, but would that be more impossible than the existence of magic and witches in the first place?" he asks me softly. "How about lycans and vampires? Humans say that the Druids we come from were nothing more than make-believe, but tell me *Osteomancer*," he practically purrs, "are they right?"

I think through his questions, unable to argue with the logic.

"Don't cast the truth aside just because you don't understand how it works," he tells me, as though he can read my mind and the struggle I'm having putting both feet firmly on belief. "Fuck, Lennox, Elon and I don't even understand how it works. But I swear it's the truth."

We stare at each other for a long weighted moment. And I feel everything settle into place in me as one resounding question flashes to the forefront of my mind. If Rogan can't die, and I'm tethered to him, what the hell does that mean for me?

"So where does Prek fit into all of this?" I ask, hoping the answer is something easier to swallow. I need a life preserver of some kind, or I'm going to drown in everything that Rogan just sloshed on top of me.

"His aunt was Kyat."

"Does he—"

"No," Rogan interrupts. "He suspects there's more to the story, but he runs into nothing but walls when he tries to look into it. Kyat was purged at the end of her inquisition. Her family were told that she was murdered along with Oront. It didn't matter that Elon's transference ceremony was weeks away and that things didn't really add up; people believed what they were told. The High Priestess said that's what happened, and that was that. All loose ends were dealt with, and Elon and I are renounced until we come to our senses and help our parents and their friends achieve what we did."

"Does this factor into why Elon is missing? Does it have to do with what happened?" I press, finally able to see the picture more clearly.

"I don't know," Rogan answers, dropping his head as though he's too tired to hold it up any longer. "I've asked myself that, but I don't see how anyone would know or why the other Osteomancers would be missing too. There would be no need for that, which makes me think it has more to do with your grandmother's vision or some other unrelated motive that we don't know about yet."

"What am I supposed to do about the Order? Are they coming for me because of my connection to you?"

Rogan looks up at me and shakes his head. "Right now, what happened to us is information less than a handful of witches know. I don't see my mother risking the secret getting out to anyone else in order to ask you outright. If you didn't know but figured it out because of something she said or hinted at…I just don't see her being that messy about it. It's possible that something's changed, that they're now more desperate for answers. Or it's possible that whatever the Order wants from you has nothing to do with me or Elon. As annoying as it is, we just have to wait on Marx for answers to that."

"Would they hurt me?" I question, needing to know what I'm up against when it comes to his mother and just how badly she wants answers from her sons. I mean, obviously bad enough to ruin their lives, but does that vitriol extend to the people around them, to the people who dare to get close?

"I'm not going to let them get near you, Lennox, you have nothing to worry about there."

"That isn't exactly an answer to my question," I point out.

His eyes drop from mine. "I want to say no, but I don't know. It's been ten years since she renounced us. The High Council has left us alone for the most part, but I don't know if their tactics are changing," he admits, and I nod in understanding, my accompanying sigh filled with anxiety and sudden exhaustion.

"So what now?" I press, needing some kind of plan or way to prepare for what might be coming our way. "Elon is missing, which may or may not have to do with the fact that he's now magically immortal. The Order wants something from me, which may or may not have to do with my connection to an immortal. I mean, I'm only a couple of days into this whole Osteomancer thing, but I think it's safe to say that I am *killing* it," I declare on a laugh that sounds hollower than I intended.

"Technically, the jury is still out on the whole immortal thing," Rogan interjects, a teasing gleam in his eye and a smile tempting the corner of his lips.

I stare up at him, confused. And then look around as though I'm searching for a witness that can confirm everything he just told me.

"Ummm...did you not just tell me about the time you and your brother died and came back to life?" I hedge, pointing around me to remind him that it all happened in this very kitchen mere minutes ago.

"Yes. I did tell you about the *one* time we came back. But we haven't gone around testing the *live forever* theory since then. There are other factors at play that could explain what happened. There's no guarantee that if we die again, we'll just bounce right back, and we're not willing to risk it at this point."

"Soooo you're *not* immortal then? You might just be some kind of fluke? Like you used your *get out of jail free* card and now you're good to go?"

He snorts out a laugh and rolls his eyes, but his shoulders lift up in a shrug nonetheless.

"Well, that's anticlimactic as shit," I observe. "Here I was trying to find the bright side to being tethered to a possible immortal. But really you might be the immortal equivalent of premature ejaculation. That's disappointing."

Rogan's eyes widen with indignation. "You did not just call me that," he challenges, and I bite back the laugh that wants to bubble out of me at the look on his face.

The oven timer dings, and it pulls my attention away. "My tea is done," I announce, but Rogan doesn't move from where he's pinned me to the counter. I look up at him and notice that his stare has grown intense again.

"It feels weird telling you all of this," he admits. "I didn't realize how much I needed to until now. I forgot what hope felt like," he confesses, and I feel my heart shatter for him.

It dawns on me how hard all of this must have been. Not just the horror of what happened to him and his brother, but what was done to them afterward by people who should have cared more and known better. I can only imagine how lonely it would have all felt, and now to have the one person who truly got it...gone without a trace.

"Thank you, Rogan," I offer and watch as uncertainty bleeds into his gaze. "Thank you for trusting me enough to tell me the truth. I want you to know that I'll never speak a word of it."

Relief seeps into his stare, but still he doesn't move.

"Also for what it's worth, I'm sorry that any of this happened to you and to Elon. You didn't deserve any of it. If I ever meet your mother, I promise to deck her," I add, hating the ache I still see floating in his eyes.

He chuckles, and the sound makes me smile. The oven dings again, and I swear it sounds irritated. I push away from the counter, rise up on my tiptoes, and peck Rogan on the lips before tapping his arm so that he'll let me out of his cage.

He freezes, and then suddenly I freeze.

What the hell did I just do?

"Oh, shit, I am so sorry," I stammer, embarrassment crashing through me like an avalanche. "I don't know why I did that. You were just there"—I gesture at his close proximity—"and it was like some weird reflex," I defend as he blinks down at me in stupefied astonishment.

"I blame the kitchen!" I declare as though it makes perfect sense and isn't completely ridiculous. "We just had this deep conversation, and the setting is kind of intimate. You're all leaning in. It's like it flipped some relationship switch in my head, and my body reacted accordingly," I explain, sounding more and more crazy by the moment. "I take it by the look on your face that this has never happened to you, but rest assured, it has happened to me. You don't need to read anything into it," I offer. "I mean, I think we've already established that I have a tendency to casually kiss and run," I point out, motioning to the note that Saxon sent, now tossed aside dismissively on the far counter.

My face is on fire with mortification. I just want to get my herbs out of the oven and then find a comfy hole to crawl into and live in for a solid twenty years. That feels like the statute of limitations on embarrassment from accidentally kissing someone and making shit awkward.

I open my mouth to apologize again when Rogan is still just staring at me, not saying a word. But out of nowhere, his body pins mine, his hands are cradling my face, and his lips are pressed against my lips in a searing kiss.

Surprise ricochets through me, but the next thing I know, I'm melting against him, my fingers threading through his hair as his mouth sends me reeling. His lips are soft and gentle at first. I can practically taste his hesitancy as he gives me a moment to decide how I feel about this. In response, I open up to him, and he wastes no time in showing me that there's nothing accidental about this.

He kisses me reverently, unhurriedly, like we have all the time in the world to get it right. His fingers dip back into my hair, eliciting a small moan that he greedily swallows down. I pull him closer, each nip and suck sending a blaze of want through my entire being. His tongue teases and then moves in to dance with mine when I welcome it. I feel like I fall into him in all the best ways, completely losing myself in the taste and feel of him. He gives me no choice, because this is the kind of kiss that changes everything. It's deep and hungry, but not rushed or frenzied. He's not just exploring, he's not testing the waters, he's staking a damn claim.

The oven timer goes off again, and I pull away for a moment as though the sound has broken some kind of spell. "Fuck off," I growl at the beeping menace, and Rogan's rumbling chuckle vibrates against me.

I stare up at him a little stunned. I was not expecting *that* at all. I mean, I've been kissed in my day, but that was something else entirely. He crushes his fingers through my curls, and I try to keep things civilized and not to close my eyes and moan.

"If you keep that up, we're going to need a safe word," I blurt.

That's it, brain, you are in time out!

He laughs and then pushes away from me, moving to pull the pans out of the oven and turn the timer off. An odd sense of loss trickles through me as he does, but I do my best to ignore it. So that was the best kiss I've ever had—it doesn't mean anything. I'm not going to go full needy-Nancy and ask for a play-by-play of what the hell it all means.

Nope. It's fine.

Casual. Just like I like it.

"What about moonstone?" he asks as he turns back to me.

I look from him to the tea ingredients spread out on the pans. "Why would I put moonstone in it?" I ask, perplexed.

"No," he chuckles. "For a safe word. I was going to go with *immortal*, but it feels too on the nose and cocky," he adds, a teasing smile on his face.

"I thought we established that you can't exactly tick the immortal box on your census form, because it's yet to be proven," I counter, mouthing *premature ejaculation* at him. "Oh I know," I volunteer excitedly. "The safe word could be *I swear that's never happened before*...no, that's too long," I note cheekily.

His eyes narrow, a playful glint alight in them as he slowly stalks toward me. Just watching him floods my lady basement, and I have to actively tell myself to keep my head in the game. As though the world decided to second that thought, the doorbell rings, and Hoot starts barking like a maniac. I swear he sounds like a dying goat, his bark caught somewhere between a donkey bray and a cat howl.

Rogan stops hunting me and straightens, his serious side shuttering down over him in the blink of an eye. I want to tell him not to answer it, not to break the moment of whatever is happening between us, but that's selfish and stupid. I'm here because people are missing. And Rogan just placed a fuck ton of other reasons at my feet as to why it's dumb to get caught up in our feels right now. He looks down at me, and it's as though I can see the same argument going off in his mind that's going off in mine.

"I think it might be Marx," he declares, as though I need a reason to be okay with popping the bubble that was just around us and letting reality snake its way in.

"We should answer it then," I encourage.

He watches me for a beat and then leans down and kisses me quickly. "I blame the kitchen too," he tells me quietly against my lips, and then he leaves to answer the door.

I chuckle softly and touch my hand to my mouth, a mantra of *holy fucking shit* repeating in my head. I take a deep breath and try to clear my mind. "Well, that sure as fuck was informative while also being confusing as hell," I mumble to myself and then chuckle. I guess that's the story of my life these days though.

I hear Marx and Rogan exchanging greetings in the living room. With a silly smile and the warm and fuzzies making their way through my body, I move to go join them. Here's to hoping that Marx has good news and somewhere pressing to be. Now to come up with that safe word.

20

I lean back against the corner cushion of Rogan's modern yet buttery soft sectional. The large lounge room is taupes and grays, and with the large windows surrounding us, I practically feel like I'm sitting in nature's fancy-schmancy living room.

I refocus on what Marx and Rogan are talking about, having been momentarily distracted by the couch that cupped my ass better than my best pair of jeans. I don't know if that's a compliment to the couch or a call to replace my wardrobe, but either way, I put this couch on the list of things I need to figure out how to take with me when I go.

"I couldn't find a registration for a witch named Nik Smelser," Marx is telling Rogan as I tune back in. "I checked the human databases as well as what we have for other supes, but nothing was coming up. I asked the desk clerk if she had any other suggestions for places I could look, and when she was showing me how to navigate some archives, that's when we got a break," he explains, a small smile sneaking across his face.

"I had been ticking the male box on all of my searches, but she didn't specify gender at all, and up popped the registry for Nik Smelser. I felt like such an idiot. I almost kissed her, I was so excited, and the woman is a bog troll," Marx admits as Rogan cringes.

"Hold up," I interrupt, lifting a finger in the universal sign that I need a minute. "Nik Smelser is a woman?" I ask, completely floored. I did not see *that* coming.

"Yep, I guess Nik is short for Nikki," Marx offers with a small shrug, like this detail isn't really worth fixating on.

The sun is just starting to peek over the tops of the trees surrounding Rogan's house, and I take in the light pinks and purples that are streaking the sky as I conjure my bag of bones. I immediately open the top and look down critically at the contents inside.

"Really?" I ask the bones, judgment dripping from my tone. "Couldn't just tack on two more letters?" I scold irritably.

Rogan smiles and shakes his head.

"To be fair, maybe she just goes by Nik, and that's what your bones were tapping into," Marx offers unhelpfully.

I level him with a warning look. "Don't defend them, Marx, they know what they've done," I tell him like some disappointed parent who doesn't want to hear the excuses for bad behavior.

Rogan chuckles, and Marx's attention snaps from me to him. He studies Rogan for a beat, like he's trying to puzzle something out.

"You okay?" he finally asks. "You seem…different," he points out suspiciously.

Rogan's brow lifts with surprise. "Yeah, I'm fine."

Marx continues to look at him as though he's not buying it. His gaze flits to me for a fraction of a second and then settles back on Rogan. "Cough twice if you're in danger," he prompts out of nowhere.

"What?" Rogan and I both ask at the same time.

"Cough twice if you need help," Marx clarifies, like it makes perfect sense.

"First of all, if I *was* in trouble, you would have just blown it, and second of all, I'm fine. What's wrong with *you*?" Rogan demands, now looking at his friend with concern.

"There's not a damn thing wrong with me; you're the one over here laughing like that's a normal thing you do," Marx accuses, and Rogan throws his hands up in exasperation.

"I laugh," he argues.

"You sure as hell do not," Marx counters.

I chuckle, completely amused by the ridiculous back and forth. Rogan fixes me with a stare.

"I laugh," he defends again.

My hands go up, palms out in a gesture of innocence. "I didn't say anything."

"I totally laugh," Rogan grumbles, looking back toward Marx and shaking his head.

My heart warms as I wait patiently for Marx to get back to his story. He's quiet for a moment like he's still not sure if he believes Rogan is fine, but eventually he just shrugs and gets back to it.

"Anyway, like I was saying, we found Nikki Smelser. Her neighbors said they haven't seen her for about a month, and her apartment looked like no one had been there in a while. We put wards all over it, so if she shows up there, we'll be on her. But I'm not holding my breath."

"Why?" I question, surprised by the conviction in that statement.

"Because someone sent a note to the Order saying that they'd trade the missing Osteomancers, and after magical analysis, the handwriting on the note belongs to one Nikki Smelser."

"She's the witch-napper?" I query, surprised.

"That's the theory the Order is working off of for now," Marx states.

I look over at my bones, feeling a little bad. Okay, maybe they could have given me a heads-up about the whole guy-girl thing, but technically they did help us find the bad guy —or girl in this case. That's certainly nothing to turn my nose up at. I reach over and pat the purple velvet bag affectionately.

"Have they assigned a team to the case now?" Rogan asks, and Marx nods.

"Yeah, after the ransom note appeared, they opened a full investigation. When Osteomancer Osseous's report was flagged as potentially useful, they brought me in for questioning."

Rogan stiffens beside him, and Marx looks over at him apologetically. "I had to tell them what you and I had been looking into. You know I can't exactly keep that to myself. It would have only been a matter of time before they questioned someone we already had and knew anyway," Marx defends. "I didn't say anything about Lennox or our insurance policy, but other than that, they now know what we know."

"So is that what they want to talk to me about? My grandmother's dream?" I query, completely confused. I suppose I can chalk up the level of aggression to Prek and Rogan's history, but why the hell not just tell me that? And why not question Rogan too, if they know Elon's missing and Rogan's been looking into everything in hopes of finding him?

Marx's eyes seem to darken infinitesimally, and he clenches his jaw at my question. "I'm sure they'll ask you about it when they question you, but no, you're on the Order's radar for another reason," he replies cryptically.

A chill runs down my spine as the High Priestess's face pops up in my mind. I saw her on the cover of a magazine once, looking cold and formidable, and from what Rogan's had to say about her, that's not just an image she portrays. I refuse to look at Rogan, not wanting to risk that it would give anything away, and knots of worry start to form in my stomach.

"Do you know what that reason is?" Rogan presses, a menacing bite to his tone that I wish made me feel better.

Marx releases a weary exhale and levels his gaze on me. "The note that Nikki Smelser sent to the Order. The one saying that she'd trade all the missing witches. Well, you're the trade she wants. The note says you for them."

I flinch back at his words as though I've just been slapped. Stupefaction swirls in my mind, and my stomach drops out the bottoms of my feet. "Why?" I demand impotently, not understanding what I could possibly have to do with any of this.

"All we have is speculation right now," Marx answers. "We don't know for sure. But that's why the Order summoned you, because we need to find out."

"Are they wanting to simply question me, or are they actually considering handing me over?" I demand, not liking that this is even a question, or the look on Marx's face.

"I can't say definitively one way or the other, but I can say that trading you is *not* off the table."

I shoot off the couch onto my feet, and both Rogan and Marx do the same. "Leni, you have to understand how the Order works," Marx defends.

"Oh, I think I understand plenty," I argue. "It's not difficult to see that it's an organization that ultimately will do what's best for them," I add.

"Maybe so, but what's best for them doesn't mean it will be what's worst for you. The Order isn't considering a trade because it personally doesn't see your value, they're considering it because that's what the Order does. They create contingencies for every possible thing," he defends.

I scoff at him in disgust.

"Leni, the Order isn't operating with a lot of information right now. We know there are missing witches, but we don't know why. We have a dream, a ransom note, and you. That's it. But right now you are their best lead. You've been summoned, and even though I won't force you to go in, someone at some point is going to."

Worry courses through me, and I look over at Rogan as I try to swallow back my panic. It hasn't been lost on me that he hasn't said a word since Marx dropped the trade bomb.

"Penny for your thoughts," I snark, and it seems to snap him out of whatever's going on inside his head. He focuses back on me and then looks at Marx as though he's getting his bearings.

"Do they know how the note got to the Order? There's not a lead there?" Rogan asks, and I can hear the desperation in his voice.

"There's a team looking into it, but they haven't found anything substantial yet," Marx replies, and his phone chirps a notification.

"Fuck!" Rogan snarls, starting to pace.

I jump at the sudden outburst, my heart aching for what he must be going through. "Do you think you and Elon know her, ran into her somewhere?" I ask him, trying to pull at the threads we have before us.

"I don't know, I'd have to see a picture, but the name doesn't ring a bell."

"I can get a picture emailed over to you," Marx assures him, sighing as he takes in his pacing friend. "The bones didn't say anything else?" he asks me, and I open my mouth to say no before it dawns on me that's not true.

"They said run," I tell him, baffled by why I hadn't thought of that until now.

"What?" Rogan and Marx both ask simultaneously.

"I was scrying, I got the name, then it told me to run. When I looked up, I saw you in the backyard," I tell them, gesturing to Marx. "I assumed you were the reason for the warning. I just didn't think about it after that," I admit, feeling a little dumb now. "Everything happened so fast. Marx wasn't a threat, but then I was dealing with what I saw from Tilda and the bones. It just got lost in the mix, I guess."

"Why would they tell you to run?" Rogan questions, but it seems like it's aimed more at himself than at me.

"I have no idea," I confess, trying to think back to that day. "I shoved magic through Elon's whole property. I didn't pick up on anything else there other than Marx lurking in the backyard."

I study Marx for a beat and notice that Rogan does the same thing.

"Do you have anything to do with the disappearances?" Rogan asks his friend.

"What? Of course I don't. How could you even think that?" he sputters, shocked.

"I'm not accusing you of anything; I had to ask," Rogan defends and then returns to his pacing.

I move closer to Marx and poke at his cheek. He slaps my hand away and levels an irritated glare at me until I back away.

"Just making sure we don't have some Scooby Doo shit on our hands," I tell him. "No bad guy wearing a good guy mask is getting past me."

Marx just shakes his head and shoos me away even more.

"This doesn't add up. Why would a kidnapper out themselves to authorities and then expect said authorities to help them?" Rogan questions, his eyes far away in thought. "How does that make sense?"

"Does it need to *make* sense?" I counter. "Nikki Smelser, or whoever is behind this, obviously has issues. There isn't a thing about any of it that *makes sense*. I don't know that we'll get anywhere other than pissed off and frustrated by trying to make sense of why anything is happening the way that it is."

Rogan sighs and runs a hand down his face. "So what do we do now?" he asks Marx, whose phone goes off again.

"We keep doing what we've been doing," Marx reassures. "We look into what leads we can and keep fitting things together until the puzzle is complete. Are you still wanting to get into the other missing Osteomancers' houses?"

"Yes, I want to get a feel for them, see if the bones can tell me anything," I confirm.

"Okay, I can try and sneak you into a couple tomorrow night. They are all being warded and guarded right now, but a couple people on the team owe me a favor," Marx reassures.

"Okay, good, because the last place I want to be is anywhere near the Order," I admit, flashes of the accident and subsequent attack coaxing a shiver to crawl up my back.

"Yeah, I think that's a wise idea. Prek and his team have been assigned to the case, and there's obviously no love lost there," Marx informs us. "I'm sorry to just drop all of this and run, but I've got to go," he announces moving toward the door. "I'll send over a picture of Nikki when I get back to the office, and I'll confirm we're good to go for tomorrow night."

"Thank you," Rogan tells him, grasping his forearm for a quick shake before seeing him out. Marx shoots me a wave and an apologetic look, and then he's gone.

Rogan and I release a tired sigh at the same time. It would be funny in other circumstances, but right now it feels like we might be taking the last gasp of air before we're pulled under by everything we just found out. I want to comfort Rogan, but experience has taught me that sometimes there isn't anything that can be said or done to make something stop hurting. So I just stand there, silently supportive, so that he knows he's not alone in this.

"I'm going to check the wards around the property and then get cleaned up. We'll leave in an hour," Rogan tells me, moving for the door.

"Leaving?" I ask, confused.

"We have that meeting with the coven today, you know, to figure out this whole tethering thing," he reminds me, and it's all I can do not to facepalm.

"Right," I declare, trying not to look like an idiot.

How the hell did that slip my mind? He just told me about it.

"Can we stop by that diner on our way so I can drop off the tea?" I ask. "You know, if it's on the way," I add, realizing I have no idea where it is in relation to where we are now or where we're going.

"Yeah, that works, let's leave in thirty then, cool?"

Rogan disappears out the door before I can so much as offer my *cool* in agreement, and despair settles around me in his wake. I can't really blame him; I'd probably need a moment to myself too if I thought my parents were plotting against me.

I look over at my bag of bones and send out a plea to them for help. I feel at a complete loss for what to do. Clearly, the Order thinks the solution is obvious, but the one interaction I've had with them could have killed me. They play too fast and loose to be trusted with something I value above all things, my life.

I sense the hot breath of some unknown danger as it

breathes threateningly down my back. I worry I won't be smart enough, fast enough, or powerful enough to keep from getting swallowed up by it. I have so many questions and so few answers. It's beyond frustrating and disheartening.

I fluff my curls and make my way upstairs to get my shoes. Hopefully, after meeting with this coven, I can check *worries about tethering* off my list. If Rogan and I can fix our magic without any long-term damage, then I'll count that as the win. And one thing I know for sure is that right now, we could desperately use one.

Sleigh bells jingle as I pull the door to the diner open, a box of homemade pain-relieving tea bags tucked under my arm. I realized as we parked outside that I didn't get the waitress's name, and I'm not sure if she'll be working today.

I scan the mostly empty diner. There's a younger raven-haired waitress refilling the drinks of a middle-aged couple sitting side by side in a booth. And at the counter, a woman with curly dark brown hair sits on a stool, casually sipping a cup of coffee. Disappointment drops like a marble in my gut when I don't see the waitress with the kind blue eyes roaming around.

I approach the counter and set the box on top of the clean surface, waiting for the raven-haired waitress to finish up with the couple. Hopefully, she'll either be willing to pass along the tea or tell me when I can stop back by to drop it off myself. The lady with the curly dark hair looks over at me, and I offer her a warm smile.

She gives me an uncertain half-grin and then drops her gaze back down to her cup of coffee. The door to the back swings open, and to my relief, the waitress with the salt-and-pepper hair and warm blue eyes walks out.

"Hello, honey," she greets me warmly. "What can I get started for you?" she adds as she settles in front of me.

"I'm so glad you're here. I brought that tea that I mentioned when I was here before," I tell her, and then I see a flash of confusion streak through her gaze. She takes me in, I'm sure searching her memory banks, and I know she's found our exchange when her eyes light up. "I'm sorry I didn't get a chance to drop it off yesterday, but as promised, there's nothing bad or illegal, and it won't make you sick," I reassure her.

"Oh don't be sorry, honey. Truth be told, I completely forgot, so this is a welcome surprise."

I chuckle and hand the box over. "I hope it helps—my grandmother swore by it—and I put my card in the box in case you ever want more."

"That's kind of you, dear, are you sure I don't owe you anything?" she asks, taking the box. I can feel her genuine curiosity and excitement.

"Not a thing, it's my pleasure to help," I tell her, pushing away from the counter.

She graces me with a beautiful smile. "Well, I think I'll brew a cup right now. I'm just starting my shift, so this will be a good test," she declares cheerily.

I wave goodbye, and she darts back through the door to the back. I turn to leave, and that's when it hits me. That uncomfortable feeling scratching just under my skin. The *need* to help someone in whatever way I can. I turn around, taking in the restaurant with new purpose. I put a hand behind my back and discreetly conjure my bag of bones.

I told Rogan I would just be a minute. Hopefully, he won't be too pissed if this takes a bit. Memories of my last reading float to the surface of my mind, and a distinct buzz of excitement-laced curiosity moves through me like a current.

Who will it be, and what will the bones have to say to them?

I look over at the couple, but this feeling isn't for them. I search for the waitress, finding her behind the counter, refilling the other patron's coffee cup. The urgency spikes in me, and I move back toward the counter, to where the bones are calling me. As I close the distance, I realize that the feeling isn't for the waitress either, but for the woman with the curly dark hair and uncertain smile.

"I'll be with you in a second if that's okay; I just need to get another pot going," the waitress tells me in greeting.

I wave her off. "You're fine, I don't need anything right now, but thank you," I declare, and she shoots me a grateful smile and then disappears to the back with the coffee pot.

I take a deep breath and pull out the stool directly next to the woman who I can feel is summoning me for help. I wait for her to look over at me in either a friendly *you're sitting too close* kind of way or to shoot me a look of discomfort, but she seems intent on staring at the counter while taking occasional sips from her bowl-sized mug.

"I'm really sorry," I start, a wide disarming smile on my face. "I promise I'm not trying to be a creeper or to interrupt your alone time, but I just got the distinct impression that you might need someone to talk to," I start, trying not to look overeager.

A thrill works its way through me, and I can't wait to find out how the bones and I can help this woman.

She turns to me, taking me in, and I notice that her eyes are more dark olive-green than the brown I thought they were from afar.

"I like men," she replies simply.

My brow dips with uncertainty. Well, I didn't see that coming, but I know the bones and I can handle anything. "Is that a problem for you, is that what you want to talk about?" I question, and she looks at me like I'm a little off my rocker.

"No, I'm just telling you that I'm not interested. You're barking up the wrong tree," she explains, and understanding flares through me.

I laugh and shake my head. "I'm not hitting on you, I swear. I legitimately felt like you needed someone to talk to," I defend kindly, but she doesn't seem as amused or disarmed by my declaration as I thought she would be.

I clear my throat and try again. Maybe I need to be more direct.

"Sorry, it's just a thing that happens to me sometimes. I get impressions about people and feel the need to try to help if I can. I usually do a reading, one that costs you nothing other than a little bit of time and a listening ear," I explain tenderly, internally fist bumping myself, because who could say no to that?

"If you'd like a reading, I would be happy to do one," I add when she just stares at me blankly.

"I don't," she answers tersely, her olive green stare returning to the black smooth surface floating inside her mug.

I stare at her for a moment, taken aback by the refusal. I'm about to open my mouth to try and approach this a different way, but the urgent buzzing crawling under my skin stops. One minute it's driving me hard to take action, and the next all that's left of the summoning is the echo of it, and even that's fading with each passing millisecond.

I reach for my phone to grab a card so I can leave it with her in case she changes her mind, but when I only feel ass cheek filling my back pocket, I remember that I lost my phone in the accident. I debate for a moment whether or not I should write my number on a napkin, but doing so makes my *I'm not hitting on you* claim seem like it's pure crap.

So instead, I shrug and turn to step off the stool. Before I can, the woman huffs and turns to me with a glare. The vitriol in her eyes makes me stop in my tracks.

"I just wanted a little quiet," she snaps, getting up and yanking a coat and scarf off the stool on her other side. "I have three boys getting out of school in twenty minutes, and two more waiting for me at home *with* my mother-in-law, who moved in two months ago. Two. Months. Ago!" she barks as she shoves her hands angrily into the arms of her coat before continuing.

"The thirty minutes I sit here to drink two cups of coffee is the only peace I get these days, and now I can't even have that, because some beautiful woman with too much time on her hands and skin that is too smooth to be real can't mind her own business or pick up on the social cues screaming that I just want to be left alone!"

She wraps the scarf around her neck and shakes her head at me furiously. "How do you keep your curls from getting frizzy?" she shouts at me drill-sergeant-style, and I jump and stammer, shocked and a little afraid.

"I use a mousse called Cork My Screw and a little bit of coconut oil on my ends," I answer hurriedly, but she just glares at me.

"Thank you," she yells angrily back and then storms out of the diner.

I watch her leave, completely dumbfounded and floundering. I look over to find the two waitresses staring out after the poor, clearly exhausted mother, with sympathy in their eyes.

"Don't take that personal, hon, she's got a lot on her plate."

I nod and close my open, flabbergasted mouth. "Well, on that note, I think I'll just go," I announce sheepishly, and then I tuck tail and practically speed walk to the door. The sleigh bells sound oddly more ominous when they jingle as I leave, and I swear it sounds like they're laughing at me. I hurry to Rogan's car and practically dive in.

"Omg, go, go, go!" I shout out, ducking my head like I'm some celebrity who's trying not to get their picture taken. I'm completely mortified and feel so bad about setting a tired mom off.

"What? Why, did you just rob the place?" he asks as he slowly puts his car in gear and pulls out at a safe and calm rate of speed.

"No, worse! I poked a mama bear on accident, and I'm lucky I got out of there alive. Now go before she changes her mind and makes the bear attack in that Leonardo DiCaprio movie look like the Care Bear cuddles," I yell, officially hitting the freak the fuck out stage of my flight response.

A low rumbling fills the interior of the car, and at first I think it's some kind of attack—until I look over at Rogan.

"This is *not* funny!" I yell as I try to duck down lower in the front seat.

Rogan pulls out onto the road and stops at the red light, the car now shaking from the force of his laughter. I punch him in the shoulder, hard, implementing every lesson Tad ever taught me growing up about how to give the deadest of dead arms, but that just makes him laugh harder.

The light turns green, but before we start moving again, a charcoal gray minivan lays on its horn as it drives by. I look over in time to see the lady from the diner flipping me off as she streaks by.

"Oh fuck, she's found us! Evasive maneuvers! Evasive maneuvers!" I order, pointing in the opposite direction of the van.

Tears drip down Rogan's face as he guffaws and revels in my misery. I fold my arms over my chest and shake my head at his insensitive, immature ways.

What an asshole.

After about five minutes and another dead arm, he starts to calm down. He releases a satisfied high-pitched sigh to signal the conclusion of his laughing fit, wiping at his eyes and opening and closing the hand of the arm that I punched twice.

"Oh fuck, I needed that," he coos, another fit threatening to sweep him away. Thankfully, he keeps it together, but the wide smile on his face is annoying as hell.

"You want to tell me what happened?" he asks in an effort to be kind, but each word gets higher and higher in pitch, and I can tell he's on the cusp of another cackling sesh.

"No, I don't. Needless to say, I think my ancestors set me up for the scolding they got earlier," I clip haughtily.

For some reason, this just sets Rogan off again. I sigh and try not to succumb to the contagiousness of his laughter. I refuse to give him the satisfaction of laughing too. But man is it hard. He has an epic laugh. I don't think I've ever heard happiness sound so good on someone. I take some consolation in the fact that he really did need this. With everything that's happened to him, he deserves all the laughing fits he can get, and as much as I want to, I can't begrudge him that.

Two dead arms are adequate punishment.

"Does Marx know what's up with you and Elon?" I ask when he starts to come down from his laugh high again.

"We've never talked to him about it, but I think he suspects there's more to the story. Elon and I always say it's a matter of time before his need to question everything has him straight up asking us. But so far, he keeps his suspicions to himself."

I nod and watch the trees streak by the window as we turn down a two-lane road, and the car picks up speed. I wondered why Rogan seemed to live out in the middle of nowhere, but it makes sense now.

"Do you run into trouble with people in the magical community? Like, this coven we're going to, or Riggs, do they not care about your status?"

"Not everybody knows who I am on sight, so I have that working in my favor in some cases," he explains. "Riggs and the lycans don't seem bothered by it. Maybe that has to do with the fact that they were outcasts for a long time in magical society, so they're more forgiving of that title or status. Or it could just be that Riggs measures people by who they are and nothing else, so if he's cool with me, most of the others are too," he goes on, and I smile. I could see that about Riggs.

"The coven we're going to today is my aunt's coven. My father's sister," he clarifies, when I shoot him a surprised look.

"Does she know?"

"She knows the kind of people my parents are. She doesn't know details about anything. In fact, she tells us she doesn't want to know, but Alora knew Elon and me well enough not to buy what was being said about us."

"Does she know why we're coming?"

Rogan shoots me a look like he's questioning how I'll react to whatever it is that he's going to say. "She knows we're coming, but she doesn't like to talk about details when it comes to anything. She's a very hippie, let-the-magic-guide-her kind of person."

"What kind of witch is she?" I ask, trying to picture which of the branches could lean more toward free love and hippie.

"My father and Alora are twins. She happens to be a Soul Witch too," he tells me, and I'm taken aback by that.

I know Rogan said that lots of older families have more

than one branch of magic in their line, but it's still weird to hear about as it's so different from how I thought it all worked.

"And what about her coven, are they all Animamancers too?"

"There's a couple others. The rest are Corium Witches," he reveals.

"Well, this should be interesting then," I mumble more to myself than to him.

"It's no being hunted by a PTA mom, but it most definitely will be interesting," he teases with a wag of his eyebrows, cracking himself up.

Nope, I was wrong. Three dead arms is adequate punishment.

21

We pull up to a stone house that looks as though it's been plucked directly from the English countryside. There's a waist-high wrought iron fence that's wrapped around the perimeter of the home, and inside the decorative iron bars is the most beautiful garden I've ever seen. It's like every witch's paradise, with planter boxes teeming with herbs, vined plants overtaking trellises, and flowers and trees dotting every inch in between. It's exactly the hippie vibe I suspected I'd find when Rogan was describing his aunt.

The sun is high in the sky and doing its best to warm the somewhat chilly day, and my stomach tightens with nerves as we pull to a stop in a little clearing to the left of the property. I take it all in and once again marvel at witches living their best life. It seems, out here in some of the less populated parts of the state and country, there's less hiding, and witches are freer to live how they want with no questions asked.

I wonder if the locals have their stories and suspicions about the people living amongst them in these parts. Although I suppose it's just as likely that they're oblivious. I find myself suddenly wanting to sit and talk with the people who live around here and see if they'll spill the tea.

I get out of the car when Rogan does, following behind him like some lamb to the slaughter as he makes his way to the gate. It opens without so much as a squeak, which I find oddly impressive. I add it to the list of weird things that excite me now that I'm a witch. It's written just under *jackalope antlers* and above *the moon*.

"Are you nervous?" I ask as Rogan leads me down a cobblestone path to the front door. I whisper the question as though the plants are spying on us, so I need to keep it down.

"Will you think of me as less of a man if I admit yes?" he asks me over his shoulder, also with a whisper.

"Obviously," I tease.

"Then no, I'm not nervous in the slightest," he replies, and I chuckle.

My laugh is a little too loud, and I almost shush myself and apologize to the plants for disturbing them, but then I realize that's crazy and stop myself.

"Um, this place is having a weird effect on me," I half warn, half observe.

"Yeah, it's the plants, they have wards and other protections woven into them. It'll get better once we're in the house," Rogan explains, but that doesn't exactly make me feel better.

He turns to look at me, amusement tilting up the corners of his lips. "Depending on what's in bloom in the garden, the effects change," he informs me. "I once found Elon laughing his ass off in a patch of pineapple weed. He said he'd been there for hours," he goes on, a full grin now stretched across his gorgeous face.

I start to giggle as I picture Rogan finding Elon like that, but then immediately slam my mouth shut. Nope. I've been ridiculed enough for one day; I don't care what happens, I'm going to keep my head on my shoulders.

I almost release a sigh of relief when we get to the door and Rogan opens it and invites himself in, but right now I'm too afraid to breathe, so I just push in after him and pull in a large inhale as soon as the door is shut.

"Ro! How are you?" a kind voice sing-songs in greeting, and before I can track where the voice is coming from, Rogan is wrapped up in a big hug from a small Asian man.

"I'm good, Dave, how are you?" Rogan volleys as he man-pats the gentleman on the back a few times before pulling away.

"I should be offended by that lie, Ro, but since Alora called all of us in today, I know you're here for something serious, so I'll let it pass."

Rogan's smile drops, and it's as though I see some of the stress and worry melt away with it. It's as if he just dropped a mask, and I can see how relieved he is not to have to hold it up anymore.

I'm not sure what to think about that. Part of me is glad that he's in a place so comfortable that he can be authentic in whatever he's feeling. But another part wonders if he's had his mask on or off for me. Uncertainty trickles into my mind, and I know it will have me examining our interactions in search of answers.

"I think the answer is a little of both, dear," Dave declares as he extends a hand in greeting. "Hi there, I'm Dave, Alora's husband," he announces.

I take his hand, not sure if he was answering the thoughts in my head, or some question Rogan asked that I missed because I was wrapped up in the thoughts in my head.

"Hi, I'm Lennox," I answer, trying and failing not to eye him suspiciously.

"Did you just read my mind?" I ask, only in my head, but Dave doesn't respond. There is something cheeky about his smile though that makes me wonder.

"Come with me, you two. Alora will be excited. She wasn't expecting to meet the new Osseous Osteomancer so soon."

Dave moves quickly down the hall, leading us into the main part of the house. My mind is reeling with questions, and I have a hard time tracking where we're going. If Alora didn't know I was coming, how does Dave know who I am? And why didn't Rogan tell anyone that I would be with him? I know he said his aunt wasn't big on the details, but does no one know why we're here and that we're hoping to undo a tether?

Dave winds us around the house, which strangely seems much bigger inside than it did outside. Eventually, we reach a large wooden door, and Dave proceeds to knock on it three times and then wait. When two resounding knocks answer from the other side, the door opens, seemingly of its own accord, and Rogan and I are ushered in.

I step into the room and freeze. It's sensory overload in all the best ways, and I'm not sure where to rest my eyes first. The walls are the same gray stone as the outside of the house, but the floors and ceiling are a pure black wood. Constellations and planets are delicately painted on every surface with gorgeous gold leaf. The front of the room is framed by large gothic-style windows, and just in front of the wall of natural light sits an exquisite gold crescent table. I count six witches sitting on the convex side of the gilded crescent, seven when Dave walks over and sits to the left of the woman sitting regally in the center.

"Alora." Rogan nods in greeting, and the woman Dave just sat next to brightens with excitement and nods affectionately back.

My mouth almost drops to the floor as I take her in. I was expecting long gray and white hair, loose flowy clothing, and lined tanned skin from tending to the garden. But what I find couldn't be further from that.

Alora is what Dita Von Teese will look like when she's eighty. Alabaster skin, almost the color of cream, with just the faintest signs of age brushing over her features. She has dark gray eyes and black hair that's side-swept and styled with finger waves that remind me of old Hollywood. She's dressed in a champagne-colored cashmere sweater that looks baby bunny soft, and I realize that I've been staring at her for too long now, and I'm pretty sure she said something to me.

Crap.

I look to Rogan, hoping he'll help me recover, but he's just staring at me too. Panic claws its way up my throat, and I can feel myself reddening with each passing second.

"I'm sorry," I start sheepishly. "I wasn't expecting you to be so beautiful. I was momentarily caught up in it, and I missed either your hello or whatever question you might have asked me," I confess.

The seven witches all start to laugh, and a stunning blonde woman to Alora's right reaches out and takes her hand. "I felt the same way the first time I saw her," she confides with a kind smile and a squeeze of Rogan's aunt's hand. Then Alora looks over at the blonde woman, her gray eyes filled with love and affection, and she squeezes right back.

I'm getting a definite vibe from the two of them, and I sneak a look at Dave, who said he was Alora's husband, to see what he thinks of the display.

Surprisingly, he's looking at his wife with such pure adoration that it makes my heart ache a little with envy.

Dave's smile grows even wider, and before I can look away, his gaze flits to mine and he gives me a quick wink.

Shock trickles through me, and I once again question whether this man can read what's in my head like it's his favorite book. When Alora looks like she's about to say something, my attention immediately snaps back to her. There's no way I'm missing whatever it is she's saying again.

"I was just welcoming you, Lennox. We're honored to have you in our home."

I smile, willing the blush that's settling in my cheeks to calm the fuck down. "Thank you. I'm honored to meet all of you and grateful for any help you can offer," I declare, feeling proud when my voice doesn't wobble with nerves.

"Have a seat," Alora commands, and with a snap, two chairs rise up out of the wood of the floor directly behind us.

As soon as they stop growing in size, Rogan sits in one. I plop my gobsmacked ass in the other, painfully aware of just how out of my league I am when it comes to this crew of magic users.

The coven quickly introduces themselves, but the only names my mind can seem to hold onto are Dave, Alora, and Harmony, the overly-affectionate blonde woman to Alora's right.

"How can I help you, nephew?" Alora asks when the introductions are over and everyone settles into their curiosity.

Rogan clears his throat, and I don't miss the blush that crawls into his cheeks as he looks from Alora to the other coven members and declares, "We need information about tethering and how to sever it."

I'm surprised when no one in the room gasps or shows any outward signs of surprise. So far, anytime anyone hears the term, they freak out, which makes the silence in the room all the more unsettling.

"And you both wish to sever that which you bound?" Harmony asks.

Rogan and I both quickly answer *yes* in unison, and she nods.

"It is not an easy thing to do or a pain-free process. We can facilitate it, but the success depends on many factors," she tells us matter-of-factly.

"Like what?" I ask, not liking the sound of that.

"It depends firstly on whether or not your magics are better off together. Or if you've already been tapping into the other's abilities, thus forging a more impenetrable connection. Each time you activate the familiar bond with the other, it strengthens it, and that can be difficult to disconnect without damage," a male witch with red hair, who I think is called Worin, explains.

"Have the two of you entertained at all the pros behind staying tethered?" Alora asks sweetly, and an alarm goes off inside my head. "You may chalk what happened up to chance, but often the threads of life weave patterns we cannot see until much later as we look back on the tapestry of our lives," she adds.

I try not to do anything that might be considered disrespectful, like laugh or scream *are you nuts?* but I'm not on board with the old school matchmaker vibe that I'm suddenly getting from her. I fidget in my chair in an effort to keep quiet, and then I give up, deciding that what I have to say matters whether they want to hear it or not.

"Please know that I'm not trying to offend you or dismiss your point," I interject, and all eyes turn to me. "But I feel like it needs to be said that this is not the era of arranged marriages and making do. Rogan and I don't know each other well enough to tie ourselves together forever. The magic in my line has always been its own entity. I'm not willing to mess with that because Rogan is a good kisser and I'd be down to play hide the wand a few dozen times before it's time for me to go home and honor the legacy bestowed upon me by my ancestors."

I feel my face turn crimson as the accidental overshare comes pouring out of my mouth. I immediately want to find a dark corner and hit my head against a wall over and over again until my brain realizes that telling a person's family that you want to do dirty things to them is weird and gross on so many levels. But instead, I just keep on going like there's no shame in my game. Even though I can practically feel the creepy nun from that show ringing a bell behind me and barking out *shame* over and over again.

"Not to mention," I hurry on, hoping everyone in the room will forget my creepy word vomit and focus only on the valid points I'm making, "life's tapestry or not, how Rogan and I became tethered in the first place was wrong on every level. Whether it could all work out for the best or not, I don't know anything good that's ever come from having your choice or your say taken away. Could I find the positives if I wanted to look for them? I'm sure I could, but I shouldn't have to. What happened was done for the wrong reasons, and it needs to be fixed."

I can feel Rogan's eyes on me, but I don't look over. There isn't a snowball's chance in hell that he's not going to make fun of me for what just happened, but I can hold him off for a little while by pretending he's not there.

The coven doesn't say anything, and I watch each of the seven witches consider and weigh my words.

"And, nephew, how do you feel about what's been said and pointed out for your consideration?" Alora asks.

He crosses his legs, the ankle of one leg resting on the knee of the other as he seems to contemplate the question.

"I think I'd like to understand more about the separation process," he eventually voices. I was expecting him to dive into how he feels about what I said, but the logistics of it all are technically valid too. "Is it dangerous? What are the risks?" he continues.

Dave studies Rogan, his head slightly cocked as though he's listening intently to something. "Well, right now the two of you are connected. You can tap into the other's abilities or use both lines of magic at the same time. You can track and apparate to one another using the tether. It will work to pull the two of you closer together, urge you to strengthen the bond and use it to protect each other."

"Tethers can manifest and develop differently depending on the magic of the bonded and how the connection is used," Alora adds. "Our tether, for example, has changed over time. Different abilities and consequences have manifested over the years. However, because there are so many variables, we can't say for certain how each one will build and blossom, or wilt and die if it be the will of the bonded."

"I'm sorry, but did you just say that *you're* tethered?" I ask, completely taken aback by the admission.

Alora gives me a warm smile. "Yes. I am tethered to both my husband and my wife," she explains as though there aren't a million things about that sentence that just blew my mind. "That's why Rogan came to us for help," she adds as though that should have been obvious.

This time I do look over at Rogan. I glare at the side of his face, but he doesn't turn to meet my eyes. I guess we're back to the *need to know* bullshit I thought we had gotten past. Irritation bubbles up through me, and I start to feel my patience for this whole Q and A session start to wane.

"If we sever the tether today, it will take time. We won't know the depth of the connections until we tap into your bond. You'll both need to be prepared for a long and trying ordeal. It's possible that your magic may fight separation. You could lose certain abilities for a period of time, or all together, depending on what kind of damage, if any, you sustain. You may have issues with loneliness afterward, or struggle to feel complete. There have been times where the breaks are clean and relatively easy, but magic is hard to predict, and we always err on the side of caution," Harmony explains.

I feel like I just listened to an ad for some prescription medication where they have to list all the fucked up side effects at the end. I mean, I should probably be grateful that anal leakage wasn't mentioned, but I'd be lying if I didn't say the rest of what could happen scares the shit out of me.

Anger unfurls in my chest and digs into me like talons. I fight the urge to rage at Rogan for putting me in a situation where I have to deal with this crap in the first place. But I doubt his family would take my tantrum well, so instead, I pull in a deep breath and tell myself, either way, it will all be over soon.

"So, what do we need to do to get started?" I ask.

"We need to gather some supplies and some spells, but we can begin in an hour's time," Alora states, watching me as though she's waiting for my cue. I take a moment and then nod my agreement. Her gray eyes move to Rogan, and he must nod too, because she smiles and then pushes up from the table.

Then everything seems to happen in fast-forward. Dave confiscates Rogan to help him get the necessary texts in the library. Harmony tells me to pretty much carb load in preparation for whatever is about to happen. I'm whisked out of the room like I'm Dorothy headed for Oz, and I feel like I was just left alone by the only person I know at a party. I'm now surrounded by a bunch of strangers, feeling awkward as hell and trying to figure out if I should just bop in place to the music until the person I know comes back for me, try to make small talk with random people, or just stare into the abyss and hope it takes mercy on me and swallows me up.

"Can you point me in the direction of the bathroom?" I ask the redheaded witch, whose name I forgot again. Warren, maybe?

He guides me to the closest lavatory, and I immediately shut myself in and try to stave off the myriad of emotions all clamoring for my immediate attention. I suddenly feel as though everything is happening too fast, and yet somehow, at the same time, not fast enough. Time feels like my mortal enemy right now.

I take a moment to get a hold of myself, to breathe through everything that's hammering at me. *I'm making the correct choice...right?*

My reflection stares back at me, answerless as I splash water on my face. I sift through my toffee-brown gaze and dive into my gut and sit with it for a moment. What is it telling me? After several beats of introspection, I focus back on my face and nod.

"I can do this," I tell the girl in the mirror, and with that shitty pep talk, I step out of the bathroom.

I look for Warren in the hall, but he's nowhere to be seen. I hesitate for a second, not sure exactly which way we came from to end up here. I step left out of the bathroom and then change my mind and backtrack going right. I jump when a head suddenly pops out around the corner. Brown eyes seem to fill with relief when they spot me, and the woman hurries toward me, her steps oddly loud against the floor.

I watch as she takes a moment to look around as though she's checking for other people before she settles a now very intense gaze on me.

"You shouldn't trust him," she whispers out of nowhere in warning.

My brow furrows in surprised disbelief, not sure how to respond to that. "Trust who?" I finally ask, not sure who exactly she's referring to.

"The renounced one," she clarifies, studying my reaction as though she's expecting me to be surprised by this news. I don't miss the shiver that seems to crawl up her spine as she delivers what she thinks is shocking information.

"You don't know his heart, Osteomancer, you should get far away from him, right now! He's dangerous," she adds, her tone suddenly scared as she once again checks that no one else is making their way to us down the hallway. "If you follow me, I can get you away, but you'd have to come *now*," she commands, moving past me hurriedly as though there isn't even time for me to consider or debate what she's saying.

At first I hurry after her, mostly because that's what you do when someone tells you to follow and then starts practically running away. But then it dawns on me that this could be a really bad idea. I don't know who this person is. Taking her word at face value suddenly doesn't make any sense.

I don't know exactly who is kidnapping witches, but someone is. And I'm not about to get myself snatched because I was too polite to say *hold the fuck up and answer some questions for me before we go any further*.

I stop and the woman looks back at me confused. "Who are you?" I demand firmly, studying her face so I can commit it to memory. Her eyes are the same dark brown as her straight, shoulder-length hair. There is a smattering of freckles dusting her nose and cheeks, and she has a small scar just above her top lip.

"I'm a friend," she offers vaguely, turning back and continuing her path down the hallway.

Yep. This is a hard pass all around.

I turn and start to run in the other direction. I force my legs to move faster as I try to listen for the telltale sound of pursuing footsteps behind me, but all I can hear is the heavy beat of my own pulse as adrenaline stomps through me like it's a Clydesdale.

I'm out of the hallway and rounding a corner in no time. I slam full speed right into a large hard body, yelping with alarm as strong arms grab me and keep me from tumbling sideways. Fear and my survival instincts kick in hard, but relief washes through me like a cool balm when I look up to find that it's Rogan that I've just bodychecked.

"What's wrong?" he asks, taking me in before pulling me into him protectively and searching around us for whatever set off the panic I know is written all over my face. "What happened, Lennox?" he demands as I look to see if the woman came running after me, but there's no one there.

"Some woman tried to get me to go with her," I explain, realizing how lame and ridiculous I sound. "I didn't recognize her, she said you couldn't be trusted and that if I went with her, she could get me out of the house. I started to follow her and then realized that was a stupid idea, so I ran until I..." I gesture between us, signaling the collision that just happened, panting to collect my breath from the impromptu sprint I just did.

Rogan's eyes continue to search around us as he pulls me tighter against him. "Okay, let's go," he orders, and then we're both jogging through hallways to who knows where.

"Do you think we're in danger here?" I ask as we hurry back in the direction of the council room. Or at least I assume that's where we're going. I'm seriously turned around in this place.

"I don't know, but I think all of this is too risky," he declares adamantly, his focus trained on getting us far away from the potential threat as quickly as possible. "This just cements that even more," he tells me cryptically.

"What do you mean?" I press as I follow him through a door that has us suddenly spilling outside into the gardens. Rogan keeps going, but I stop, completely confused. "Rogan, what are you doing?" I demand, bewildered by why we would be in the garden and not holding up in the house where it would be safer.

"Lennox, we need to go," he barks at me, closing the distance between us like he's prepared to carry me away if he needs to.

"You're not making any sense," I snap at him. "We need to sever the tether. We can only do that in there," I point out, gesturing back toward the house.

"No, we need to use it," Rogan states matter-of-factly, his eyes hard and filled with determination that all at once makes me feel uneasy. "My aunt was right; things happen the way they are supposed to. This bond could be the thing that saves Elon," he declares, and my stomach sinks as panic floods me.

Rogan must see in my eyes the moment I decide to run. I don't take more than a step away from him before he's pulling me against him and locking himself around me. My magic flares angrily, but before I can do anything, Rogan marks me with blood and calls out, "*Seno.*"

Betrayal shatters through me, the treacherous shards ripping me open from the inside out. I fight the blackness that tries to take root in my mind, refusing to let it take over. I pull on my magic as hard as I can, desperately trying to stave off unconsciousness by wrapping power protectively around me. And that's when I see the tether, the bastard connection that started all of this shit in the first place.

I know I'm not supposed to mess with it, but if it's the difference between me passing out or fighting, I'm going to fucking fight. I pull the tether closer, suddenly siphoning Rogan's blood magic into me. Immediately the blackout spell fizzles into nothing, and I pull on both magical reserves, ready to fuck Rogan up.

I don't think I've ever been so mad and hurt in my life. Not even after reading my dad's note, and I thought nothing would scar me the way that did. Sorrow moves through me, tainting things that I thought were good and happy. I feel so completely stupid that I let Rogan in, that I even tried to trust him, and now here he is, once again deciding what's best with not a care or concern about how I feel, or a thought to ask me.

Well, I just hit my limit with Rogan fucking Kendrick. I throw my elbow back hard, nailing him in the side of the face. I shove magic into him, trying to overload him enough that he's forced to loosen his hold on me. I snarl and growl as I push and kick to get away, and just as I feel Rogan's arms loosen, a familiar face steps into view in front of me.

Seemingly out of nowhere, Prek strides toward us. Alarm sucker punches me in the mouth, and I wait for him to attack without hesitation like he did before. Confusion and fear settle over everything inside of me, and I hate that the Order member's presence sets off an involuntary reaction that has me worried for Rogan *and* for myself. I shove that useless concern away and try not to get pulled under by the trepidation and turmoil that's crashing through me.

Prek doesn't attack Rogan like I expect he will. Instead, he opens his fist and blows a powder into my face. Satisfaction fills his russet-brown gaze, his smile widening as I start to panic and hold my breath. Rogan's arms tighten around me as I throw my head back in an effort to break his nose with the back of my skull and evade the mist of magic still floating in the air around me.

Magic spills out of me like some feral beast intent on

ripping everything in its path to shreds, but in a blink, my connection to it is severed. I reach for both branches of magic again, but it's as though I hit a wall within myself that keeps me from reaching my power. I feel terrified and exposed as I try over and over again to the same end. I can feel my magic right where it's supposed to be, but no matter how I try, I can't get to it. I'm left hollow and reeling, as my head starts to feel hazy and dread takes up residence in my chest.

"I thought a little payback was in order," Prek says to me, brushing the rest of the powder off his hands as my head lolls to the side, my muscles one by one no longer able to answer my commands. An impotent keening spills from my lips as I lose all control of my body and slump against Rogan, the cage of his arms the only thing keeping me from falling.

"I would say you acted admirably by calling us, Kendrick, but it's you we're talking about. Hand her over, I'll take it from here," Prek orders arrogantly.

"If you think I'm just going to leave her in your care, no questions asked, then you're dumber than I always thought you were," Rogan growls out, pulling me closer to him. "I'm coming with her Prek; that's the deal I arranged with the Order, and you know it."

Silence envelops me, and I feel like I'm breaking into so many pieces that there's no hope I'll ever be whole again. Rogan called the Order. Rogan, who hates them with every fiber of his being, who was betrayed by them at the highest level and in the deepest ways. *He* invited them here to hand me over like I'm nothing more than the ticket he needed to the investigation.

"I'm aware of the bullshit you and Marx negotiated, but you don't run the show, Rogan. I don't take orders from you," Prek snaps back. "Now hand her to me."

"Not happening, Prek, and if you ask one more time, I'll do everything in my power to make sure the only thing you do for the Order from here on out is clean dried shit out of the toilet bowls. The agreement was that I would hand her over only if I was brought in on the case too. Either honor that or call a team here who will. We both know what will happen to you if you go back on what was already promised to me by witches farther up the ranks than you."

Treachery hits me like a freight train. I'm nothing more than a bargaining chip. Rogan knows I'm not safe. He knows what they might do to me. But there isn't an ounce of concern in his voice about anything other than getting what he wants. I've always heard that blood is thicker than water; Elon will be grateful to hear that, for his brother, that's true.

Agony rips me apart, and although I can't move, I can feel a tear as it spills down my cheek. I was such a dumbass. I thought I could trust him.

Rogan adjusts his hold on me, lifting me until he's secured me bridal style against him. I'm disoriented as he repositions me like an inconvenient sack of flour. The next thing I know, my cheek is pressed against his shoulder, forcing me to breathe him in far too intimately, more than I'll ever want to do again.

Prek doesn't say a word or try to take me from him anymore. He walks away from Rogan and me, but I can't turn my head to follow where he goes. I assume that means Rogan won this round of petty bullshit. My eyes focus on Rogan as he brings his face into my unblinking line of sight. Another tear slips down my cheek as his green eyes take me in.

"It's okay, Lennox, I'm here," he reassures me, but nothing could be further from the truth.

I can't yell, or rage, or make him hurt as badly as he's made me hurt in this moment. But I let my eyes fill with promises of suffering and retribution. I don't give a fuck what I have to do, I will make him regret the day he ever laid eyes on me. I feel the prick of a needle in my neck, and then just like the first time Rogan Kendrick betrayed me...everything fades to black.

The End, for now...

ALSO BY IVY ASHER

Urban Fantasy Romance
The Osseous Chronicles

The Bone Witch

The Blood Witch

The Bound Witch

Dark Shifter Romance Standalone
The Savage Spirit of Seneca Rain

Rabid

Paranormal Romance RH
The Sentinel World
The Lost Sentinel Series

The Lost and the Chosen

Awakened and Betrayed

The Marked and the Broken

Found and Forged

Shadowed Wings Series

The Hidden

The Avowed

The Reclamation

More in the Sentinel World coming soon.

Hellgate Guardian Series

Grave Mistakes

Grave Consequences

Grave Decisions

Grave Signs

Shifter Romantic Comedy Standalone

Conveniently Convicted

Dystopian Romantic Comedy Standalone RH

April's Fools

ABOUT THE AUTHOR

Ivy Asher is addicted to chai, swearing, and laughing a lot—but not in a creepy, laughing alone kind of way. She loves the snow, books, and her family of two humans and three fur-babies. She has worlds and characters just floating around in her head, and she's lucky enough to be surrounded by amazing people who support that kind of crazy.

Join Ivy Asher's Reader Group and follow her on Instagram and BookBub for updates on your favorite series and upcoming releases!!!

- facebook.com/IvyAsherBooks
- instagram.com/ivy.asher
- amazon.com/author/ivyasher
- bookbub.com/profile/ivy-asher

Printed in Great Britain
by Amazon